"In *Hunt Them Down*, Gervais has crafted an intelligent and thoughtful thriller that mixes family dynamics with explosive action . . . the possibilities are endless in this new series, and this will easily find an enthusiastic audience craving Hunt's next adventures."

—Associated Press

"[An] action-packed series launch from Gervais."

—*Publishers Weekly*

"Nonstop action meets relentless suspense . . . the blood flows knee deep in this one as Gervais uses his background as a drug investigator for the Royal Canadian Mounted Police to bring a gritty authenticity to his latest thriller."

—The Real Book Spy

"Gervais dishes out lavish suspense to keep a reader glued."

—Authorlink

"Superbly crafted and deceptively complex . . . this is thriller writing at its level best by a new voice not afraid to push the envelope beyond traditional storytelling norms."

—*Providence Journal*

"From the first page, *Hunt Them Down* is a stick of dynamite that Simon Gervais hands you, masterfully lights, and then dares you to put down before it explodes. Don't. It's worth a few fingers to read to the end."

—Matthew FitzSimmons, bestselling author of *The Short Drop*

TRAINED
TO
HUNT

TRAINED TO HUNT

A PIERCE HUNT THRILLER

SIMON GERVAIS

THOMAS & MERCER

Text copyright © 2019 by Simon Gervais

Published by Thomas & Mercer, Seattle

www.apub.com

Amazon, the Amazon logo, and Thomas & Mercer are trademarks of Amazon.com, Inc., or its affiliates.

ISBN-13: 9781542004923
ISBN-10: 1542004926

Cover design by Kirk DouPonce, DogEaredDesign

Printed in the United States of America

This book is dedicated to my parents,
Céline and Raymond.
Thanks for teaching me that books are portable magic.

CHAPTER ONE

French Quarter
New Orleans, Louisiana

Pierce Hunt watched his target exit the small bookshop. The man climbed down the three steps that led to the sidewalk and turned around, as if he was waiting for someone else. To Hunt's surprise, a tall, slender, and seemingly athletic woman in her early forties walked out of the store and joined the man on the sidewalk. When his target had entered the bookshop ten minutes ago, he'd done so unaccompanied.

That complicates things.

His target, a man named Pascual Andrade, was supposed to be alone. Hunt grunted inwardly. From a safe distance, Hunt followed Andrade and the woman as they strolled down the streets of the French Quarter, holding hands, swinging them lightly. In the span of twenty minutes, they stopped only twice. Once to share a long, passionate kiss and the other to buy ice-cream cones. Was she Andrade's wife? A mistress perhaps? What did she know about Hunt's target?

From Andrade's respectful and caring attitude toward the woman, it was hard to imagine that the man had had anything to do with the abduction of Hunt's daughter four months ago. But he had. He was a high-ranking member of the Black Tosca's cartel. And now, he was about to pay the price.

What Andrade was doing in New Orleans, Hunt had no idea. Nor did he care. Tom Hauer—the administrator of the DEA—had given him the tip about Andrade's location. Where Hauer had gotten it from, Hunt hadn't asked. The encrypted file Hauer had sent his way had contained enough pictures of Andrade posing with Valentina Mieles—a.k.a. the Black Tosca—and other cartel members to convince Hunt the man might know where the remaining members of the cartel might be hiding. Hauer hadn't given him any specific instructions. Just the tip and the photos. And these four words:

You have three days.

Three days before what? Was Andrade set to be arrested by the DEA in three days? Was he traveling back to Mexico? Was there another agency planning to make a play? Hauer hadn't said. Using an alias backstopped by Hauer, Hunt had purchased a one-way ticket from Miami to New Orleans. Using a second alias, he had rented a nondescript four-door economy car and had paid cash for a tiny room in a small hotel on the edge of the French Quarter. The hotel he had chosen might have been shady, but it was less than one hundred feet from the more luxurious hotel where Andrade was staying. It was perfect for keeping track of Andrade's comings and goings.

Hunt had used the first two days to familiarize himself with his new environment and to look for an opportunity to get Andrade one on one. So far, he'd had no luck. He had, at maximum, thirty-six hours left before his *three days* expired. If Andrade didn't give him an opening, Hunt would have to create one.

Hunt shadowed the duo as they took a side street, a feat made more difficult by the evening's unseasonably warm weather, which had encouraged gobs of people to leave their overpriced apartments. The streets were crowded, and music blared from the open doorways of jazz clubs. The smell of food, beer, and garbage soaked the already-humid air as the horde of tourists made their way to the bistros and cafés that were just beginning to get busy. After a few minutes, Andrade and the woman entered a restaurant. Over the entrance dangled an enormous neon sign in the shape of a palm tree. It burned bright green with flashing brown coconuts.

Hunt spotted a bistro across the street from which he could keep watch. He was about to cross the street when Andrade came out of the restaurant, holding a cell phone to his ear. He looked directly at Hunt, and his face betrayed a split second of surprise.

Hunt averted his eyes and kept walking, praying Andrade would second-guess himself and decide he hadn't recognized Hunt after all.

That hope evaporated the moment Andrade bolted.

Hunt raced after him, but Andrade was fast and had a decent lead. Andrade glanced over his shoulder, then darted left, down a narrow and poorly lit alleyway. Hunt surged after him. The alleyway was really just a driveway behind a building occupied by bars and restaurants. Andrade ducked behind a large garbage can.

Hunt pulled his SIG Sauer. He didn't want to use it, at least not yet. As much as he wanted to kill Andrade for what he had done to Leila, Hunt wasn't about to take him down in a public place with so many witnesses—and so many civilians who would be caught in the cross fire if Andrade had a weapon of his own.

Hunt was twenty feet away from the garbage can when a door popped open, and a young woman in a red summer dress stepped out of the building. Hunt saw Andrade shove aside the woman and rush through the door.

Hunt darted after him, taking only a moment to ensure that the woman was all right, and yanked the door of the building open. Hunt raced inside, leading with his SIG Sauer. He found himself at the end of a long hallway opening into a crowded bar, where people were bunched in small groups talking and drinking from plastic cups. Blues music was playing in the background. Hunt quickly lowered his handgun, keeping it close to his thigh. As he studied the crowd, his stress level rose steeply at the thought of the disaster if anyone fired in here, and he decided to holster his weapon.

Too many people. Too dark.

Then a flash of movement, quickly followed by a yelp. Forty feet in front of him, Andrade barreled through a group of people, sending drinks flying. Hunt elbowed his way past outraged bystanders, looking . . .

There. Andrade was making his way to the exit. Hunt dodged a group of drunken men, one of them yelling something unintelligible at him. Then, someone or something tripped him, and Hunt crashed to the floor. The smell of spilled beer immediately filled his nostrils.

"I think you had too much to drink," yelled one of the men. Hunt heard his companions laughing.

He had no time for this bullshit. He swallowed his pride, got up, and was about to head out of the door when a pair of strong arms reached from behind and grabbed him in a suffocating bear hug.

"I said you drank too—" a man started to say.

Hunt drove the heel of his right foot into the man's shin. The man yelled in pain and let go. Hunt spun around and delivered a sharp jab to the point of the man's jaw, driving him backward. The man was tall, at least one or two inches taller than Hunt's six-two frame, and must have weighed over 250 pounds, not all of it muscle. The man's eyes were wide with drunken fury.

Ducking the man's flailing blows, Hunt stepped forward and inside the sweep of the big man's arms. He drove a two-punch combination into the man's soft stomach and finished with a powerful left hook to the man's face, sending two bloody teeth on a brief voyage across the floor. Without another sound, the man folded up. Hunt stepped out the exit—and not a moment too soon; the man's companions were starting to approach.

The whole encounter had lasted less than eight seconds, but it was enough for him to have lost sight of Andrade. Hunt cursed. Then a distant scream, shrill and terrified, caught his attention. He took off toward the scream, dashing across the road and cutting through a corner yard. He forced his burning legs and calves to keep going.

A shot rang out. A bullet zipped past him. Hunt threw himself forward and rolled to his right. Flat on the sidewalk, he pulled out his SIG Sauer.

Damn it!

Where the hell was Andrade? Ahead of him was a large brightly lit parking lot, but the number of cars made it impossible to see much. Hunt belly crawled toward the lot. Reaching the first row of vehicles, he peered under the cars, trying to spot where Andrade had taken cover.

Nothing.

A car horn blared nearby. Hunt jumped to a crouch, heart thundering. He searched for the source. Three rows away, Andrade was pointing his gun toward the windshield of a white Honda Civic. Hunt brought up his SIG Sauer, aimed, and fired.

Andrade's hand flew to the bicep of his other arm. His pistol dropped to the ground. By the time he turned in the direction of the shot, Hunt was slamming into him with the force of a speeding freight train, sending him reeling backward.

He landed on his back, hard, and Hunt heard the hollow sound of Andrade's skull hitting the pavement. The man's eyes rolled back in his head. Not wanting to take any chances, Hunt spun Andrade onto his stomach and bound his hands securely behind him with a flex-cuff he removed from his back pocket. Hunt heard the whine of the Honda Civic's engine as it sped away behind him.

With the Black Tosca cartel member no longer an immediate threat, Hunt grabbed Andrade's pistol, stripped the magazine, and ejected the round from the chamber. He then slipped the pistol into his waistband. Slowly but surely, Andrade was regaining consciousness. Hunt grabbed him under the armpits and sat him up against a parked car.

"Hey, asshole, you know who I am, right?" Hunt said.

"I . . . I had nothing to do with your daughter's—"

Hunt grabbed Andrade's wounded bicep and squeezed. Andrade opened his mouth to scream, but Hunt used his other hand to clamp his mouth shut. Andrade convulsed, his eyes bulging from their sockets. When his face looked as if it would explode, Hunt released his grip. "That was for being stupid, dipshit," Hunt said. "You kidnapped the wrong girl."

Andrade coughed, gagging for air. Blood poured down his sleeve.

"What do you want, Hunt?" he gasped. "You here to kill me?"

"Don't tempt me," Hunt growled.

Hunt grabbed his phone and was about to dial 911 to identify himself to the first responders he knew were coming—one of the many witnesses would have called the cops—when he felt a presence come up behind him. Hunt turned swiftly, his SIG Sauer appearing in his hand while he was still halfway through the turn.

"Don't shoot," the woman said coolly.

It was the woman he'd seen walking with Andrade earlier.

"Keep your hands where I can see them," Hunt said to her. "Who are you?"

"Ivanka! Don't listen—"

"Oh, would you shut up, Pascual?" the woman said, condescension lacing her words.

"Hey!" Hunt intervened. "Who are you?"

"It doesn't matter," she replied. "Just don't kill him, Mr. Hunt." She smirked. "He's quite valuable."

Hunt met her eyes, which carried a steely gaze. They were even more unsettling than the fact that this woman knew his name.

"The cops are coming," Hunt said. Police sirens wailed close by. "Your boyfriend's safe."

The woman's brows rose in amusement. "He's not my type."

While they'd been talking, she'd taken a few retreating steps while making sure to keep her hands visible to Hunt.

"Stay here," Hunt ordered. A police car turned onto the street outside the lot.

"You won't shoot me, Mr. Hunt. And please, ask our friend Pascual about Paraguay." She turned her back on him and disappeared into the maze of vehicles.

Hunt swore. Who was that woman? He had a feeling he'd see her again.

He holstered his SIG Sauer, then raised his hands over his head and waited for the cops to arrive.

CHAPTER TWO

MacDill Air Force Base
Tampa, Florida

Hunt hugged his sixteen-year-old daughter until she shrieked for mercy.

"Be careful out there, Dad." Leila kissed him once more on his cheek. "I love you."

The words went straight to his heart, disengaged every defense he had, and for a moment Hunt questioned if his decision to work as a consultant for the DEA had been the right one. This was his second trip outside of Florida in the last two weeks. He didn't mind traveling, but he loathed being separated from his daughter.

"I love you more," he said, his throat tightening. "Thanks for being here. Means a lot to me."

"You'll be back in time to catch Jack's next game, right? It's on Friday."

"You bet," he said.

Leila gave him a doubtful look, as if he were a disobedient child who kept making promises he couldn't keep.

"I swear," he said, instantly regretting his words. He thought about adding something that would get him off the hook, but the delight on his daughter's face sucked away his very breath.

Now you really have no other choice but to make it to the game.

This trip to Paraguay stemmed from the intelligence the DEA had obtained from Pascual Andrade after a thorough grilling by a joint team from the CIA and DEA. It appeared that the mysterious woman Hunt knew only as Ivanka had been a senior CIA case officer who had been close to turning Andrade into an asset before Hunt had inadvertently torpedoed her operation. It was nobody's fault, just the way the cards had fallen.

Hunt looked in the direction of his ex-wife. Jasmine DeGray was standing a dozen feet away, flanked by her towering husband, Chris Moon, and Leila's boyfriend, Jack Cameron, who was only a couple of inches shorter than Moon. Moon, the star quarterback for the Miami Dolphins, gave Hunt a quick nod of acknowledgment. It had been nice of them to make the four-hour drive to Tampa.

"I need to check on a boat I'm thinking of buying," Moon had said. "It's docked at a marina close to Saint Petersburg. It's fifteen minutes from MacDill. We'll be there to see you off."

Hunt appreciated the gesture. He knew his daughter didn't need him for her day-to-day activities, that she was doing just fine with Jasmine and Chris, but it was weighing on him that the minute they had started growing closer, Tom Hauer had come begging for Hunt's help. An undercover DEA asset embedded deep within the Venezuelan government had claimed that surviving members of the Black Tosca's cartel—the cartel both Hunt and Leila had nearly lost their lives to a few months ago—were about to close a deal with Lieutenant General Euclides Peraza, a.k.a. the Spider, the commandant of the Venezuelan armed forces' Operational Strategic Command. But until two days ago, the DEA had had no idea how they were going to do that. If they were to believe Andrade, the Black Tosca leadership planned to meet with General Peraza's representative in Paraguay in three days' time.

So when Hauer asked Hunt to tag along with a CIA hunter-killer team led by Ivanka, Hunt had been unable to refuse, despite knowing the mission would take him away from his daughter.

Unable, or didn't want to refuse?

Hunt believed that anyone who'd had a hand in his daughter's kidnapping deserved to be caught and punished. As personal as the stakes were, though, there were other priorities to consider. The recent and sharpened aggressive anti-American rhetoric of Venezuela's president Capriles had done nothing to appease the building tensions between Venezuela and the United States. Learning more about the potential alliance of the Venezuelan government with the Black Tosca's cartel was a necessity, not a luxury. Such an alliance would be the first step in a global legitimization of organized crime and terrorist networks hostile toward the United States.

That was why Hunt was going to South America. That was why he was leaving Leila behind.

Again.

"Be kind to your mother, Leila," Hunt told her. "And don't spend too much time playing with your machine, okay?"

"Why do you keep calling my iPhone a machine, Dad? It's a phone, not a machine. Got it?"

"One more thing," Hunt said, grasping one of his daughter's hands in his. "There's no rush, okay?"

Leila looked at him in a strange way. "About what?"

"You know," Hunt said, a tad uncomfortable. "With Jack."

Leila rolled her eyes heavenward. For an instant it looked as if she was about to snap back with a sharp reply, but she held her tongue. "Don't worry, Dad."

Moon, who knew Jack much better, had taken him under his wing. Jack certainly knew how to throw a football. Moon had told Hunt in confidence that if Jack continued to perform on the field with his high school varsity team—the Carol City Chiefs—he was almost guaranteed to be offered a position with the Miami Hurricanes, one of the most storied teams in college football history.

Hunt bade them farewell, and the foursome walked out of the terminal's double glass doors together.

Hunt let out a long sigh. He was going to miss his little girl.

And what about Anna? Where was she? Anna had promised him she'd meet him inside the terminal prior to his flight. He hoped she hadn't changed her mind. They'd had a small argument the night before. Nothing serious—he couldn't even remember what had started it—but just knowing they had quarreled distracted him. It had been their first squabble since they'd gotten back together. He had broken her heart once, years ago, by betraying her trust when she'd learned that he was a DEA agent who'd used her to infiltrate her family's crime syndicate. At the time, he hadn't expected to fall so passionately in love with her. They'd had to join forces when the Black Tosca had kidnapped Leila and her best friend, Sophia—Anna's niece. Taking both of them by surprise, the foray had reignited their hunger for each other.

There was no way he could leave for South America before he knew they were okay. He had messed up so many things in his life; he didn't want his relationship with Anna to suffer the same fate.

He had tried to call her twice, but she hadn't picked up. He glanced at his watch and saw that he should already be on the plane.

Where the hell are you, Anna?

CHAPTER THREE

Tampa, Florida

Anna Garcia gripped the steering wheel of her Range Rover so hard that if it had been alive, it would have screamed in pain. The next traffic light turned yellow. Her reflex was to press the gas pedal to make the light before it turned red, but the delivery van in front of her stopped, and she had to slam the brake to avoid rear-ending it.

Anna banged the steering wheel in frustration. Hunt's flight was in thirty minutes, and she was still a good ten-minute drive from MacDill Air Force Base. She forced herself into calmness by taking three deep breaths. She rolled her head in circles in an effort to relieve the stiffness in her neck. It didn't work.

Pierce won't leave before saying goodbye, she thought. *He won't.*

She knew she should have driven with him to the airport, but she'd had two important conference calls scheduled. Neither call had gone well. Mauricio Tasis, her right-hand man, was in Miami trying to seal a deal on a piece of commercial real estate she wanted to buy. But just like the three deals before it, the seller had changed his mind at the last minute. He still wanted to sell, but with a premium she didn't feel was warranted. The deal was about to fall through. It seemed that whatever she did, it wasn't good enough. The Garcias, once one of the most powerful crime families in Florida under the direction of her father and then her brother, were slowly but surely imploding.

That was fine. That was exactly what she wanted.

Her deal with the DEA had given her one year to clean everything up. With Hunt's help, she had convinced Tom Hauer that she'd be able to peacefully break up the organization she'd inherited. In return, Hauer had promised to indefinitely postpone any new DEA investigations into the Garcia family, but with the clear understanding that he wouldn't impede another agency's investigation and would only hold to the deal if no new criminal acts were committed. That had been five months ago.

At first, Anna had made quick progress. Not everyone in the organization agreed with the path she had chosen—to funnel the family's massive fortune and payroll into legitimate businesses that would replace the money her employees earned from trafficking drugs with aboveboard employment—but it had been working. Then, all of a sudden, her commercial real estate deals had started to fall apart.

It was as if the deals were being sabotaged. But by whom?

Anna looked down at her phone on the empty passenger seat, yearning for a message from Hunt that would bring her some respite from the mounting stress.

No calls. No texts.

She noticed that the phone's battery had already lost more than half its charge. Strange, since she'd charged the phone overnight. She reached over to plug the phone into the SUV's USB port, but before her fingers could touch the device, the car behind her honked. She looked up and saw that the light had changed and the delivery van was already through the intersection. She cursed and stomped her foot on the accelerator, sending the Range Rover leaping forward with a roar. Nothing was going her way today.

———

"What is she doing?" Alejandro Mayo asked out loud. "You think she spotted us?"

"No way," his brother replied between bites of the protein bar he was holding in one hand. "She probably realized she's late."

Their vehicle was stuck eight cars behind Anna's Range Rover. With Anna's slow reaction to the traffic light, there was no way they were going to make it across the intersection. That didn't bother Alejandro. By way of a carefully crafted text message containing malware code, he had remotely installed an application on Anna's personal phone that allowed him to listen to her voice calls and monitor her emails. While the app was invisible to its target, it had a tendency to drain the battery of the device it was running on, so Alejandro used it judiciously.

"I don't think she'll make it," Santiago said.

Alejandro couldn't care less if she made it to MacDill or not. The only thing that mattered to him was that Pierce Hunt would finally be gone. He'd never admit it to anyone, especially not to his brother, but the former DEA agent scared him to death. What Hunt had done in San Miguel de Allende was impressive—Alejandro had to give him that. To directly challenge the Black Tosca and win? That took big *cojones*. Not only had Hunt left a throng of dead bodies in his wake, but he had managed to rescue his daughter and her friend. At best, Hunt was dangerous. At worst, he was insane *and* dangerous. Not a good mix. Hunt wasn't the kind of man you crossed willingly. That was why Alejandro and his brother had shadowed Anna and Hunt from Miami to Tampa. They wanted to make sure Hunt was overseas before moving on Anna.

Anna Garcia could handle herself, but thanks to Alejandro's efforts to undermine her at every turn, her grip on the Garcia crime family was slowly fading. He had listened with great pleasure to her phone conversations this morning. The offer on the small shopping mall she wanted to buy in Aventura had been turned down. A threat to the lives of the present owner's family had been enough to convince the man to ask for a premium he knew Anna wouldn't pay.

The Garcia crime family needed someone at the helm who could lead them to an even bigger share of the drug market, not someone who wanted to turn them into managers at a shopping mall. Alejandro was that person. And with Hunt's imminent departure, the biggest obstacle to his ascension to the throne was about to vanish.

In a few hours, Anna Garcia would be dead. The new deal Alejandro had struck with the Venezuelans would put the family back on the map. But it wouldn't be called the Garcia crime family anymore, would it? By the end of the day, it would be renamed the Mayo cartel. What about that?

Alejandro had planned everything. His men were waiting in Miles City, ready to abduct her on Alligator Alley on her way back to Miami. They only needed his word to make Anna Garcia disappear. The only question still lingering in Alejandro's mind was, Once he was done with her, who would get to Anna first: the alligators or the crocodiles?

CHAPTER FOUR

MacDill Air Force Base
Tampa, Florida

Hunt dialed Anna's number one more time. After six rings, the voice-mail came on, and he hung up, frustrated.

Why wasn't she answering her phone?

With a sigh, Hunt grabbed his oversize gear bag and weapons case and headed down the small terminal. He was about to step onto the hot tarmac where a C-17 Globemaster was waiting when someone yelled his name. Hunt turned to see Anna running toward him.

"Pierce! Wait!"

"You made it!" he shouted back, relieved to see her.

Hunt dropped his bag and weapons case, and Anna ran into his open arms, squeezing him tightly. A jolt of electricity shot through him as she grabbed his head and pulled him closer. Her lips touched his with a light, feathery kiss. For a few precious seconds he forgot where he was. He forgot who he was. Hunt deepened the kiss, not wanting to let the moment go. Anna wrapped her arms around his broad shoulders and buried her head against his neck.

"I'm sorry about last night," she said.

"Me too."

"Don't go," she whispered in his ear. "Stay with me, Pierce. I really need you to."

Her words tore him apart, her vulnerability even more so. Tension was visible in Anna's shoulders, and her heart pounded against his chest. Hunt rubbed the back of her neck with one hand while he ran the fingers of his other hand through her hair. He leaned in close and kissed her lips once more. He explored her face with his hands, like a blind man memorizing every surface, saturating his memory so that he would never forget the feeling.

"I can't. I'm sorry," he said, holding her tight. "Hauer needs me to do this."

Anna took a deep breath and let it out slowly before speaking.

"I know, and I have work to do too. I just wish you could stay a bit longer. You'll be back in a few days, right? Nothing has changed?"

Hunt stroked her hair back from her face and tipped her chin up.

"I'll be back before you know it," he said, intentionally staying vague about his exact return date. He didn't want to repeat the mistake he had made with his daughter. On the odd chance he wouldn't make it before the weekend, he didn't want the two most important women in his life to be pissed at him at the same time.

"I can't wait for all this to be over," Anna said. "There's nothing I'd like more than to disappear for a week somewhere with you. To a quiet beach, maybe?"

"That'd be nice," Hunt admitted. He could easily picture the two of them lying on a beach somewhere, lazily warming their uncovered bodies under the hot sun before inevitably turning and pressing against each other. Hunt shook himself out of his daydreams before his thoughts could distract him further.

"We're almost there," he continued. "Everything you've done in the last few months is nothing short of a small miracle. I doubt your brother and father could have done the same so gracefully."

"We'll never know, will we?" she replied, her eyes darkening at the mention of her deceased family members.

"What I do know is that you're the most courageous and audacious woman I've ever met."

"The shopping mall deal is falling apart," Anna said, changing the subject.

"What? I thought that was in the bag. What happened?"

"The owner is asking for a premium. A big one. Millions."

"What changed his mind?" Hunt asked. Then he said, "Someone got to him."

"That's what I think," Anna said. "The next few weeks will be crucial. That's why it would have been nice to have you around."

"I will be, baby. This is just one op. Won't take long at all, and for what it's worth, I know you'll be fine. You're good at this. Just don't push too hard. Know when to quit."

"Quit?" Anna cocked her head to the side. "What are you talking about? Did you ever quit anything?"

"You can't push the men too hard, Anna. At some point, every man needs to decide what's best for him."

"Meaning?" Anna asked. Hunt could see she was getting angry. Like last night. Now he remembered why they had quarreled. The last thing he wanted before boarding his flight was to leave Anna angry. He chose his next words carefully.

"What I'm trying to say is that this isn't a game, Anna," Hunt warned her.

"Don't you think I know that?"

Hunt raised a hand in surrender. "I know you do. I'm sorry," he said, pulling a small piece of paper from his pants pocket. He gave it to Anna.

"What's that?"

"My Iridium satellite phone number. With this you'll be able to reach me anywhere, anytime."

She pocketed the number. "I'll see you when you return. Then we'll talk. About us."

"I'd like that very much," he said, smiling. He liked the sound of *us*.

What he couldn't know, though, was that Anna would be soon fighting for her life.

CHAPTER FIVE

Five miles west of Miles City
Alligator Alley, Florida

Alejandro Mayo had both his hands resting on the steering wheel, his fingers tapping lightly to the upbeat song playing on the radio.

"Where is she?" he asked his brother, who was seated in the passenger seat of the Audi S7.

Santiago didn't seem to mind that Alejandro had asked him the very same question less than thirty seconds ago. His eyes were glued to his phone's screen, blindingly bright in the dark car. Santiago replied, "She's two miles in front of us and about six miles west of Miles City. She's almost there."

At last.

Alejandro turned down the volume of the radio and focused on the job at hand. They'd been on the road for a little more than two and a half hours, departing Tampa just before sunset. The little shopping spree Anna was currently on had taken him by surprise. Didn't she have things to do in Miami? In Alejandro's opinion, if it wasn't for Mauricio Tasis's support, there was no way Anna could have lasted so long as the head of the crime family. It wasn't a secret that Anna hadn't really been involved in the organization prior to the kidnapping of Sophia. In Alejandro's mind, Anna's only role had been to let Pierce Hunt in.

That dumb bitch! Her brother, Tony, had been killed five months ago, and since then, the whole organization had been in a virtual free fall. Her stubborn insistence on transitioning the family into something it was never meant to be was putting them all at risk. Sensing weakness, rival criminal organizations were trolling around, ready to pounce at the first slipup. It was getting harder by the day to maintain the facade of invulnerability. That was why he had joined forces with the Venezuelans. They understood the business. She didn't.

It was up to Alejandro to show real leadership. And he was about to.

During the night, while her Range Rover was parked outside her hotel, Alejandro had placed two small explosive charges near the front of the SUV. Just enough to blow holes in the run-flat tires. He didn't want to kill Anna, not yet anyway. First, he needed her to reveal the passwords of the accounts in which she was keeping the organization's money hostage. Alejandro had money of his own—quite a lot, actually—but he needed more if he was to take full control.

He suspected that Tasis might know the passwords, too, since he'd been indispensable to Anna's father, Vicente, and Tony. But the chances that Tasis would betray Anna while she was still alive were slim to none. If Alejandro went to Tasis with the deed already done, though, he had a feeling Tasis would join him . . . and so would all the men loyal to Tasis. Alejandro just needed to play his cards well.

Seeing that his brother was already on the phone with their crew, he asked, "Are they ready?"

Santiago smiled. "We all are."

Alejandro reached across Santiago, opened the glove compartment, and grabbed a shiny silver object that looked like a small television remote. There were two round blue buttons in the center. Directly above the buttons were two indicator lights. One was green; the other was red. The green light was glowing, indicating that the explosive devices on the Range Rover were armed. His thumb hovered above the red button.

"Let's get this over with," Alejandro said, jamming the button hard.

The green light of the remote detonator went off. The red light ignited.

———

Anna couldn't remember the last time she'd taken a real vacation. The idea of getting away with Hunt to a deserted island somewhere in the South Pacific was enticing. Not for the first time today, she thought about his physical reaction back at the airport and smiled. Clearly, that was something he desired too. A strange fluttering started up inside her. She was getting addicted to Pierce Hunt. She'd have to tread carefully with him. She had been hurt before.

Isn't it a bit late to wonder about that? You're already committed.

They had shared so much in the last five months that it would be impossible to distance herself from him. Truth was, she didn't want to. She was at her best when he was around. He was the only man with whom she felt she could truly be herself. With Hunt, there was no need to play the role of the tough crime-boss lady. It was like unfastening a belt that was too tight. With him, she could breathe normally.

After their goodbyes at the airport, Anna had decided to linger a bit in Saint Petersburg before heading home. Tasis was more than capable of handling things back in Miami. For the space of an afternoon, she wanted to be free to do as she pleased. She had a lovely lunch, then spent the next two hours zigzagging around Beach Drive, checking out the little shops and art galleries. She'd felt relaxed for the first time in weeks.

Suddenly, cold reality flooded over her. Hunt was gone. Moreover, she had a business to run. She couldn't afford to be distracted.

Not yet.

She pushed away the last images of deserted islands and white sandy beaches. Outside, the Range Rover's headlights picked up a traffic sign indicating that the junction with Florida State Road 29 was five miles away. In two hours she'd be in Miami, where a myriad of problems was begging for her attention.

A loud pop and a sharp, involuntary jerk of the steering wheel made her gasp.

What the hell?

At sixty miles an hour, the SUV might as well have been on ice. Anna wrestled with the steering wheel, but to no avail. The Range Rover swerved violently to the right, then to the left. She tried to recover, but she overcorrected, spinning the SUV out of control. The Range Rover made a complete revolution and skidded off the road, slamming into the ditch sideways with a sickening thud.

———

Alejandro had just given the go-ahead to his men when his vehicle's Bluetooth displayed an incoming call.

What now? He had gone over the plan three times with them. There had been no questions. It wasn't a difficult plan to execute, was it? He released an irritated sigh and pressed the call button on his steering wheel. "What do you want?"

The voice on the other end didn't belong to one of his men.

"What are you doing, Alejandro?" the caller asked, his voice laced with anger. "Anna Garcia isn't to be touched. Wasn't I clear enough?"

Shit! Jorge Ramirez. Ramirez was his main contact with the Venezuelans. He was a broker of some sort, but Alejandro had the impression the man wielded considerable power in Caracas.

"What are you talking about? I—"

"Don't play this game with me," Ramirez hissed. "Whatever you're doing, it stops now. Understood?"

"It's too late," Alejandro barked back. "I've already—"

"Then we're done," Ramirez said. "Goodbye, Alejandro."

Hijo de puta! As General Peraza's envoy, Ramirez wasn't a man to be trifled with. People who crossed General Peraza the wrong way had a tendency to disappear.

"Wait!" Alejandro shouted.

"Yes?"

"Very well, I'll do as you say," he said, flushing with anger and embarrassment. "I thought you'd be pleased if I—"

"Leave the thinking to me," Ramirez said. "No more transgressions."

Alejandro swallowed his pride and said, "No more transgressions."

"I'm glad to hear that," Ramirez replied before severing the connection.

So close. He'd been so damn close. Why did Ramirez, or whoever was pulling *his* chain, want to keep Anna Garcia alive? She was the weak link. Why couldn't Ramirez see that? In order for the Mayo cartel to rise and eclipse the Garcia name, the traitorous bitch had to go.

Permanently.

The problem was that without Ramirez's support, Alejandro's scheme wouldn't work. The Garcia crime family was too fragile to climb back to the top on its own. Thanks to Anna's decisions, most of the family's South American distributors had already found new partners to move their product along the East Coast.

Without the Venezuelans, there'd be no crime family for Alejandro to take over. He would bow to his new master's wish.

For now.

———

Anna was jarred forward abruptly. Then the airbags deployed, shoving her back against her seat and momentarily depriving her of oxygen. Pain radiated through her face and chest. She was conscious of a searing pain where her seat belt cut across her chest. Her heart was hammering; her mouth was dry. She felt sick. She batted the airbag away.

To her left, two dark vans screeched to a halt. The rear doors of the vans flew open, and several masked men jumped out and ran toward the Range Rover. They were all armed.

And then she understood. They were coming for her. This wasn't an accident.

Her mind raced ahead, trying to think of a way out of this. She reached into the glove compartment, fumbling for the pistol Hunt had insisted she keep there. She glanced left, and for a moment she was blinded by panic. The men had already reached her SUV.

She screamed. Her fingers touched something cylindrical, metallic—the barrel of her pistol. She grabbed it and jerked it free from the glove compartment just as one of the men wrenched open the door. As the interior light of the Range Rover blinked on, Anna screamed with a renewed intensity. A fist slammed into her face, splitting her lip, making her drop the pistol. She hurled herself toward the passenger seat, but it was too late. The man grabbed her by the hair and began hauling her out of the vehicle.

Anna's hand found the pistol, which had fallen on the floor beneath the steering wheel. She didn't hesitate. Grabbing it by the barrel, she swung the pistol toward the man's head. The butt caught him just below his left eye. His head snapped sideways. He growled. He tried to grab her arm, but she tore it free.

"You fuckin'—"

She hit him again, driving the butt of her pistol into the side of his head. The man fell. Onto his knees at first, and then all the way, tumbling to his side.

"Back off!" she howled to the other masked men surrounding her, her cheeks wet with tears. She swung her pistol back and forth. "I'll kill you all!"

She was hysterical now, unhinged. She knew she couldn't shoot them all. She didn't care.

But to her utmost surprise, instead of opening fire, the men began retreating. One of the masked attackers approached her, his gun hand lowered to his side, his other hand held high.

"We're taking him," he said.

Her pulse skyrocketed. She had heard this voice before.

"Who are you?" she screamed. "Who the fuck are you?"

The man didn't respond. Instead, he grabbed his fallen comrade under the armpits and dragged him back to one of the vans. The rest of the men climbed inside the vans and left.

Anna was overcome with dizziness, her head spinning so badly that she fell to her knees right outside the damaged Range Rover. Then she threw up.

CHAPTER SIX

The Triple Frontier
Paraguay

Hunt's lungs were burning. The humidity in Paraguay was crushing.
The pack on his back was soaked from the sweat that rolled down his
spine under his shirt. His feet throbbed and burned from the nonstop trek across the punitive terrain. He wished they could have driven
the four-wheel-drive SUV a bit closer to the objective, but the early-
morning downpour had transformed the steep stretches of unpaved
roads between Ciudad del Este and their objective into hilly mud baths.
Three times they had to climb out of the SUV to winch it free from
the axle-deep mud bogging it down. At some point, the road conditions had deteriorated so much that their team leader—CIA senior
case officer Ivanka, the woman with whom he'd crossed paths in New
Orleans—had pulled over to the side and cut the engine. So far, Hunt
had been impressed at her operational skills, especially for a case officer:
this wasn't her first rodeo.

"We're six miles out," she'd said. "We'll do the rest on foot."

Logistical support for the covert operation was minimal. There was
a safe house in Ciudad del Este and a couple of vehicles parked strate-
gically to facilitate their exfil, but that was pretty much it. Hunt kind
of liked it. There were no higher-ups whispering commands in his ears

or second-guessing his every decision. Hunt, Ivanka, and the two CIA paramilitary operations officers were on their own.

But flying solo without oversight and operational support had its downfalls too. They were now twenty-four hours behind schedule because their first SUV had been stolen while parked on the street.

Hunt, tasked with purchasing a new vehicle, had walked two miles to a used car lot. The salesman on duty, an emphatic and doubtless trustworthy soul with slicked-back hair and a thick mustache, had laughed at him when Hunt had inquired about import papers and a bill of sale for the Chevrolet Spin he was looking at.

"It has air-conditioning, stereo, and even a first aid kit," the salesman had said. "No extra charge for the first aid kit. Five thousand US dollars for the keys."

This being his first mission with the three CIA officers, Hunt knew them only by their call signs. The leader, Ivanka, was Ms. Red, her second-in-command was Mr. Brown, and the junior man was Mr. White. Hunt was Mr. Green. Hunt was convinced that Mr. Brown and Mr. White were both members of the Special Activities Division. By the way these two guys operated in the jungle, Hunt wouldn't be surprised if they had gone through Ranger School, just like he had done nearly two decades ago.

Rangers, lead the way!

While there were many triple borders in the world, this one was different. This particular border between Paraguay, Argentina, and Brazil was formed naturally by the convergence of the Paraná River and the Iguazu River. Despite the small number of people calling the tri-border area home, the region was notorious for narcotics, weapons smuggling, and clandestine meetings. The DEA had long ago lost its appetite for working in the region due to the high level of police corruption. If something went wrong here, Hunt knew he'd be on his own.

As good as the CIA officers were, he also didn't trust them entirely. He felt like a third wheel rather than part of the crew. He didn't blame them. The three CIA officers had probably operated together in some capacity for years, and it was normal that they saw him as an outsider. But there was something else. Something deeper. He couldn't quite put his finger on it yet, but the feeling kept him on his toes, even now, in the jungle.

Their objective, based on the intel provided by Pascual Andrade, was the Mbaracayú Lodge, a small family-run hotel located at the entrance of Mbaracayú Forest Nature Reserve, a thirty-minute drive from the closest town. The hotel consisted of a medium-size reception building and several fairly well-maintained annex buildings. The intel hadn't specified if the bad guys had rented the whole lodge or just one of the buildings, though Hunt was confident there would be no other guests staying at the property. Cartel members and corrupt government agents weren't known to enjoy the company of witnesses when conducting their business.

The initial plan had called for twenty-four to thirty-six hours of surveillance prior to hitting the lodge. The holdup with the stolen vehicle had denied them their reconnaissance time. Ms. Red had asked the rest of the team their opinion about whether they should go ahead with the raid. They had all agreed to continue, which had been a relief for Hunt. He'd been after these Black Tosca cartel bastards relentlessly for months. Now that he was so close to getting payback, he didn't want them to disappear.

A few feet in front of Hunt, Ms. Red signaled a halt. They all gathered around her.

"We're less than a quarter mile from the objective," she whispered, reaching for her water canteen. "Let's take two minutes to hydrate and to check our gear. This is our rally point."

Hunt gently dropped his rucksack from his back. The relief to his shoulders was immediate. To know that some of the people responsible for his daughter's abduction were nearby played with his psyche.

What would have happened if he had not intervened in San Miguel de Allende?

Leila and Sophia would have been shipped God knows where to do unspeakable acts for despicable men.

A shiver ran along his spine at the thought. Hunt shook his head to clear the images out. He closed his eyes and took a deep breath. He held it for as long as he could, exhaled slowly, then repeated the process three more times. A sensation of calm energy and strength filled him. Hunt felt more alert, not only to his surroundings but also to himself and his body.

"Mr. Green, you ready?" Ms. Red asked, a touch of wary concern in her eyes.

"All set," Hunt replied.

Ms. Red kept her eyes on him for a few seconds, then said, "We'll proceed with a quick recce of the objective. Chances are that our marks are already there. Mr. White, you go first. Mr. Brown, you're next. Mr. Green, you're last—you leave two minutes after White. Back here in twenty. All copy?"

They confirmed that their watches were synchronized. Hunt approved of the decision to run a quick recon prior to moving ahead with the actual raid. Sure, the recon would eat some precious time, but it was better than walking into an ambush. Mr. White and Hunt would surveil the left side of the hotel property. Mr. White would cover the six to ten o'clock area, while Hunt would check out the ten to two o'clock. Mr. Brown, who would cut to the right of the property, would cover the two to six o'clock position.

Once Mr. White and Mr. Brown had disappeared into the thick jungle, Ms. Red grabbed Hunt's arm.

"I know what these assholes did to you and your family," she said. "But I need you to stay focused."

Hunt didn't bother asking her how she knew about his link with the Black Tosca's cartel. But it made him angry that she would challenge his readiness. Hunt was about to reply but bit his tongue at the last second. Ms. Red, as the team leader, was only doing her job.

"Roger that."

"One more thing," she added. "If someone shouts the phrase *Queen Bee*, you don't shoot. Got it?"

Did the CIA have an asset close by? More importantly, why was he learning of this only now? Hunt didn't like it one bit. Clearly, he wasn't the only one with a trust issue. But now wasn't the time to make a scene.

"Queen Bee. Got it."

"See you in eighteen minutes," Ms. Red said.

CHAPTER SEVEN

The Mbaracayú Lodge
Paraguay

Jorge Ramirez looked at the five men seated in front of him. They bored him. He was done listening to them. It had been a mistake to accept their invitation. They had nothing new to bring to the table. General Peraza had thought it was worth a shot, but he had been mistaken. With the untimely deaths of its gutsy—some would say crazy—leader, Valentina Mieles, and her cousin Hector, the Black Tosca's cartel had essentially been reduced to a toothless bulldog that could bark but couldn't bite.

What little the men from the cartel had to offer, Ramirez didn't need. He would have to go to plan B.

He sighed. Plan B meant his associates would need to stay in Afghanistan a little while longer since the Black Tosca cartel couldn't guarantee their safety in Mexico.

Afghanistan. A country he disliked, but a country he understood better than most people. It was easy for the West to think of Afghanistan in the one-dimensional terms portrayed by the mass media. Many saw Afghanistan as a land populated entirely by fundamentalist tribesmen who were bearded, turbaned, and armed. Such superficial images clouded the truth. Afghanistan was a complex land with a rich history. And in Ramirez's mind, the major powers bore a responsibility for its problems—especially the United States and the former Soviet Union.

When the Soviet Union fell apart and the Cold War came to its conclusion, the United States shifted its attention to other regions, leaving the habitants of one of the world's poorest countries to suffer in silence, its economy completely torn apart by the war the two superpowers had waged within its borders. It was hard for Ramirez not to see a similarity between Afghanistan and Venezuela. If things didn't change soon in Venezuela, the country would fall apart.

Some pseudoexperts thought it was already too late. But they didn't know what Ramirez knew. General Peraza's plan could save his nation. Operation Butterfly could work. The ball was already rolling; Ramirez just needed a bit more time to bring the general's plan to fruition.

As the men around the table droned on, he stifled the urge to sigh again. The Black Tosca's cartel had nothing to offer, but at least the deal he had struck with the Garcia crime family was solid. Their distribution network along the East Coast of the United States was exactly what Ramirez needed. But he'd have to keep an eye on Alejandro Mayo. The man was ambitious. Maybe a little too ambitious.

A young woman wearing a school uniform—she couldn't be older than fifteen or sixteen—walked into the room carrying a coffeepot. As she poured coffee into the men's mugs, Ramirez could see she was nervous, her hands shaking. He could only guess that she wasn't used to seeing men with guns standing guard on the hotel's terrace. Poor girl. She wouldn't enjoy the next few minutes.

"So what do you think of our proposal?" asked the group's leader once the young woman had left the room. The older man had a dark complexion, broad lips, and a crown of white hair around his head. In his younger years he would have been a confident man, someone not to mess around with, but now, he was just old.

"I don't think it's gonna work out," Ramirez said truthfully. He could see from the man's body language this wasn't the answer he had expected, but Ramirez didn't see any reason why he should lie to him.

They would all be dead very soon. Ramirez closed his laptop and stood up, his chair scraping across the floor.

"Where are you going?" the older man snapped. "We're not—"

With astonishing speed, Ramirez drew his pistol and shot the older man once in the head. Before anyone could react, Ramirez aimed at the two Black Tosca bodyguards, both standing in the same corner, arms crossed against their chests.

Bad form. Unprofessional, Ramirez thought as he squeezed the trigger four times, double-tapping both men's center mass. They weren't on the ground yet when another cartel member rushed into the room, weapon drawn. Ramirez dropped to his knees, angled his body to his right, and pulled the trigger again. The man, hit once in the forehead, fell face-first, his pistol sliding under the conference table where the remaining four cartel members were still seated. They all had the same look of horror and disbelief etched on their faces.

Ramirez knew there were four more cartel bodyguards patrolling the outside perimeter of the building. The sound of AK-103s told him the mercenaries he had hired were earning their pay. Seconds later, it was over.

"Please—" one of the remaining men started before Ramirez pumped two rounds into his chest.

"C'mon, nobody's going for the gun?" Ramirez asked, his eyes on the pistol under the table. Maybe if they had armed themselves, the outcome would have been different, but Ramirez doubted it. Their arrogance and condescension toward the people who actually did their dirty work was now biting them in the ass. Their pampered and privileged lives had made them forget what it was like to be outside their walled compounds and armored SUVs. Ramirez didn't make those kinds of mistakes.

The three cartel members realized the trouble they were in, and their eyes were now filled with pure hatred. They knew that nothing they could say would matter. They were going to die today.

Ramirez was about to execute them when he heard a high-pitched scream.

CHAPTER EIGHT

The Mbaracayú Lodge
Paraguay

Hunt walked slowly through the jungle weeds, cocking his head to catch the slightest sound that would betray the presence of an enemy ambush or patrol. The soft mud and jungle litter squirmed under his combat boots, slowing his progress even more. Moving silently through the spongy jungle floor wasn't easy, and it was time consuming, but damn if he didn't love every minute of it. As a former Army Ranger, Hunt was in his element. All his senses were alive, sharpened by the danger around him. To his right, he saw the trail Mr. White had used to get to his position. It took Hunt another seven minutes to reach his position at the edge of the tree line that ran parallel to the complex. From there, he could see the main building and two armed sentries patrolling the rear of the annex building. Six dark SUVs were parked next to the main building, though Hunt couldn't be sure what color they were since they were covered with mud.

He'd been in position for less than ten seconds when he heard the first gunshot. It was quickly followed by five more, four of them in quick succession.

Shit! Where is the fire coming from? Hunt's first thought was that a member of his team had been spotted. He trained his suppressed M4 on the closest of the two sentries and flipped off its safety, his fingers moving to the trigger. His target was about 150 feet away. Then, startling Hunt, one of the sentries fired a three-round burst into the other sentry's torso.

What the hell?

Three more bursts were fired, but Hunt couldn't see where they had come from.

"Brown, this is Red, sitrep, over." The team leader's voice came through Hunt's earpiece.

"This is Brown. I just saw two guards shooting at two other guards," Mr. Brown replied, sounding confused. "Both are down. Not sure what's going on."

"Red, this is Green," Hunt said. "Just saw the same thing. One guard down at the twelve o'clock position. Shot by another guard."

"Roger that," Red said. "White, anything on your side?"

"Red, this is White. I got one guard down too. Same scenario."

The rear door of the main building burst open, and a young man wearing a school uniform rushed out. The sentry, caught by surprise, swung his rifle in his direction.

Hunt didn't hesitate, did not waste a single brain cell pondering what would happen next. An innocent young man—about the same age as his daughter—was about to get slaughtered right in front of him. Whatever the cost, he wasn't going to allow that to happen.

He pulled the trigger. A metallic cough echoed. His 5.56 round hit the sentry in the right eyeball, blowing the contents of his skull across the outside wall of the building behind him.

The young man, oblivious to what had just happened, continued to run away from the building.

"Red, this is Green. I just took out the sentry at the twelve o'clock position. Rear door of the building is open."

The response was immediate. "Copy that, Green."

"Red, this is White. The three remaining sentries are entering the main building using the front door."

"Red, copy."

"Red, this is Green. There are no windows at the back of the building. This could be our entry point," Hunt offered.

This time it took a moment for Ms. Red to reply, but once she did, her voice was decisive and commanding. "All call signs, this is Red. Regroup at Green's position, and begin the assault. I'll stay in reserve and cover the exit road."

A bunch of acknowledgments followed. Then Hunt heard a scream coming from the open door of the main building. A scream so high, so piercing, that it could have come only from a child. The sound chilled Hunt's soul. His heart thundered in his chest as images of his daughter flashed in his mind.

This could have been Leila's fate.

Hunt couldn't wait any longer. He had to break cover. His professional training told him to wait for the rest of the team, but his inner voice—the one he had always associated with Leila—told him that the person screaming inside the building couldn't afford for him to wait any longer.

"Red, this is Green. I'm moving in."

"Negative, Green. Stay in position. I repeat, stay in your position."

But Hunt was already on the move, the butt of his M4 locked into his shoulder. Hunt moved swiftly across the deadly open ground. He was fifty feet away from the building when a tall bearded man carrying a rifle appeared in the doorway. The man's eyes met Hunt's just as he was about to pull the door closed. For a split second the man paused, a look of confusion crossing his face. His slight hesitation was enough for Hunt. He squeezed the trigger twice. The rounds hit the man, propelling him back inside the building. The man's index finger compressed, squeezing the trigger and letting loose a three-round burst.

Hunt quickened his pace, knowing he had just lost his biggest advantage. Surprise.

———

One of his mercenaries dragged the young woman who had just poured them coffee into the room, and for a moment, Ramirez lost his concentration. The mercenary grabbed her by her hair and shoved her to the ground, her head bouncing off the tiled floor.

"What are you doing?" Ramirez growled. His eyes moved to the girl. She had stopped screaming and lay half on her side, curled up with one arm outstretched toward the door.

Movement to his left caught his eyes.

The gun. One of the three cartel members was under the table, reaching for the gun that had slid beneath it. Another man had lunged over the table and was already halfway across when Ramirez fired. He hit the man in the head, but his body had too much momentum and crashed into Ramirez, slamming him into the wall behind him.

Then a shot rang out, and another. Ramirez saw the mercenary take a few steps back. Ramirez fired at the shooter under the table just as the mercenary raised his AK-103 and opened up on full automatic on the two remaining Black Tosca cartel members. Two seconds later, they were dead, but the young girl had started screaming again. The mercenary, hit twice in the chest, dropped his empty rifle and staggered a few steps until his shoulder came in contact with the wall. He drew his pistol, and Ramirez watched in astonishment when he aimed it at the child. Before the mercenary could pull the trigger, Ramirez shot him in the head just as the fourth mercenary entered the room. Seeing his dead comrade on the floor, he raised his rifle and aimed it directly at Ramirez.

"You wanna be dead, or you wanna get paid?" Ramirez asked.

The mercenary lowered his weapon. "I can't reach Javier on the radio," he said.

The echo of a three-round burst outside told Ramirez he wasn't out of the woods yet. With all the Black Tosca cartel members dead, who was his man outside shooting at? It could mean only one thing.

They weren't alone.

It didn't matter who was coming for him. He had to go. He looked at the young girl. She'd be all right. He inserted a fresh magazine into his pistol and pocketed the half-spent one.

"Lead the way," Ramirez said to the mercenary. "We're headed to the vehicles."

———

Hunt entered the building, sidestepping to his right as he crossed the threshold. Designed for the tropics, the building was open and airy, with high ceilings and open doorways. In front of him was a long corridor with rooms on both sides.

Damn!

Not exactly the kind of building Hunt wanted to clear by himself. Hopefully the rest of the team would be joining him momentarily. He stormed into the first room to his left, his M4 leading the way. It was the kitchen. He cleared the hard corner first, then swept his rifle from left to right, scanning for threats. With the exception of a coffeepot and a full tray of cheese and crackers, the kitchen was empty. He exited the kitchen as a single gunshot reverberated across the hallway. Hunt automatically took cover behind the doorframe. He thought the gunshot had come from one of the rooms at the opposite end of the hallway.

"Green, this is Brown. We heard another gunshot. I'm coming in with White by the same entry point you took. How copy?"

"Good copy, Brown. I'm in the first room to your left. It's the only room I've cleared."

"Roger that. We're three seconds out."

The girl's high-pitched screaming had resumed, and the blood in Hunt's veins ran cold. He cursed again. It went against all of his training to rush down a hallway without clearing every open room along the way. If it were Leila in that room screaming for her life, what would he expect a highly trained operator like himself to do?

Fuck it.

With the muzzle of his M4 up, Hunt stepped into the hallway just as a hail of bullets peppered the walls around him. Hunt retreated into the room.

"White's hit," Mr. Brown said. "Flesh wound to the left arm."

"Brown, this is Red. Copy that."

Someone was making a move. Hunt sneaked a peek into the hallway. A tall black man dressed in jeans and a T-shirt was walking down the corridor, followed by a medium-height Hispanic man dressed in a business suit. The tall man was aiming a rifle in Hunt's direction and fired a couple of three-round bursts that forced Hunt to scurry deeper into the room. A moment later he heard the muffled shots of an M4. Mr. Brown and Mr. White had finally joined the fight and were returning fire.

"Red, this is Brown. Another guard is down. One got away and might be heading out by the main entrance."

"Copy that, Red."

Hunt knew that Ms. Red had positioned herself to cover the only access road leading in and out of the Mbaracayú Lodge. Not only would this allow Ms. Red to warn them if any reinforcements were to arrive, but it would also allow her to thwart any attempt to escape. Hunt took another peek into the hallway. The man with the rifle was sprawled on the floor, arms flung out, half of his head blown off.

Hunt made eye contact with Brown, who nodded. Hunt took the lead down the corridor with the two CIA officers close behind him.

———

Ramirez saw the mercenary's head explode. Ramirez ran toward the main exit and pushed the doors open. He sprinted to his parked SUV, half expecting to be taken out by a sniper. Surely the attackers had left men around the perimeter. He was less than twenty feet away from his vehicle when he realized that he had left his laptop on the conference table. There was no way to retrieve it now. Fortunately, all his files were heavily encrypted, and he could erase the entire contents remotely once he was back in Venezuela. Worst-case scenario, after three failed log-in attempts, the security application would nuke all the data. Not great, but all in all, this was a manageable situation. Not one he needed to share with General Peraza.

He opened the door of the SUV, slid behind the wheel, and started the engine. He placed his pistol on his lap, making it easily accessible. Ramirez gunned the engine, and the SUV leaped to life. He accelerated quickly down the path running toward a dirt road, the only way out of the site.

He was a quarter mile away from the main building when he heard a loud pop. For a fraction of a second, Ramirez wondered what it was. Then he heard another one and saw two holes in his windshield, each with a dozen cracks spidering outward.

Sniper. If Ramirez had had a passenger, he'd be dead.

Another pop. This time the headrest of the front passenger seat burst apart. Ramirez had no idea of the shooter's location, but the sniper's message was clear: *Stop the vehicle, or you're dead.* Ramirez brought the SUV to a stop and raised his hands so they were visible through the windshield.

Something moved in the tree line to his right. Someone dressed in jungle fatigues and body armor came out, an M4 aimed in Ramirez's direction. By the way the sniper moved, Ramirez knew he was dealing with a combat-hardened warrior. *American? British?* As the figure moved in closer, Ramirez cocked his head. The sniper was a woman.

"Keep your hands up!" the woman shouted in Spanish once she was about thirty feet from the SUV.

Ramirez obeyed.

"Keep your left hand in the air. With your right hand, turn off the engine," the sniper said once she had almost reached the SUV.

The woman's Spanish was excellent, but no amount of foreign language training hours could completely make her American accent disappear. Instead of turning off the engine, Ramirez lowered his window.

The sniper sent two quick rounds through the windshield, the rounds zipping past mere inches from Ramirez's right ear.

"Turn off the engine!" the sniper yelled. "Now!"

"Don't shoot," Ramirez said in English. "I'm American. I'm Queen Bee."

The woman nodded but didn't lower her weapon. Ramirez hadn't expected her to. There was protocol to follow. But he had been right: the assaulters were Americans. They were CIA.

"Show me your left hand, and cut the damn engine," the sniper said. "One false move and the next one goes through your brain."

Ramirez nodded. He slowly lowered his right hand, but instead of reaching for the ignition, he wrapped his fingers around the butt of his pistol. It would be an impossible shot. The woman was standing next to the front left tire of the SUV. In order to make the shot, Ramirez would have to bring his arm up above the steering wheel, angle his body, and shoot through the already-cracked windshield. That wasn't going to work. He let go of his pistol and turned off the engine.

"Now open the door, and get out of the truck."

Ramirez slowly opened the door with his left hand, once again holding his pistol in the right one. He placed his left foot on the ground. Then his right. Then he made his move.

Action is faster than reaction.

Ramirez dived to his left and fired four times before his left shoulder hit the ground, feeling something bite into his right leg as he fell. White-hot pain shot through his leg. Gritting his teeth, he pushed the pain aside and got to one knee, aiming his pistol at the sniper. The woman was on her back, groaning in pain while trying to propel herself backward with her legs. Upon seeing Ramirez, she tried to grab her pistol from its holstered position on her chest rig. Ramirez shook his head.

"You're done," he said. "Don't fight it. Say a prayer."

But the woman didn't quit. Finally, she managed to get her pistol out.

Ramirez shot her in the head.

With a sigh, he limped back into the SUV, started the engine, and drove off.

CHAPTER NINE

The Mbaracayú Lodge
Paraguay

Hunt and the two CIA paramilitary officers cleared the rest of the building in less than three minutes. Midway through, they received a brief communication from Ms. Red letting them know she had intercepted a vehicle with a single male occupant. Once the building was secured, Mr. Brown tried to contact Ms. Red to give her a situation report, but the team leader didn't reply.

With the exception of two scared young women hidden in a broom closet, they didn't find anyone else inside the building until they reached the small conference room at the other end of the corridor. That room was filled with dead bodies.

And a young woman.

She looked to be about sixteen and was curled up in a ball on the floor, rocking back and forth in fear, her school uniform and face covered in blood. Hunt knelt next to her.

"Are you injured?" he asked in Spanish, trying to make his voice as gentle as possible.

The girl looked up, her swollen eyes holding a hollow, haunted look that told Hunt she had seen too much. "Please don't kill me."

Hunt was taken aback by her fear but then realized how he must look dressed in dirty jungle fatigues and his face covered with camouflage paint. He'd be afraid, too, if he were a fifteen- or sixteen-year-old boy who had just witnessed a multitude of murders.

"Hey, it's okay. Don't be scared. I'm not gonna hurt you."

Big tears started to roll down her cheeks. "He saved my life," she said in a broken, shaky voice.

"Oh yeah? Who's that? Who saved your life?"

The girl used the sleeve of her blouse to wipe her face, her body still quivering.

"He's . . . he's gone now. He shot that man," she said, her eyes moving toward the body of one of the dead men. "He shot that man when he tried to kill me with his gun."

Hunt turned to look. He had trouble imagining what had caused the carnage in this room. Clearly two opposing factions had met. The Venezuelans on one side, the Black Tosca cartel members on the other. Hunt had seen two men trying to make their escape. The driver Ms. Red had intercepted would know what had transpired here. They needed to talk with him.

"Green," Mr. Brown said. "I still can't reach Red. Give it a try on the alternate frequency."

Hunt did. No response.

"Nothing," he said to Mr. Brown.

"All right," Mr. Brown said, a concerned look on his face. "White, check their clothes for cell phones or other intel. Green, take pictures of all these assholes, and see if you can identify who's who. I'll make my way back to the rally point and try to reestablish our comms with Ms. Red. Let's meet there in ten minutes."

"What do we do with her?" Hunt asked.

"What do you mean?" Mr. Brown replied.

"We can't leave her and the two other girls here," Hunt said, growing impatient. "There might be other cartel members on their way here as we speak."

"They aren't the mission, Green," Mr. Brown said, exiting the room. "You can't save them all."

Asshole.

Mission or not, there was no way Hunt would leave these three girls behind.

He patted the girl on the shoulder, reassured her that she should wait and he'd help her get to safety, and then spent the next minute taking pictures of the dead men while Mr. White busied himself searching them. Hunt recognized five of the men, all high-ranking members of the Black Tosca cartel. A strange sensation of peace washed over him. With the deaths of these five men, the organization that had nearly killed his daughter was no more. Almost their entire leadership was dead. It was possible midlevel players would attempt to take over, but the knowledge and contacts these five men had were irreplaceable.

Hunt couldn't identify the rest of the men, but the minute he had access to a secure link to the DEA, he would send their pictures to Tom Hauer. With the help of facial-recognition software linked to the DEA's database, the dead men would be quickly identified.

In Hunt's book, this mission was a success.

"You ready?" he asked Mr. White, who was perched over a laptop.

"Yep. Let's go, and I'm taking this with me." The CIA paramilitary officer closed the laptop and tucked it under his chest rig.

Hunt turned toward the exit, and his heart jumped when he realized the girl was gone. She must have taken advantage of his distraction to get away. He quickly exited the room and ran to the other room where they had found the two other girls hidden in the broom closet. They were gone too.

Damn it!

"This is Green. The girls are gone," Hunt said over the radio.

Where were they? Why had they left? *Because they don't know you. They don't trust you.* How could he blame them? He hadn't really given them a chance, had he?

"Copy that," Mr. Brown replied. "This is a family-run hotel. There's a house three-quarters of a mile due east, accessible by a small pathway. The girls' parents probably live there."

Hunt breathed a sigh of relief. The young man he'd seen bursting out of the back door earlier had been running that way.

"White, Green, this is Brown."

"Go for Green."

"Forget the rally point. Grab the keys for a vehicle, and make your way along the dirt road."

"Copy that, Brown," Mr. White said, brandishing a pair of keys as he walked past Hunt. "Found them in one of the dead men's pockets."

Outside, Hunt covered Mr. White as the CIA man sprinted to a parked Mercedes ML he had remotely unlocked. Once Mr. White had the engine running, Hunt joined him and took a seat in the front passenger seat.

"Brown, this is Green. What's your location?"

"Green from Brown. Just follow the dirt road. You'll see me soon enough."

Hunt got the feeling something was wrong, but he kept his mouth shut. A minute later, his intuition was proved right. Mr. Brown, standing in the middle of the empty road, gestured them to stop the vehicle. Hunt climbed out of the Mercedes SUV and jogged to where Mr. Brown was standing. His breath caught in his throat at the sight on the ground. Ms. Red was sprawled on her back, one of her legs folded under her. Multiple gunshot wounds were visible, one of them in her forehead. Her M4 lay a few feet in front of her, but her right hand was still grasping the butt of her pistol.

"Maybe the shooter is still around," Mr. White said, joining them. He trained his rifle around the edge of the jungle.

Hunt shook his head. "He's long gone," he said. "When we left the main building, there was one less vehicle than when we came in."

They loaded the body of Ms. Red into the back of the SUV. As they drove back to their safe house in Ciudad del Este, Hunt couldn't help but think about the traumatized girl they'd found in the conference room. Why would someone willing to kill to save a teenager execute Ms. Red? From what Hunt had been able to deduce from his time with Ms. Red, she had been a fine operator. Whoever had killed her was no average mercenary. Maybe she'd been tricked.

Hunt looked out the car window. The sun had risen over a dark bank of clouds that stretched across the eastern sky. The pleasant scenery stood in sharp contrast to the bleak ambience inside the SUV, where each man was lost in his own thoughts. Mr. White and Mr. Brown had just lost a colleague in combat. Hunt knew the feeling. Coming face to face with your own mortality wasn't fun. Hunt thought back to what Ms. Red had told him at the ORP.

If someone shouts the phrase Queen Bee, *you don't shoot,* she had said. Hunt hadn't come in contact with anyone claiming to be Queen Bee. Had Red? Could the person who had escaped be Queen Bee? Was one of the dead men Queen Bee?

"Who's Queen Bee?" Hunt asked.

Mr. White, who was applying a layer of antibiotic ointment on his arm injury, replied, "No clue. I don't think Red knew either. We were told not to shoot anyone claiming to be Queen Bee."

"You were told by whom?" Hunt asked.

"Dorothy Triggs."

"For God's sake, White. What the hell's wrong with you?" Mr. Brown growled. He turned his attention to Hunt. "Forget what he just said."

Hunt nodded. "Yeah. No worries."

Dorothy Triggs. The deputy director of the Directorate of Operations, the clandestine arm of the Central Intelligence Agency. Hunt had never met her, but he knew her reputation. A real hard-ass who had her fingers in most covert operations the United States undertook.

"Can I have a look at the laptop you seized?" Hunt asked.

"Why?" Mr. Brown asked. "You're here because of the Black Tosca angle. Whatever's on that laptop is our property now. It doesn't belong to you or the DEA. Capisce?"

Hunt wasn't happy about it, but the CIA man was right. With the deaths of the Black Tosca cartel members, his job here in Paraguay was done. He could finally go back home to his daughter, and he'd even be on time to catch Jack's football game. Queen Bee and Dorothy Triggs weren't his concerns.

Still, Hunt couldn't shake the feeling that he was letting something very, very important slip away.

CHAPTER TEN

La Gorce Island
Miami, Florida

Hunt stopped his Ford F-150 next to the security guard manning the main entrance of the gated community where Jasmine and Chris Moon's opulent residence was located. He lowered his window.

"Hey, Mr. Hunt," the guard said, approaching Hunt's pickup. "Nice to see you."

"Could you do me a favor?"

The guard straightened his back. "Of course. Anything, Mr. Hunt."

"I'm here to pick up my daughter," Hunt said. "I'm a day early, and I'd love to surprise her. You think you can let me in without calling it in?"

The guard gave him a knowing smile. "You got it."

Though Hunt had been to the house many times, he still wasn't immune to the sheer beauty of La Gorce Island. A private residential gated community along the shores of Biscayne Bay, La Gorce Island consisted of only fifty-nine custom luxury homes, most of them on the waterfront. Just last month, Jasmine had told him one of the neighboring houses had sold for $45 million, a far cry from Hunt's $2,000-per-month apartment.

As Hunt drove his Ford into the circular driveway, he wondered how Leila would react to seeing him a day early. He parked his F-150 next to Moon's Maserati Quattroporte and climbed out. As he closed the door behind him, Hunt caught sight of his reflection. He didn't like what he saw. Bleary blue eyes stared back at him, along with an unkempt beard and dark brown hair that needed a trim. He looked like a bad advertisement for an adventure magazine. He hadn't gotten much sleep on the flight back to Florida.

"Daddy?"

Hunt turned. His daughter was standing at the front door. Leila surprised him by taking the stairs two at a time and running straight into his arms. He wrapped his arms around her and pressed her against his chest.

"Didn't I promise you I'd be back in time for the game?"

She grinned. "Thank you for keeping your promise, Dad."

"So what are you guys up to this evening?" Hunt asked, leaning back.

"We were about to head out to Fort Lauderdale to pick up Jack for dinner," she said as Moon walked out the front door.

"How are you, Pierce?" he asked as the men shook hands.

"I'm just glad to be here, to tell you the truth."

"Listen," Moon said, "Jasmine's out grocery shopping, and Leila and I were about to get on our way to pick up Jack. Why don't you go with her instead? I have a few things I need to do here at the house. You'd do me a favor."

Hunt appreciated the gesture. Moon was a terrific guy. "Would it be okay if I bring her back after dinner?" he asked.

"Absolutely."

He turned to his daughter.

"Only if I can cook," Leila said.

"Where did you learn to cook?" Hunt asked.

"Food Network," she said, laughing.

"Seriously?" Hunt asked.

"That, and I started taking cooking lessons with Sophia," Leila said.

"Speaking of Sophia, would it be okay with you if I invited her and Anna over for dessert?"

Leila looped her arm through his. "It's a plan."

———

Hunt picked up the empty plates and carried them over to the sink. "I'll take care of the dishes. Go enjoy the outside."

"You sure?" Leila asked.

"Go before I change my mind and ask you to dry the dishes," he said with a smile.

He watched Jack stand and pull her chair out. Earlier, he'd eaten three helpings of Leila's chili and told her, "You cook like a goddess." His comment had made Leila's cheeks turn deep red. Any man who saw how special Leila was, was an okay guy in his book.

He had just finished cleaning the countertop when his phone chimed with an alert that Anna and Sophia had arrived. He unlocked the building's main entrance door by pressing a key on his phone. Two minutes later, there was a gentle knock on his door.

He opened the door, and there she was, the most beautiful woman he had ever laid his eyes on. Medium height with the build of a professional dancer, Anna had dark hair and emerald-green eyes set in the most perfect face he had ever seen. Her skin had a golden complexion that no amount of suntanning could match.

Anna jumped into his arms and held him tight. She gave him a light kiss on the lips. "I'm so pleased you got back early."

"Where's Sophia?" he asked.

"She spotted Jack and Leila as we were coming in. The bodyguards are in the truck."

Hunt stepped away from the doorway. "Come in."

He let her in and closed the door behind her. "Coffee?"

"We need to talk, Pierce." Her tone surprised him, and he instantly knew this was serious. "Before the kids get back."

Hunt sat down on the couch next to her. "I'm listening."

"The day you left for South America, I was ambushed by two dark-colored minivans."

Upon hearing this, Hunt jumped to his feet and grabbed a notebook from one of the kitchen drawers. "Talk to me, Anna. Tell me exactly what happened."

For the next fifteen minutes, he listened as she described the attack, his blood pressure climbing higher and higher. He asked a few probing questions and had her go over her story again.

"Who else knows about this?" he asked.

"Mauricio Tasis. Sophia has no idea."

"Smart move. Did you enhance your security package?"

"Mine and Sophia's."

"I'm so sorry you had to go through that," Hunt said.

"I thought they were going to kill me. As I've said, I'm sure someone called them off midattack."

Hunt wanted to hold her in his arms and shield her from ever having to experience that kind of situation again. He had warned her many times that her plan to restructure her family business was fraught with perils. It was time she put a stop to this madness.

"Why don't you leave the cartels behind? Forget about new investments; just shut the family business down, and let the men scatter where they may. Would some of them try to start up their own cartel? Sure, but it wouldn't be your concern anymore. You could even move in with me," Hunt offered. "It's not fancy, but you and Sophia are welcome to stay for as long as you want."

She narrowed her green eyes at him, and he could see her stubborn streak coming to the fore. "Thanks, but we've talked about this before. I want to do this."

"Think about Sophia," he said gently. "What's best for her?"

"I know what I'm doing, okay?"

"Okay. If you need me, I'm here."

Anna squeezed his hand. "Didn't you mention dessert when you called?"

———

Hunt had just taken the ice cream out of the freezer when his work phone vibrated in his jeans pocket. He signaled Leila over.

"Do you mind scooping?" he asked her. "I need to take this."

"Sure thing, Dad."

Hunt took the call in his bedroom, making sure to close the door behind him. "How are you, sir?"

"Where are you exactly?" Tom Hauer asked without preamble.

"I'm home," Hunt said. "I'm having dinner with the family. Everything all right?"

"When can you get to Weston?"

At these words, Hunt's heart sank. He knew he was about to receive an assignment.

"I'll be there on Monday," Hunt said, crossing his fingers like a teenager.

Hauer snorted. "My question should have been, How fast can you get your ass to HQ?"

"I just got here, for God's sake. Can I get a couple of—"

"This is serious, Pierce. The agency called. The laptop you seized in Paraguay is a gold mine."

Hunt sighed. "Where am I going?"

"Afghanistan, and the minute I hang up with you, I'm calling Simon Carter and a few others."

Afghanistan. Things were going from bad to worse to worst. At least he would have Carter to back him up.

"I'll be there in an hour," Hunt said. With a heavy heart, he made his way back to the kitchen. Everyone was having a good time. Even Sophia was laughing out loud. Anna glanced at him and smiled. She blew him a kiss.

Shit. He didn't want to go. He'd much rather stay with them, drink another glass of wine, and go to Jack's game the next day.

Like a real person.

The hardest thing would be to tell Leila he wouldn't be there for Jack's game. His daughter must have sensed something because she approached him.

"You okay, Dad? You look like you've seen a ghost. What's going on?"

He didn't even have to say it. With her, he was like an open book.

"You're leaving. Again." Her grudging tone indicated she hadn't decided yet whether she was pissed or just unsurprised.

"When?" she asked. Hunt noticed that the smile on her face had vanished, replaced by a tightened jaw and knitted brow.

"Tonight."

"How long?"

"I don't know."

She nodded, then turned on her heels and stormed out of his apartment.

Goddamn it! "Leila, wait!"

Seeing his girlfriend leave, Jack excused himself and followed her. "Thank you for dinner, Mr. Hunt. We'll take a cab back to Mr. Moon's place. See you tomorrow, yes?"

"I don't think I'll make it," Hunt admitted. "Something came up. I'm sorry."

Jack nodded. He looked disappointed, but he didn't say anything. He headed toward the door, but just as he was about to step out of the apartment, he turned as if to say something. Hunt half expected Jack to tell him that he was about to lose his daughter's trust or that he really sucked as a father, but after a moment, Jack simply nodded again and left.

"What happened?" Anna asked. She was still seated at the table, a spoon filled with chocolate pudding and vanilla ice cream hanging halfway between her bowl and her lips. "You gotta go?"

"Afraid so."

She placed the spoon in her bowl, untouched. "I'll be here when you get back. Don't worry."

CHAPTER ELEVEN

Traz Powell Stadium
Miami, Florida

Leila DeGray stuffed a handful of caramel popcorn in her mouth and closed her eyes, enjoying the sweet taste of her favorite halftime snack. After a brief moment of hesitation, she tilted the bag toward Sophia.

"Want some?"

"I don't know how you can eat that crap." Sophia Garcia frowned at the humongous bag of popcorn and pushed it away.

Leila shrugged. "Suit yourself," she said, then offered some popcorn to Sophia's two bodyguards, who were sitting behind them, hoping they would decline.

They did. Leila breathed a sigh of relief. She wasn't keen on sharing. It was funny, she thought, how quickly she'd gotten used to two fierce-looking strangers following them everywhere. After the kidnapping incident, Anna had insisted that her niece be accompanied by a protective detail everywhere she went, football games included.

Beside Leila, Chris Moon's leg pumped up and down. Leila thought it was hilarious that an athlete with Chris's reputation—he had a Super Bowl ring to prove it—was anxious about the fate of her boyfriend's football game. Though she had to admit the game wasn't going how it was supposed to. Jack's team, the Carol City Chiefs, was trailing the Northwestern Bulls 14–7 at the break. The game was the first in a series of neighborhood battles, and Miami Hurricanes recruiters were rumored to be in attendance. So far, Jack had played an okay game by completing ten of his fourteen pass attempts. But he had also been intercepted twice on deep throws, including one that had set the Bulls up on the Chiefs' thirty-yard line, leading to a Northwestern touchdown.

"You really care about him, don't you?" Leila asked.

"I care about you, young lady. That means that, at least for the time being, I care about him too. Got it?" Moon scooped an alarmingly large handful of her popcorn. "And so does your mother, by the way."

Leila stretched her neck around Moon and glanced at her mother, whose face was happy and relaxed. Sipping at a giant Diet Coke, her mom was doing her very best not to join the conversation. Leila was aware of her mom's reticence about the boyfriend situation.

"Is that so, Mother? You like Jack?" No way Leila was giving her mother a break on this one. Moon had opened the door wide, and she intended to put her mother on the spot.

"He's okay, I guess," she replied, but she was smiling. "He's cute."

Cute? That was a first. "Try gorgeous, Mom."

As she said the words, she realized it was the sort of thing she'd say to her friends, but his looks weren't what really mattered the most. Jack was a good listener, too, which was surprising since most of the other players on the team didn't seem to care about anything but their own image and winning the next football game. Jack wasn't like that. He was one year her senior and exactly what she needed in her life. Talking with shrinks was fine, but it was her late-night conversations on the phone with Jack that had alleviated her anxiety after the kidnapping. Every time a dark thought entered her mind, she could count on him to talk her down.

Jack had taken good care of her for the last few months, and tonight she'd take care of him. Just before the game, she had spent an hour grocery shopping with her stepdad to find all the ingredients she needed to make a pot roast. Six pounds of beef, butter, parsley, onions, dried mushrooms, turnips, and carrots would do the trick. The recipe called for a wineglass of brandy, but she'd need her mother's permission for that one. For appetizers, she would prepare duck confit crostini with parsnip puree and fig. It was an elegant way to start dinner, but it was also easy to make—or so it seemed on the Food Network. However the dinner turned out, it was going to be an enjoyable evening.

Especially if the Chiefs win.

The only dark spot was that she wished her dad were there at the game to share this moment with her. She was still pissed at him for breaking his promise. Okay, she admitted, before the terror of the kidnapping, she'd never imagined how much evil there was outside her cushy, sheltered life. The world needed men like her dad to keep that evil at bay. But even if her current problems didn't compare to the issues and dangers he faced overseas, didn't she need him too? Wasn't she entitled to spend time with him? The more difficult question was, Did he want the same thing? Did he want to spend time with her? She wasn't so sure anymore.

"Here they come," Moon said, startling her back to reality.

As the two teams entered the stadium, a low but audible "Beat the Bulls"—*bump-bump*—"beat the Bulls" echoed across the bleachers. Jack was first in line, trotting toward his starting position, his fist in the air.

"C'mon, Jack!" Sophia cheered next to her.

"Come on, baby!" Leila yelled, her hands cupped around her mouth. "Beat the Bulls!"

As if Jack had heard her, he stopped and turned to face her side of the bleachers. She watched as he scanned the crowd for her. Seconds later, his eyes found hers. Her heart fluttered when he winked at her in that audacious way he had.

Oh my God. I love this guy. I really do.

Then Jack's eyes rolled back in his head, and he collapsed to his knees, and Leila started screaming.

EIGHT WEEKS LATER

CHAPTER TWELVE

Jalalabad, Nangarhar Province, Afghanistan

Hunt kicked at the frozen dirt and blew into his cupped hands. The early-morning cold pressed against him with an intensity he hadn't expected. While the Afghan capital of Kabul often got very cold during the winter months, Jalalabad rarely got below the freezing point. Being outside in crisp weather was simply part of life in Afghanistan. Hunt didn't mind it a bit. The fresh morning wind helped clear the fog that clouded his mind more than an energy drink ever could. Hunt wore a full beard, and his dark hair was the longest he remembered keeping it. At six foot two and just a few pounds away from two hundred, Hunt had a commanding presence, but dressed in his ACU—army combat uniform—in operational camouflage pattern, he didn't stand out from anyone else in sight. Despite the early hour, he felt rested and energized. His impending thirty-ninth birthday seemed a decade removed, not one month away. His thoughts, though, usually clear and well defined, were whirling around and around in fruitless circles, trying to justify the $4 million he and his team had already burned through since the beginning of their deployment eight weeks ago.

The door behind him creaked open, and Simon Carter appeared at his side, carrying two cups of steaming coffee.

"Thanks, brother," Hunt said, accepting the hot beverage.

"My God, it's cold," Carter muttered.

Hunt wrapped his fingers around the warm mug. It felt good in his hands. "How's your back this morning?"

"Are you gonna ask me the same damn question every morning?"

"Don't be so cranky, big guy. Emma asked me to take care of you, okay?"

Carter and his wife, Emma, had been together for sixteen years. In Hunt and Carter's line of work, where the divorce rate was close to 80 percent, this was exceptional. Simon Carter was Hunt's best friend and had been his second-in-command when Hunt had commanded one of the DEA rapid response teams—or RRTs. Not only had they kicked down hundreds of doors together, but Carter had also put his life on hold and risked everything to help Hunt rescue Leila and Sophia. Despite Carter getting critically injured, they had succeeded in freeing the girls. But for the unsanctioned actions they had taken in Mexico and all the bodies they had left behind, Hunt and Carter had been officially shown the door at the DEA.

Three months later, though, Hauer had surprised Hunt with a job offer as a contractor. Hunt's initial tasking—to track, arrest, or otherwise neutralize the last of the Black Tosca's leadership—had quickly morphed into something else following the successful raid in Paraguay. Based on the intel the CIA had acquired, Hauer had determined that the Venezuelans the Black Tosca had met with were involved in some scheme to manufacture a new drug in Afghanistan. What sort of drug was unclear, but the multinational scope of the operation worried Hauer. He had asked Hunt to spearhead Task Force Victor, a small but well-financed task force reporting only to him. No red tape. For a man like Hunt, this was the perfect job. And of course, Carter, along with Dante and Abigail Castillo, two DEA agents stationed at the Guadalajara office whom Hunt had called upon for help, were the first people Hunt had solicited for his new team.

In addition to paying for the salaries of Hunt's team, Hauer had used some of the funds from his black budget to provide the task force with a crew chief and two pilots to fly the Super Huey, along with two DEA intelligence research specialists and all the equipment, hardware, and software Hunt would need.

Given the substantial resources, Hunt wished he had something more to report to his boss by now than "I need more time."

"What's the plan for today?" Carter asked.

"There are a few more poppy-field owners I'd like to talk to," Hunt said. "Maybe one of them will have seen or heard something about this secret drug lab."

"Yeah, maybe."

Clearly, Carter wasn't convinced. Hunt wasn't confident, either, but he wouldn't go back to the States until he had looked under every rock.

Unless Hauer decides to cut his losses and send us packing.

It was entirely possible that there was no team of scientists developing a new drug in the Nangarhar Province. Hunt certainly hoped so. New drug or not, he had to find a way to prove or disprove it. Maybe today would be the day.

"Thanks again for the coffee," Hunt said, heading back to the steel shipping container Task Force Victor used as a tactical operations center. "Briefing's in ten."

CHAPTER THIRTEEN

Nicklaus Children's Hospital
Miami, Florida

Leila drew in a shaky breath, held it in for two seconds, then let it go
with a shudder. Her mom was rubbing her back, doing her best to calm
her down. But how could she be calm? What had she done to deserve
so much pain in her life? She sucked in another labored breath. Leila
could hear Jack's mother's soft cries.

*Oh my God! I'm so selfish. Jack's parents just lost their only child, and
here I am thinking about myself.*

For the past eight weeks, the hospital had been Leila's life. She'd
spent all day, practically every day, sitting by Jack's bedside, keeping up
a constant string of chatter. Every weekday, Sophia came by with class
notes and homework, which Leila worked through out loud with Jack.

Five football players had collapsed at the same game. Five. Two of
Jack's teammates had died. Two had recovered. For eight weeks, Jack
had hung on valiantly. Long enough for Leila to pretend he was going
to be okay. To hope.

Would it be less painful now if he'd died right away?

A sob escaped her.

The Carol City Chiefs' coach had been arrested almost immediately
and accused of giving the players drugs. Coach Harris had sworn they

were only amphetamines. That he gave them to the players regularly. That he hadn't given them anything different this time.

When Moon questioned her, at first Leila had denied that Jack had ever taken drugs—it was as if they wanted to blame him for his own death, to diminish what a good player he'd been. She wouldn't let that happen. Moon had been patient with her, assuring her that the truth would help them punish whoever did this, and finally she'd admitted that yes, Jack had told her the coach sometimes gave them pills—but only to help with the pressure so they didn't screw up while the scouts were watching.

Should she have done something? Told someone about it? Was this her fault?

Across from her chair, Jack's father was pacing the floor, his eyes red and puffy, with dark shadows under them. His wife was lying on her side on a love seat, weeping. Her legs were curled up against her body, her fingers digging into her hair.

Leila stood and took a step toward them. Then she froze, incapable of another one. By sheer will, she forced one foot forward. She felt like a cripple learning to walk again. Her knees were stiff and unstable, giving her the impression they could give out at any moment. Jack's mother looked up at her. A vacant but terrified look transfixed her face. Leila's tears were coming fast now, but she didn't brush them away.

"I'm sorry," Leila mouthed. Her throat burned and ached. This was all too much to bear. She couldn't take it.

With a sob, she turned and ran down the hallway. She could hear her mother calling her, but Leila needed fresh air. She needed to be somewhere else. She needed Jack. She ran as fast as she could, tears spilling down her face.

A little farther down the hallway, she could see her stepdad on the phone. Leila slowed down to a walk. Though she couldn't hear what he was saying, Moon's demeanor suggested he wasn't happy. She watched in a stupor as he slammed a fist into the nearest wall, sending out a small cloud of white, chalky debris into the air. His words carried as she inched closer.

"Our boys aren't the only ones, Tom. The doctor told me over one hundred young athletes have been transported to different hospitals in the past few weeks."

Leila sucked in a breath. *Over one hundred athletes sick—or dead, like Jack?* This was no accident. Someone was purposely targeting kids.

"And what's the name again? Yeah, Santiago Mayo. You're sure Coach Harris said he works for the Garcias? Christ, Tom, did Anna do this? Sophia is Leila's best friend—do we force her to cut off contact with her best friend when her boyfriend has just died? Are you going to arrest Anna?"

Anna? Leila thought stupidly. *Anna killed Jack?*

Of course not, she thought. The Garcia family? No, it couldn't be. She refused to believe it. Didn't want to. Her father had told her that Anna had walked away from all of that. That she was making things right, putting the family on a legitimate path. A sense of helplessness and betrayal enveloped Leila. Did Sophia know?

Leila felt guilty for even entertaining the thought. Sophia was like a sister to her. Should she tell Sophia that her aunt was still a drug dealer?

I need to call Dad. Dad will know what to do. She slipped silently down another corridor. He'd given her the number for his satellite phone, though it was supposed to be for emergencies only. She'd wanted to call him weeks ago, right after it had happened, but Moon had convinced her not to. Her dad could be in the middle of something dangerous, he said, and worrying about her would only distract him. If a player's mom died on Super Bowl Sunday, Moon said, the coach would wait to tell him until after the game. That was what she should do for her dad.

But this was too important to wait.

She was about to slide her phone out of her pocket when another thought occurred to her. If she confronted her parents, they'd only tell her to let the DEA handle it. That was who Moon had been on the phone with, hadn't it? Now she started to worry. Tom Hauer was his boss, but her father wouldn't hesitate to defy him, right? And he might love Anna, but if it came down to taking sides, he'd choose Leila's—wouldn't he?

I know what I need to do too, Leila thought, a plan forming in her head.

CHAPTER FOURTEEN

Venezuelan jungle

Peter Godfrey loathed the jungle. He hated everything about it: the damp green smell of the undergrowth assaulting his nostrils, the incessant hum of insects, the putrid odor of the swamps, even the endless tweeting of birds as they settled into trees for the night. Godfrey didn't belong in that environment; he much preferred his air-conditioned office in Caracas, where he could do what accountants did in comfort. But for this one night, Godfrey hated the jungle a little less. In fact, the birdcalls piercing through the canopy and the ceaseless jabber of the monkeys served his purpose.

Godfrey and the two bodyguards assigned to him by his boss, General Euclides Peraza, had departed Caracas at noon. Godfrey was among the twelve high-ranking members of General Peraza's inner circle who would convene at a secret gathering somewhere deep in the eighteen million hectares of the Amazon rainforest. After a five-hour ride south aboard a military SUV, they had been instructed to finish their journey on foot using a narrow trail that meandered through the thick jungle. Their final destination was ten miles deep into the jungle and only accessible by foot, motorbike, or helicopter. With the exception of a few daringly steep spots, it was easy going. The high temperature made Godfrey's hair slick with perspiration and glued his white shirt to his back. Why General Peraza hadn't seen fit to provide him with a helicopter, Godfrey had no idea. Peraza sometimes operated in mysterious ways that made sense only to him.

"How long till we get there?" Godfrey asked the bodyguard in front of him, even though he knew exactly how long it would take to reach the camp. He had studied the map with care prior to their departure.

"Not long, Mr. Godfrey. Another couple of hours at most," the lead bodyguard replied in heavily accented English.

Godfrey glanced at his watch. "Can we take a five-minute rest? I'm exhausted."

"We don't want to be late," the man warned. "We better keep going."

"I need water." Godfrey's mouth felt like the bottom of a parrot's cage. "Give me another bottle. Mine's empty."

The bodyguard dropped his oversize backpack to the ground and placed his AK-103 assault rifle beside it. He retrieved two water bottles, one from each side pocket, and handed one to Godfrey. Godfrey unscrewed the cap and took a long drink. The lukewarm water tasted unreasonably good to his parched mouth. He tried to pace himself but failed. He tossed the empty bottle to the bodyguard, who caught it with one hand while answering a call on his satellite phone with the other.

Nervousness made Godfrey thirsty. It always had. For a second, Godfrey wondered if he should take advantage of the distraction offered by the phone call to kick the bodyguard in the crotch, grab his rifle, and shoot both men dead. He was confident he could find his way out of the jungle alone and be out of Venezuela by morning. But if he were completely honest, he wasn't absolutely sure he could take down both bodyguards at the same time. It had been a while since he'd gotten his blood pumping with a good fight.

He'd stick with the plan. For now.

It was silly to worry that anyone had discovered his secret. If they had, he wouldn't be included at this meeting. The unexpected death of Valentina Mieles, the head of the biggest and most influential Mexican drug cartel, the Black Tosca, had left a major power vacuum in the underworld. General Peraza wanted to fill the void.

Needs to fill the void would be more accurate, Godfrey thought. Without a large influx of hard currency, Venezuela would continue its economic downward spiral. But after today's meeting, General Peraza, also known as the Spider due to his vast web of spies and informants, would become one of the top suppliers of cocaine to the United States.

As the general's personal accountant, Godfrey was well positioned to see what others couldn't. He knew how big of a threat Peraza really was. As ruthless and brutal as Valentina Mieles and her cousin Hector had been, her organization never had the support of the Mexican government—corrupt officials excluded. Peraza, on the contrary, had the blessing of the Venezuelan government. Peraza's growing power was unchallenged, and Godfrey doubted that Leopoldo Capriles— Venezuela's president—could do without him even if he wanted to. Peraza not only controlled all branches of Venezuela's military, but he was also the brain behind the political decision-making process. Godfrey had concluded long ago that President Capriles would fall within a week if Peraza ever decided to loosen his grip on the daily lives of the Venezuelan people.

Consolidating his power and controlling the South American drug trade wasn't Peraza's endgame, though. Rumors had it that Peraza wanted to strike at the very heart of America.

But how did Peraza intend on attacking the United States? And with what? Godfrey didn't have all the answers yet, but he had his suspicions, and with a little luck, he'd be able to confirm everything during today's meeting.

One way or the other, he had decided this was going to be his last night in Venezuela and had downloaded all the intelligence he could onto the encrypted flash drive he was carrying.

He just hoped his ride home wouldn't be in a coffin.

CHAPTER FIFTEEN

DEA Headquarters
Arlington, Virginia

Tom Hauer terminated his call with Chris Moon and walked into the waiting elevator that would take him down to the tactical operations center. His conversation with Moon had put him in a sour mood, and with the Venezuelan operation at full speed, he had enough on his plate.

He thought about Hunt's daughter. *Poor girl.* Not only had she just lost her boyfriend, but it was possible that her father's girlfriend had facilitated the distribution of the drug that had killed him. If that were indeed the case, Hauer's head would roll. He was the one who had given Anna Garcia the necessary breathing room to "restructure" her organization.

Against his best judgment, he dialed her number. She picked up on the second ring.

"I've held up my end of our bargain, Anna," Hauer barked. "What the hell have you been up to?"

It took a few seconds for her to reply. "I don't know what you're talking about. Care to explain this sudden burst of aggression?"

"You've played me for a fool," he said. "Tell me you don't have anything to do with what's been happening to our young athletes."

"I . . . I really don't know what—"

"Over one hundred of them, Anna! How could you?"

"Listen, Tom—"

"Our deal's over. You're going down, Anna. I'll have your head for this." Hauer severed the connection.

That's what you get for playing fair with a criminal.

He stepped out of the elevator into the tactical operations center. As soon as he was done here, he would call Hunt; then he'd transfer Anna Garcia's case to his deputy to launch a full investigation.

And if he had to, he'd arrest her himself.

———

"Is this real time?" Hauer asked, his eyes glued to one of the four massive flat-screen TVs perched on the wall of the tactical operations center. As the administrator of the DEA, Hauer wasn't usually so actively involved in an operation. But this operation was different. The intel their informant was about to smuggle out of Venezuela could possibly be a game changer regarding diplomatic relations between the two countries. If the intel Godfrey had in his possession proved that there was a concerted effort from within the Venezuelan government to harm the United States, President Reilly had made it clear that no options would be off the table. Including boots on the ground.

"Yes, sir," the drone operator replied.

"Why are they stopping?" Hauer said out loud to no one in particular. "They need to get moving, or they won't get there in time."

Apart from Hauer and the drone pilot, there were five other people inside the operations center, including Linda Ramer, the director of the Intelligence Division, who was also Godfrey's handler. Ramer's reputation was stellar. Straightforward and utterly reliable, she was one of Hauer's favorite people. He was glad she was in the TOC overseeing the operation.

The screen showed that Godfrey and two unidentified men were now stationary. Assault rifles were clearly visible, and for a second,

Hauer marveled at the modern technology. These new drones could almost read the serial numbers on the rifles. Earlier that day, a DEA two-man team had been inserted into the region to cover Godfrey during the meeting and to run point on the exfil. Godfrey was a good agent and a fantastic accountant, but he wasn't a precision weapon like Pierce Hunt.

For the last four years, Godfrey had provided crucial intelligence about the Venezuelan drug trade. For some time now, Hauer had the impression that something far more sinister than drug trafficking was going on within Venezuela's borders, and Godfrey was the DEA's best chance to figure out what it was. Three days ago, Godfrey had made contact and informed Ramer that he would be attending a critical meeting with General Peraza and most of the important players who were taking part in the Venezuelan general's plan. Godfrey had also mentioned that he had the impression that his cover was getting thinner. He wanted out.

"Check this out, sir," one of the analysts said, pointing at a still image on his screen.

Hauer's heart jumped, and he turned to Ramer. "When was this taken?"

Ramer looked at her tablet. "It came in four hours ago."

Hauer's blood turned cold. *Shit!*

"Why are we only seeing this now?" he asked, his fists clenched at his side, his knuckles already turning white.

"The feed isn't ours, sir," Ramer replied defensively. "It came from the NRO."

The National Reconnaissance Office, often considered one of the big five US intelligence agencies, was headquartered in Fairfax County, Virginia. Its job was to design, build, and operate the reconnaissance satellites of the US federal government. Among other things, it provided satellite intelligence and imagery intelligence to the DEA. Satellite surveillance was useful, but its drawback was that unlike with real-time drones, vital and time-sensitive intelligence was often delivered too late.

Like now.

The feed the NRO had sent showed half a dozen pictures of a large meeting taking place in the middle of the Venezuelan jungle. The exact same meeting that Godfrey was on his way to attend. Only the meeting had taken place four hours ago. Which meant Godfrey's cover was blown.

Ramer's face turned pale as the implication sank in. "We need to get him out of there," she said.

"Are we in communication with the ground team?" Hauer asked.

"Yes, sir," one of the analysts replied, handing Hauer a headset. "The team leader's call sign is Papa-One."

Hauer nodded his understanding and took the headset from the analyst. "Let's hope we're not too late."

CHAPTER SIXTEEN

Ministry of Defense
Caracas, Venezuela

Lieutenant General Euclides Peraza, commandant of the Operational Strategic Command—OSC—of the Venezuelan armed forces, sat behind his wide polished wood desk, reading field reports submitted by his military commanders. The more he read, the more his mood darkened. The Venezuelan armed forces were in poor shape. Arrests for rebellion and desertion had continued to rise sharply in the last quarter amid discontent within the ranks about food shortages and dwindling salaries. The official position of the government run by Venezuelan president Leopoldo Capriles was that the dissent within the military was isolated to a few individuals rather than being a systemic problem, but Peraza knew better.

Peraza's humble beginnings had taught him to listen to the men and women serving under his command. Two years ago, he had asked his driver to take him to an army base to personally talk to fellow officers below the rank of general. Upon entering an army captain's house, he asked the officer's wife to walk him to the kitchen, where he wanted to inspect the fridge. When Peraza saw that the only items were two cartons of eggs and a half-empty bottle of milk, he demanded to know where the rest of the food supply was located. With tears in her eyes, the poor woman had replied that they couldn't afford anything else.

"What's happening in the slums is now happening on our military bases," Peraza had said to President Capriles on his way back to Caracas. "Our soldiers are going hungry, and their families are suffering."

"What do you propose?"

When Peraza had presented his plan to his president, he had expected some kind of resistance. There hadn't been any.

"Whatever you need, I'll provide," Capriles had promised him.

Capriles wasn't stupid. Venezuela had a history of coups and attempted overthrows at times of crisis. Peraza was pretty sure Capriles was wondering if this was one of those times. Whatever Capriles needed to do to stay in power, he would do. He had proven it again just last week by promoting two hundred officers to the rank of general. By Peraza's count, there were now more than two thousand Venezuelan generals in the armed forces. Militarily speaking, that didn't make any sense. Politically, though, it made complete sense since generals enjoyed a wide range of privileges, from lucrative control of the food supply to advantageous rates for trading dollars. Generals had a stake in preserving Capriles's control over the country. Peraza wasn't a fool either. He was aware that with more generals, each general's influence was diminished, making it virtually impossible to effectively rebel against Capriles.

What infuriated Peraza to no end was that while the generals and political elites were living large, the country's population had lost an average of nineteen pounds of body weight in the last year. Just two years after his visit to the captain's house, Venezuela's money was worth less than toilet paper. When a Venezuelan citizen needed 2.6 million bolivars to acquire a single roll of toilet paper, actions—not words—were needed.

Still, before Peraza executed the plan the president had approved—because once he did, there would be no turning back—he had sought to appeal to the international community one last time by pleading for the opening of a humanitarian channel that would allow the most basic medicine and food supplies to enter the country. With the $55 billion line of credit that Russia and China had extended almost depleted, Venezuela's back was against the wall. But Peraza's plea hadn't received the international echo he was looking for. Instead, it had backfired. Believing that the crisis was man made, the international community had found it difficult to agree to a unified response. So in lieu of providing financial relief, the international community had focused on condemning the illegal imprisonment of activists opposing President Capriles.

As a last resort, and without specific approval from Capriles, Peraza had risked his life by getting in touch with the American CIA. Peraza had done his best to explain to the CIA station chief that the American president's fiery rhetoric against Venezuela only gave Capriles a sturdier rationale for amalgamating his power to fend off the perceived American menace. Peraza's suggestion that the US Navy stop, or at least tame, its training exercises just outside Venezuela's territorial waters had fallen on deaf ears. Not only had the CIA dismissed him as a power-hungry general, but they had threatened to denounce him as a dissident.

Fuck the Americans!

If the richest country the world had ever known didn't want to help his impoverished countrymen, Peraza would make them pay. He would become a thorn in their side and find a way to make the unwilling Americans contribute to the next Venezuelan revolution in a manner they had never expected.

Just like President Capriles, there was nothing Peraza wouldn't do to give Venezuelans back their pride. Months ago, in a Hail Mary attempt to turn the country around, Capriles had announced an increase of 3,000 percent to the minimum wage and a plan to peg the bolivar to the Petro, a new state-backed cryptocurrency the Americans and most European nations considered a scam. Capriles's plan had failed quickly, and Venezuela's central bank had had no choice but to devalue the bolivar by an additional 96 percent.

Sensing mounting dissension within the ranks, Capriles had given Peraza carte blanche to bring in hard American currencies and to proceed with his scheme.

With Capriles's sanction, Operation Butterfly had begun. The means Peraza was using to reach his objective weren't the purest, but his conscience was at peace. He had given the Americans a chance, and they had spit in his face.

This morning's meeting at his jungle camp with the principal actors of his plan had gone even better than he had predicted. After the initial failure to team up with the Black Tosca's cartel, it was surprising that everything was falling into place so smoothly. Dealing with Hezbollah, the Taliban, and his American allies from Florida was actually enjoyable. Amazing what an ad hoc group of people with little in common could accomplish when they combined their strengths and assets in order to defeat a common enemy.

So far, the only real setbacks outside of Paraguay had been Peter Godfrey's betrayal and the realization that the new amphetamine pills he'd been producing in two secret labs in Afghanistan weren't ready for distribution—an understatement, given the deaths they'd caused, but not what was bothering him the most. It wasn't until today that Peraza had had his suspicions confirmed about Godfrey. Fortunately, Godfrey's access to the overall stratagem had been limited—he'd been led to believe their plans had to do with run-of-the-mill cocaine—but there was still a chance he had put enough of it together to jeopardize the final objective.

What had worried Peraza the most was the news of an unidentified American unit on the ground in Afghanistan. If the Americans had found the secret labs where his Hezbollah partners were producing the new synthetic amphetamine pills, Operation Butterfly would have ground to a halt before he could have distributed the product. In an abundance of caution, Peraza had pulled his team from Afghanistan sooner than he had wanted.

Was it Godfrey's doing that the Americans were in Afghanistan sniffing around? Peraza believed so. How else could they have known? There were fewer than fifty people who knew about the Afghanistan portion of Operation Butterfly, and only a handful of them had the clout to convince the Americans to send a team to investigate.

The Americans had forced his hand. The time for diplomacy had come and gone.

Now we go to war.

Peraza picked up the phone to fire the first salvo. And Peter Godfrey would be its recipient.

CHAPTER SEVENTEEN

Venezuelan jungle

Peter Godfrey hadn't survived so long as an undercover officer by being oblivious to what was going on around him. He had noted a not-so-subtle shift in his two bodyguards' demeanor following a phone call one of them had received. For the last fifteen minutes, they had quickened their pace. They had tightened their grips on their rifles, their eyes constantly darting here and there, scouring the immediate area in all directions.

"Is everything all right?"

"Nothing to worry about. Just be quiet," snapped the lead bodyguard.

Godfrey didn't believe a word of it. Something was going on. His stomach contracted into a knot. A cold sweat came over him despite the outside temperature reaching new highs. Did General Peraza know? Had the general somehow found out who he was? Godfrey tried to keep his mind on what he was supposed to be doing, but it wasn't easy. He had seen with his own eyes how General Peraza dealt with traitors. He didn't want to suffer that fate.

Godfrey was still considering his best course of action when his peripheral vision caught movement. His whole body tightened. The lead bodyguard must have seen it, too, because he stopped, his fist in the air. A fraction of a second later, half of the bodyguard's head disappeared in a spray of fine red mist.

Godfrey didn't hesitate. He hit the deck and crawled to the fallen bodyguard and relieved him of his AK-103. Behind him, the other bodyguard had also dropped to the ground. Had they stumbled into a rebel ambush? Godfrey hadn't heard the shot that had taken out the lead bodyguard. The rebels likely didn't have many weapons fitted with suppressors.

"Did you see anything?" Godfrey asked the surviving bodyguard.

Anxiety joined confusion on the man's face. His eyes filled with fear. "Nothing," he whispered, his breath short. "I've seen nothing."

A branch cracked off to their left. The bodyguard panicked and jerked toward the sound. He popped to one knee and squeezed the trigger of his AK-103. With the rifle having a rate of fire of six hundred rounds per minute and at such a close range, the noise was deafening. When the AK-103 fell silent, Godfrey's ears sang. Two men dressed in camouflage uniforms emerged from the jungle, their weapons pointed in their direction.

"Keep your hands where we can see them," one of the camouflaged men said in English. "We're DEA."

Like a tidal wave, relief washed over Godfrey, temporarily causing him to feel faint. But the reprieve was short lived. Peraza's bodyguard shot him a quick hate-filled glance and said, "You're dead."

Then, in an act of defiance, the bodyguard drew his pistol from his belt holster. Before the pistol was fully drawn, one of the camouflaged men's rifles spat once. The round punched through the bridge of the bodyguard's nose and mushroomed into his brain.

"Are you okay, Mr. Godfrey?" the taller of the two DEA agents asked.

"Yeah, I'm okay." Godfrey was slightly confused as he processed what had just happened.

"Do you know how to operate one of these?" the agent asked, while the other one scanned the surrounding area.

"What?" Godfrey asked.

"Are you familiar with the AK-103? Can you operate it?"

In all the chaos, Godfrey had forgotten that he was still holding the lead bodyguard's rifle. Godfrey removed the magazine; pulled the operating handle fully to the rear, releasing the round that had been chambered; and inspected the chamber and receiver to confirm they were cleared. He then inserted the magazine back into the receiver and chambered a round.

"I'm good," Godfrey said.

The DEA agent nodded. "I'm Papa-One, and this is Two," he said, pointing to the other agent. "We've been keeping track of you all day. We've been told you've been compromised, and our orders are to bring you back stateside."

"What about the meeting?"

"Not going to happen."

"How did they—"

"There's no time for that now," Papa-One said, pulling a satellite phone from one of his plate carrier pockets. "I'm going to call HQ; then we go. We have a six-mile trek in unfamiliar and hostile terrain."

Damn!

Still, if his identity had indeed been compromised, a six-mile hike in the jungle was nothing compared to what would have happened to him if the DEA hadn't come to his rescue.

"Search them and grab their ammo," One told Godfrey as he extended his satellite phone antenna and inserted a foam-covered earpiece into his left ear.

Godfrey frisked the lead bodyguard first and didn't find anything of value except the two spare magazines he snagged. He went through the second bodyguard's pockets and pulled out a wallet and a set of car keys. After examining the wallet and finding nothing of interest, he slipped his hand into the inner breast pocket of the dead man's shirt and discovered a cell phone. He looked at the cell phone display. His heart sank.

Oh shit.

The line was open and had been so for the last fifteen minutes. Whoever had called in had instructed the bodyguard to keep the line open. Godfrey placed the phone against his ear.

"Hello?"

"Ah, Peter, my good friend."

Peraza.

An icy clamminess settled at the back of Godfrey's neck. The air around him turned fetid.

"I'll see you very soon," Peraza said before hanging up.

Godfrey forced back the bile rising from his stomach. He popped open the back of the cell phone and removed the battery. He walked to Papa-One, who was twenty feet away and still talking on the satellite phone.

"What's up?" he asked Godfrey, seeing him approaching.

"We have a big problem."

"Whatever it is, we'll figure it out."

"You don't understand," Godfrey replied. "Peraza knows where we are. And he's coming for us."

The color drained from the DEA agent's face. "Fuck."

CHAPTER EIGHTEEN

Miami, Florida

Anna hung up with Tom Hauer and looked at her phone in complete disbelief.

What the hell was that about? A knot formed in her stomach, slowly crawling its way up to her throat. Hauer was a good man. A fair man. A man of his word. For him to turn on her like he had meant something had gone terribly wrong. But what?

Hauer had said, "Tell me you don't have anything to do with what's been happening to our young athletes."

Jack? Was he talking about Jack? And who else?

The knot in her throat threatened to make her vomit. Anna had to admit that she'd been preoccupied the last few weeks. Other than accompanying Sophia to the hospital and offering Leila what comforting words she could, she hadn't followed the details of the investigation into what had caused Jack and his teammates to collapse. A bad batch of amphetamines, she thought she'd heard. Those sorts of drug had many sources. Maybe some of the Garcias' low-level street dealers had sold amphetamines—in the past, not anymore—but that hadn't been the family's bread and butter.

Was there more to Jack's death than that? She thought about texting Sophia to ask her to join her in her office, but the poor girl was so devastated—part sadness about Jack and part empathy for Leila—that

Anna couldn't bear to make her talk about it. She reached for the TV remote instead and tuned in to a local news station.

There was only one thing the anchor was talking about. *More than a hundred reported cases . . .* She switched to CNN. Same thing. Anna's blood turned to ice.

Oh shit.

———

The day only got worse.

Following her dreadful phone call with Hauer, Anna had looked into the matter personally. Was she or her organization in any way involved with what had happened to those student-athletes? It hadn't taken long for her to discover that something was amiss. One of her distributors, who owned a small warehouse that the Garcia crime syndicate had often used in the past to stockpile drugs and other illegal products, had admitted he had continued to deal with Alejandro Mayo and his brother, Santiago. The distributor had apologized profusely, but he had been convinced that Alejandro had Anna's full authority and blessing. Anna had sent three of her trusted men to go inspect the warehouse and find out what kind of shit Alejandro and Santiago were pulling.

Now her men were dead. All three of them. Somebody had been waiting for them, just like someone had been waiting for her on Alligator Alley. With the exception of Mauricio Tasis, who had been a loyal employee of the Garcia family for decades, she wasn't sure who she could trust anymore.

Anna buried her face in her hands, refusing to lose control as she forced herself to find a solution to this newest crisis.

"This is crazy," she whispered through her fingers. "Are you sure Alejandro did this?"

Tasis exhaled loudly. "Yeah, I'm sure."

"How can you—"

"He called me, Anna," Tasis said, cutting her off.

"The bastard. He had the guts to brag about it?"

"I think his call was meant more as a warning than anything else. I'm afraid more violence is coming our way if we don't back off."

"Shit! So Hauer's right? We're involved in these kids' deaths?"

"Alejandro isn't listening to your instructions anymore, or to mine for that matter. He's gone rogue, and he's definitely involved. Why else would he have murdered our guys for snooping around the warehouse?"

That meant she had played an active—albeit unwilling and unknowing—role in the death of Leila's boyfriend. She cursed and slammed her fist against the desk.

This can't be happening.

Driven by a vision of making the family business entirely legitimate, Anna was under siege from people within her own organization who disagreed. The Garcia family, once the most powerful crime syndicate in south Florida, was on the verge of disintegrating. Without the authoritative figure of her brother, Tony, at the helm, discontent factions were plotting against her. Could Alejandro be the mastermind behind the ambush that had nearly cost her her life too? If Alejandro had the guts to murder her men, surely he'd be willing to murder her as well.

"What if I voluntarily step down and let Alejandro and his brother run the show?" Anna suggested.

Tasis shrugged. "Alejandro wants you gone. That much is clear."

Since she had taken control of the syndicate, she'd always said she'd do the right thing, no matter the cost. But the assassination of three of her men by rebellious members of what she had always considered her family was not a cost she had anticipated. Nor were the deaths of so many young athletes. She wasn't sure she could live with that on her conscience. At the thought of Jack Cameron, her heart flipped, and her whole body trembled.

"I know what you're thinking," Tasis said.

"Do you really?"

"You wish *he* was here."

Anna knew exactly who Tasis had in mind. He wasn't referring to Tony or her late father, Vicente. Tasis was talking about Pierce Hunt. Funny how drastically things had changed between her and Hunt. A year ago, she would have murdered him for all the pain he had caused her. She had wanted Hunt to suffer as she'd suffered. She'd wanted him to know the pain, the hunger, and the hopelessness she had felt when he had betrayed her and her family years earlier. But everything had changed the day her niece had been kidnapped by an enemy of her family. Caught in the cross fire was Leila DeGray.

"Anna?" Tasis asked, bringing her out of her reverie. "What do you want to do?"

"I don't know, Mauricio, okay?" she howled. "I don't know. I'm not my brother, and I'm not like my father either. Sorry if I keep disappointing you too."

For a fleeting moment, a flash of fury subsumed his entire face. An instant later it had disappeared. Tasis took a step back, raised his hands in surrender, and said, "I'm not disappointed, Anna. That's unfair. I've always had your back."

Damn it! Tasis was right. She shouldn't have pounced on him. But what about that look he had just given her? Even though it had been for the briefest of moments, there was no denying it: Tasis was annoyed with her.

No, not with you. He's annoyed with the situation. He has to be. The opposite was too scary to consider. Maybe transitioning the family business into a legitimate entity had been a bad idea from the start. The Garcia crime syndicate had always operated outside the law. She had been naive to think everybody would follow her lead. Hunt had told her that much. He had warned her that it would be challenging, even dangerous.

"Contact Alejandro," she said finally. "Let him know I got his *message* and that I'd like to meet."

Tasis's gaze, openly and irritatingly skeptical, roved over her. "He might take that as a sign of weakness."

"I don't care how he sees it, damn it!"

"Why don't you let me take care of Alejandro? Once I'm done with him—"

"No, you will not *take care* of Alejandro," she said, her tone indicating that there would be no more discussion on the subject. "I want to know why he's doing this."

"I know his reasons," Tasis said.

Anna cocked her head. "I'm confused, Mauricio. What are you saying?"

"Alejandro is greedy and power hungry. He and the men loyal to him are afraid you'll turn on them."

"Why would they think that?"

"C'mon, Anna—the men aren't blind. They know about you and Hunt. He's DEA, for God's sake!"

"Not anymore," she protested, but Tasis had a point.

"Men like Alejandro don't become property managers," continued Tasis. "It doesn't matter how much real estate you buy or how many corner stores and gas stations you acquire; managing legitimate businesses isn't what they do. Heck, it's not what I do. And it never will be."

Anna sighed. Hunt had told her that much, too, but she hadn't listened.

"What about you, Mauricio? Why are you sticking with me?" She was not entirely confident she wanted to hear his answer.

Tasis didn't hesitate. He looked her straight in the eyes and said, "I took an oath many years ago. I swore allegiance to your father. I'll never betray my word."

There was no hint of evasion in what he said. She swallowed hard, relieved.

"Thank you."

Tasis nodded. "If you still want me to contact Alejandro, I will."

Anna reached for her cell phone. The battery was dead again.

What's wrong with this damn phone?

"No, I'll do it," she said, plugging her phone into her laptop. "I'll figure a way out of this mess."

CHAPTER NINETEEN

Jalalabad, Nangarhar Province, Afghanistan

Hunt used his laser pointer to indicate their current location on the map and continued using it to show the route they would take to reach the Helmand Province. The entire team was gathered in the windowless briefing room located behind the task force TOC—tactical operations center. The briefing room was small, but the lack of any furniture except for the eight wooden chairs made it look bigger. At the front of the room, a large two-dimensional map of Afghanistan was projected onto a flat-screen monitor mounted on the wall. On either side of the map were smaller screens with maps displaying important data and imagery like deployment of friendly force units in the area.

"We'll refuel in Kandahar before making our way here," Hunt said, the red beam of his laser pointer stopping over the city of Marjah.

"I've already prearranged everything for the pit stop, boss," DEA intelligence research specialist Colleen Crawford said.

"And I've secured extra ammunition in case you encounter any problems on your way," added IRS Barry Pike.

Crawford and Pike were Hauer's gift to Hunt. In addition to having more than a decade conducting and managing multifaceted research into drug cultivation and production, Pike was a logistics and computer whiz who had full access to most national intelligence databases. While Pike had more field experience than Crawford, the thirty-eight-year-old woman had earned a master of arts in international security and was at ease operating in complex and variable environments like Afghanistan. Even if they weren't special agents, they were an integral part of the team, and Hunt valued their insights.

"Let's hope we won't need those extra rounds," Dante said, his chair propped against the back wall.

"Cheers to that," Abigail said.

Hunt nodded to them. Since Dante and Abigail were married, Hunt had had to convince only one of them to join the group to get both. Abigail had jumped at the opportunity, which had pleased Hunt very much since she was a logistics mastermind. Just as he had planned, Dante, who happened to be an army Black Hawk pilot before joining the DEA, had followed his wife's lead.

"I'm not expecting a hot landing zone, but we all know not to take anything for granted in that region," Hunt said. "There's been a resurgence of Taliban activity in the last month, so I want you guys to keep your heads on a swivel the moment we touch down."

"Oh, that's just great. I hate this freakin' place," Carter said, shaking his head. "I never thought we'd go back there."

Hunt wasn't a fan either. He and Carter, while still in the DEA, had spent quite a bit of time in the Helmand Province, especially in and around Marjah, conducting raids on known secret laboratories used by the Taliban to convert raw opium into heroin. Marjah, a midsize agricultural town in southern Afghanistan, was geographically situated in one of the country's major belts of poppy fields.

"This will be a long day, folks," Hunt said, "but Hauer is counting on us to deliver."

"Why *are* we going to Marjah?" Abigail asked. "We spent pretty much all our time in Nangarhar so far. Why the change of heart?"

"You've said it yourself," Hunt replied. "We've spent the last couple months in Nangarhar. Did we find any solid leads? Are we any closer to finding that goddamn drug lab?"

Abigail and Dante both shook their heads.

"What did Hauer have to say about that?" Carter asked.

"He didn't chew my head off, if that's what you're asking," Hunt replied. "He's meeting POTUS this week, and he'd appreciate it if we had something to report by then."

"And that's why we're going to Marjah," Carter said, nodding. "You want to talk to that guy Azfaar."

"Yep," Hunt said, smiling. "I think it's worth a shot."

"Who's Azfaar?" Crawford asked, opening her notepad.

"He's a farmer who had some issues with the Taliban," Carter said. "Pierce and I, with the rest of our team, protected him and his family on our last visit to Afghanistan."

"So he's a friend?" Abigail inquired.

"We'll find out when we get there," Carter replied.

"What do you mean? He owes you guys, right?" That was from Dante.

Hunt saw that Carter was hesitating, so he explained. "It was our job to protect Azfaar. He was the first farmer in Marjah to voluntarily give up cultivating poppies in favor of growing wheat and corn."

"And that didn't please the Taliban," Carter said.

"I can see why," Dante said. "So what happened?"

"The Taliban tried to destroy Azfaar's crops a few times," Hunt said. "We fought them off and killed enough of them for the attacks to stop. So after a month without any attack, and thinking the Taliban and drug dealers had learned their lesson, the DEA decided to redeploy our team somewhere else."

"Shit," Pike said. "The Taliban returned, didn't they?"

"You got it. Two days after our departure, they launched an assault on Azfaar's property while he was in Kandahar." Images of the massacre were still vivid in his mind. "The Afghan soldiers tasked with protecting Azfaar's family were mowed down. Azfaar's wife and seven children were executed."

"My God," Crawford said, covering her mouth with her hand. "Those bastards."

"My thoughts exactly," Hunt said. "Of course, and rightfully so, Azfaar blames us for what happened. All this to say that I have no idea how receptive he'll be when he sees me. Any other questions?"

Hunt scanned the faces of his team, holding on to every pair of eyes for a second or two. He was looking for any sign of uncertainty. He found none.

"We're wheels up in fifteen."

———

Hunt was on his way to the bathroom when his satellite phone beeped in his pocket.

"Good morning, sir," Hunt greeted the caller. "We're on our way to Marjah to speak with an old contact of mine."

"I'm not calling to get an update," Hauer replied somewhat dryly. "And I only have a minute—there's an operation in Venezuela that requires my attention."

"Okay . . ."

"I'm afraid there's something I need to share with you, and this one is personal."

Hunt frowned, but he wasn't overly concerned. He hadn't received a call from Jasmine, Leila, or Anna—any of them would have called him in an emergency. Everyone he cared about was accounted for, or so he thought.

How bad could it be?

"What is it?" Hunt asked.

"The investigation is still ongoing, and what we have is preliminary at best . . . ," Hauer said.

"What is it?" Hunt growled. If the administrator of the DEA felt the need to beat around the bush, something was definitely wrong. Now he was worried.

"Jack Cameron, and four other players on his team, collapsed on the field a few weeks ago. Jack died earlier today."

What? That sounded so far-fetched he wondered if he had heard Hauer correctly. Hunt's immediate thought was of Leila. Had his daughter been in attendance? Was she okay?

"Is Leila okay? How? What happened?" Hunt asked, holding his breath, his hand tightening around the satellite phone.

"Leila's fine, Pierce. Your whole family is fine. Don't worry," Hauer replied.

Hunt exhaled loudly, relieved but angry.

"The deaths were drug related," Hauer continued. "The players, Jack included, took some amphetamine pills."

Hunt felt like he had been sucker punched.

"What the hell, Tom?" Hunt asked. "Since when do those pills kill people?"

"The lab is testing the pills we recovered. It could have been a bad batch. We don't know yet. Jack and his teammates weren't the only student-athletes affected."

Hunt's mind was still reeling from the death of Leila's boyfriend. He tuned out the rest as Hauer explained that he was the one who had made the decision not to call Hunt earlier to explain the situation.

He needed to speak with Leila. He needed to know she was okay.

Of course she's not okay. She just lost her first boyfriend. Hunt felt like shit for not being at her side. Once again it would be Chris Moon who'd play *his* role. It would be Moon who'd comfort Leila, look out for her.

Leila. His daughter had never called him on the satellite phone; she knew the number was for emergencies only. But if this didn't count, what did? The moment he disconnected from Hauer, he called her.

"Hey, baby girl. What's up?" he asked, trying to hide the anxiety from his voice. "I heard—"

"What's up? Really?" Leila spoke so loudly Hunt had to hold the phone away from his ear. "Jack's dead, Pierce. That's what's up. Where the fuck are you?"

Her words hit him like a bucket of cold water, but now wasn't the time to address her foul language. He'd never been good with words or at comforting others. That was remarkably true with his daughter.

"I'm so, so sorry about Jack, Leila. Hauer just told me—"

"Did he tell you it's Anna's fault?" Leila interrupted him, her voice steadily rising in pitch and volume. "It's her, Dad. She killed Jack. She killed Jack!"

"What? Leila, you're not making any sense. Slow down for a minute, will you?"

Had Leila just said that Anna had killed Jack? She had to be mistaken. But before he could collect his thoughts, Leila continued. "Just listen to me, Pierce. For once in your life, listen to me."

Hunt swallowed hard. "Okay, Leila. I'm listening."

CHAPTER TWENTY

Miami, Florida

Leila stood in her bedroom, clutching her phone so tightly her fingers began to cramp. She was furious at herself. What had she hoped for—that her dad would believe her? Her father was in love with Anna. Of course he'd pick Anna's side instead of hers. Wasn't it exactly what he had done when he'd gone undercover inside the Garcia crime family? Wasn't it true that his affair with Anna was the reason her parents had divorced? Her dad always chose Anna over her and her mom. Always.

Talking to him was a waste of time. He'd never understand what she was about to do.

"Leila, I said I was listening," her father said. "Please tell me what's going on."

She sighed heavily. "Coach Harris told the DEA that he bought the drug that killed Jack from someone working for Anna," she said, examining the butcher knife she'd taken from a kitchen drawer. "She lied to you, Dad. Can't you see that? She's a fucking liar!"

"Leila, I understand that you're upset, but Anna couldn't have done—"

Leila hung up. When it came to Anna, her dad was a lost cause. She would have to take matters into her own hands.

She texted Sophia.

Hey—Are u awake?

Sophia's reply was almost instantaneous. Yeah. Can't sleep. Can't stop thinking about Jack. You okay?

U trust me, right?

You r my BFF. I trust u.

Leila typed. Can u keep a secret? Her heart was hammering in her chest as she awaited Sophia's reply.

Yes. U know that.

For a second, Leila hesitated. Was she sure of what she was about to write to Sophia? Could she be wrong? No, she had heard what Chris had said on the phone. She took a deep breath and let her fingers type the words. Then she read her sentence. Anna is responsible for Jack's death. Her index finger hovered above the send button.

This wasn't right. Sophia was her best friend. They had gone through so much together. She deserved better than a text. Leila deleted the text. Instead she typed, Don't tell anyone. I'm coming to your place. I'll text you again when I'm at the gate. Ok?

Ok sis. Can't wait.

Leila dressed rapidly, leaving her pajamas on the floor. She opened the door of her bedroom with great care. Prudently, she peered around the doorframe. Nothing. Complete darkness and not a sound. Her mom and Chris were probably asleep. *Perfect.* With the butcher knife in her right hand, she tiptoed down the hall, feeling her way along the walls until she reached the broad staircase. She crept gingerly down the steps. At the front door, she jammed her feet into a pair of sneakers, grabbed her backpack, and had her hand on the door when she remembered the alarm.

Better not go that way.

She made her way to the kitchen instead. She opened one of the large windows and was about to climb out when she realized that she still had the knife in her hand. That wasn't going to work. She grabbed a rainbow-colored dishcloth and used it to wrap the knife before placing it against her laptop inside her backpack. Satisfied she wouldn't cut herself, she climbed out the window, eased it shut behind her, and slipped into the Floridian night.

CHAPTER TWENTY-ONE

Jalalabad, Nangarhar Province, Afghanistan

His brief conversation with his daughter had shaken Hunt to his core. He had tried to call her back numerous times but had managed only to get her voicemail. He understood that she was having a hard time coping with Jack's death, but to blame it on Anna? That wasn't right. He considered calling Chris and Jasmine to discuss the matter with them.

She lied to you, Dad. Can't you see that? She's a fucking liar! His daughter's words were like blows delivered with a silk-clad sledgehammer. Could she be right? Was Anna capable of such a betrayal? Hunt was feeling nauseated.

Notwithstanding his deep feelings for her, his relationship with Anna was complicated at best. It was through her that Hunt had infiltrated the Garcia crime syndicate during his early years with the DEA. Two years later, he had sent her father to jail in what was, at the time, one of the biggest arrests of the decade. His betrayal had broken Anna's heart. But it had broken his too. During the two years he had spent undercover, Hunt had fallen madly and irrevocably in love with Anna, and she with him. It was at Vicente Garcia's trial that Hunt's wife, Jasmine, learned of his infidelity. The next morning Jasmine packed her and Leila's suitcases and left Hunt. Hunt had never blamed her for doing so. He was the one who had fucked up. She was only protecting herself and their daughter.

Was Anna now returning the favor by betraying *his* trust? Had she only used him to give herself some breathing room from the DEA?

Goddamn it!

Hunt had no time for this shit. He had a mission to run. He would deal with it later. He walked into the weapons vault located across the briefing room. He was about to press his thumb against the biometric reader when the reinforced door opened. Behind the door stood Simon Carter. Carter was all geared up. His helmet was fitted with an infrared strobe at the rear and night-vision goggles at the front. An M4 rifle was strapped across his plate carrier, and a Glock 17 was secured in a drop holster.

"Abigail and Dante are ready. They're waiting by the helicopter," Carter said.

"Ask the pilots to warm up the engines and complete their diagnostic procedures," Hunt replied. "I'll be out shortly."

Carter must have noticed something because he gave Hunt a second look.

"You okay, brother?"

"Yeah, everything's fine. I'm just running numbers in my head, and I want to make sure I have all my i's dotted and t's crossed for the mission. I'm good, man."

"All right then." Carter slapped him on the shoulder and exited the vault.

Hunt pinched his nose. He and Carter had shared so much together; it was normal to sense when your partner wasn't 100 percent.

Get your head in the game.

The vault was divided into seven cages, each packed with guns and other tools of war. Hunt walked to his cage and spun the combination lock. He kitted up and, last, reached for his earpiece. Every member of his team was capable of communicating via high-tech Bluetooth throat microphones linked to a personal radio protected with 128-bit encryption. Hunt secured the throat microphone around his neck and powered on the radio.

"To all call signs, this is Victor-One, comms check, over," Hunt said.

By the time everyone had checked in, Hunt could hear the Super Huey's main rotor spinning. When he came outside, the crew chief was waiting by the Super Huey's door, wearing a flight helmet with the black eye shield down. A long cord running from the side of his helmet back into the belly of the Super Huey allowed him to remain in contact with the pilots.

"We're good to go, boss," the crew chief yelled.

Hunt climbed aboard the helicopter, and the crew chief took his position manning one of the two door-mounted machine guns. Carter took care of the other one. Hunt strapped himself in. One of the pilots twisted in his seat and looked at Hunt. Hunt gave him a thumbs-up.

The two 1,828-horsepower engines roared to full power, and the Super Huey's frame began to rattle. The pilot pulled back the helicopter's collective pitch control, and the Super Huey rose effortlessly. Hunt felt his stomach drop as the Super Huey leaped off the makeshift helipad, banked hard, and accelerated rapidly over the bleak, unforgiving terrain of the most dangerous province in Afghanistan. As someone who'd been an Army Ranger before joining the DEA, Hunt was accustomed to riding in helicopters, but familiar feeling or not, the exhilarating sense of flying at 150 miles per hour so close to the ground was something he relished. A quick look in Carter's direction confirmed his good friend was enjoying the ride as much as he was.

The same couldn't be said about Dante. When Dante saw that Hunt was looking at him, he averted his eyes.

"What's wrong?" It wasn't the first time he'd noticed that Dante seemed uncomfortable in the Super Huey.

"Nothing. All's good, man."

"He hates flying," threw in Abigail.

Hunt laughed. Dante was a former Black Hawk pilot who had flown combat missions in Iraq. On his fifty-third mission, a surface-to-air missile had found its way into his Black Hawk engine's exhaust over Latifiya, a small town south of Baghdad. Despite multiple hydraulic system failures and having almost no flight controls, Dante had succeeded in crash-landing his helicopter on a sand dune. Luckily for him, Hunt had seen the chopper go down and, with six other Rangers, had charged five hundred feet across open ground to provide suppressive fire. With the enemy combatants pinned down by his team's fire, Hunt had called in an air strike on the enemy position, saving Dante's and the rest of his crew's lives.

"He's a decorated Black Hawk pilot," Hunt said, "so unless I saved someone else's ass in Iraq, I don't believe you."

"Why do you think he left the army and never flew again?" said Abigail.

"That's why you joined the DEA?" Hunt asked Dante. He had no idea Dante had never piloted again after the crash.

"Really, Pierce? You want to talk about this now?" Dante asked, clearly not happy with his wife's comment.

"We have a two-hour flight to Kandahar. Why not?"

"Hey, Dante," joined in Carter with a big smile, "we won't judge."

Dante gave him the finger but nonetheless said, "I'm not afraid to die, in case that's what you're all thinking. It's how I might die that scares me shitless."

"Tell us," Carter said. "How would you prefer to die?"

"With a bullet to the head. There's no pain, and you die instantly. How long would it take you to die by burning or drowning in a chopper crash? One or two minutes? Believe me, those final and painful minutes would leave me more than enough time to find a hell of a lot of things to regret in my life. I don't want to die miserable. I'd like to die happy—you know, like getting your head sliced off clean by Captain Hook at Disney World."

Abigail watched him, bemused. She'd clearly heard this before.

"Oh man, you're sicker than I thought," Carter said.

"Not at all," replied Dante. "Because wherever I ended up after I died, I'd be able to laugh my ass off at how I must have looked to the five-year-old waiting to get Hook's autograph . . ."

Hunt wasn't listening anymore. His mind was somewhere else. Dante's talk about being engulfed in flames brought back painful memories of Valentina Mieles's basement. The pain of being shot, Sophia's screams . . . it was all coming back.

"Hey, boss? You okay?" Abigail asked, her voice penetrating Hunt's fog-shrouded brain. "Your hands are shaking."

Hunt cursed under his breath. He had let his mind drift away to a place that had nothing to do with today's mission. He couldn't let that happen again.

"I'm good. Dante's voice put me right to sleep," he said, forcing a smile.

Before Abigail could follow up with another question, Crawford cut in from back at the TOC, where she and Pike were monitoring the mission. "Victor-One, this is Echo-One, over."

"Go ahead for Victor-One."

"Just received a report that a suicide bomber rammed his vehicle into one of the gates at the Kandahar Airfield. Two US casualties are reported."

Hunt's heart sank. "Copy that, Echo-One. Are they keeping the airfield open?"

"That's affirmative, Victor-One, but coalition forces are cordoning off the area."

"Thanks for the heads-up, Echo-One. Victor-One out."

The mood inside the cabin had changed drastically. The deaths of two US servicemen was a hard thing to digest. It also put their own vulnerability in perspective.

Hunt closed his eyes and offered a silent prayer to the fallen American soldiers. It didn't matter that he didn't know the soldiers personally. They were Americans, and that was all that mattered.

He opened his eyes and checked the GPS strapped to his left wrist. They were fifty miles northeast of Kandahar.

"Echo-One from Victor-One," Hunt said.

"Go ahead, Victor-One," Crawford replied from three hundred miles away.

"We're fifteen minutes out of point Whiskey, over."

"I have you on my screen, Victor-One."

"Copy that, Echo-One. Victor-One out."

Hunt had no doubt that Crawford and Pike had been keeping a sharp eye on their progress. Still, it didn't cost anything to make sure the intel specialists had a fix on them. In this part of the world, you never knew when the next shit storm was going to sucker punch you.

Like Anna just did?

He still couldn't wrap his head around Jack's death. It was inconceivable that Anna had willingly played a role. Hunt considered himself a good judge of character. His experience leading Rangers in combat and serving in an undercover capacity had honed his instincts about people. There was no way Anna was playing him. The more he thought about it, the more he was convinced she was a victim. Anna needed his help. Leila needed his help.

And they need it now. How am I supposed to do this from Afghanistan?

Hunt cursed. Anna had asked for his assistance, pleaded for him to stay before he left for Paraguay, and he had brushed her off. Same thing for Leila. He wasn't by her side when she needed him the most. That couldn't continue. And what about Anna? The jackals were at the gate; she needed every friend she had by her side in order to keep her enemies at bay. What Hunt needed to do was to wrap up this mission and get back to Florida pronto before he lost Anna *and* Leila for good.

He forced himself to ignore the little voice in his head that told him he was already too late and that he'd have to choose between one woman or the other.

CHAPTER TWENTY-TWO

Miami, Florida

Anna gritted her teeth at the sound of Alejandro's voice coming through the speaker of her phone. It was late, and her tolerance for bullshit was almost gone.

"Oh, hello, Anna. Glad you called."

Anna wanted to scream at him, but at the last moment she held herself back. Alejandro's voice was warm and unconstrained, and it pissed her off. It was as if nothing had happened—as if he hadn't sent men to assassinate her. If he had been there in person, she would have ripped out his vocal cords with her fingers. As if he had sensed her internal struggle, Tasis, who was seated across from her on the opposite side of her desk, signaled her with a wave of his hand to remain calm. She wasn't sure she could.

"You could have come to me instead of murdering three members of our family."

"Our family?" Alejandro laughed. "You're kidding yourself if you think that everybody you've wronged will simply forgive you and go on with their life."

"You're making no sense. I've listened to your concerns and—"

"And you proceeded in dismantling everything your father, your brother, and I have built over the course of two decades," Alejandro barked back. "You're an ungrateful little bitch who needs to be put down."

"I'll have your head for this," inserted Tasis, his voice a block of ice. "I'll chop it off myself."

"Ah! You're there, too, old friend. Well, you're welcome to try," replied Alejandro.

Anna shushed an angry reply from Tasis by raising her hand. It was her turn to calm him down.

"What's the point of all this?" she asked Alejandro.

"Why don't I explain it to you in person?"

"It's getting late. Why don't you come to the estate, and we'll talk," Anna replied.

Alejandro chuckled. "So that our friend Mauricio can chop off my head? I don't think so."

"Where then?"

"At the old warehouse in Wynwood."

Anna knew the place. She'd been there many times when her father was still the head of the family. The Garcias had used the location to break down large cocaine shipments into smaller quantities for street-level distribution. She thought her brother had sold the warehouse following Vicente's arrest. Obviously, there was a multitude of things going on in her own organization that she wasn't aware of.

"I'll be there."

Tasis was shaking his head vigorously in disapproval.

"Out of respect for Vicente and Tony, I'll give you one chance to make things right, Anna. You'll kiss my ring and instruct everyone still behind you to fall in behind me. You've seen what I'm prepared to do, so don't fuck me over," Alejandro warned.

"You mean killing young athletes?"

"I'm prepared to continue the transition process peacefully," Alejandro said, not taking the bait. "It's up to you to decide how you wanna play this. I'll see you there in one hour. Don't waste my time. Think about Sophia."

Anna wished she could have slammed a receiver back into its cradle, but since she had called Alejandro with Tasis's cell phone, that was impossible. Anna had to bite her cheek not to say out loud the curse that was on her lips.

"How dare he threaten Sophia!"

Tasis grunted. He placed a comforting hand on her shoulder but didn't speak.

"I'm so tired of this shit," she murmured more to herself than to Tasis. "What are you thinking?" she asked him.

"I don't trust the son of a bitch."

"Neither do I. Do you think it's a trap?"

Tasis folded his arms across his chest and said, "If you had asked me this question three months ago, I would have said no. But with what happened today, who the hell knows?"

"It's not like I have any choice."

"I disagree," Tasis said. "We can leave."

"And leave behind the men who are loyal to me?"

"Alejandro is growing stronger by the day. It's only a matter of time before he takes over."

Tasis's assessment was correct. If she elected to stay and fight, more men would die. She had started this whole process to offer the men and women who'd been loyal to her family a way out. But if a life without crime wasn't what they wanted for themselves, who was she to force it upon them?

"Is there any chance that if I relinquish control of the organization to you—" Anna started, hoping to find a way not to abdicate to Alejandro, but Tasis cut her off midsentence.

"It's too late for that, I'm afraid. We'd only be pushing down the road what's inevitable."

"Shit," she said. "I'm sorry."

"Don't be. You did what you thought was right. It was worth a try," he reassured her.

Was it? The execution of her men at the hands of Alejandro was a harsh reality check. She should have listened to Hunt and Tasis and renounced her place at the head of the Garcia family the moment Hunt had saved Sophia. Poor Sophia deserved better. Her mom had died in a freak skiing accident when she was still a little girl, and her dad had been killed trying to rescue her from kidnappers. What Sophia needed wasn't a strong woman at the head of a criminal enterprise. No, what she needed was an aunt who would love and support her no matter what.

And it's up to me to do just that.

"I'll meet with Alejandro and hope it will bring an end to this madness," Anna finally said, resigned. "Then Sophia and I will leave."

"Let me come with you when you run," Tasis said. "I'll protect you."

"That won't be necessary, Mauricio. But thanks."

For a second Tasis looked shocked, even hurt, but then he seemed to figure out what she had in mind. He smiled. "You're sure Hunt will leave with you?"

She wasn't, but she refused to entertain the thought she had misinterpreted his signals, so she nodded.

"Where will you go?"

"Far away from here."

CHAPTER TWENTY-THREE

Miami, Florida

Leila thanked the Uber driver. "Right here's fine." She had texted Sophia two minutes ago to let her know she was almost there.

At the gate, Leila texted again.

Ok. Gimme a minute, came the reply. A guard will meet you. Sorry.

Leila knew that Sophia had an application on her phone that could open and close the front gate. A moment later, the gate opened. Leila walked in. A man was waiting for her. He was only a few inches taller than her five-foot, three-inch frame. He had short dark hair. Despite the night air being quite warm, the man wore a light windbreaker.

"Sophia's waiting for you, Miss DeGray. Go right ahead."

Leila was glad the man didn't ask to check her backpack. She hadn't prepared a story to justify the butcher knife. She walked down the long driveway leading to the house. Sophia was waiting by the front entrance, a big smile on her face.

"What are you doing here so late?" she whispered. "Anna's gonna be pissed at us if she finds out."

"Where is she?"

Sophia pointed behind her. "In her office."

Leila walked straight past her friend. "Let's go to your room. We need to talk."

———

Anna wasn't looking forward to her meeting with Alejandro tonight. The man was a snake. The more she thought about it, the more she was convinced that he had been behind the ambush on Alligator Alley.

But why had his men retreated?

Anna had replayed the scenario a hundred times in her mind. Nothing made sense. Someone had called them off at the last minute—but she got the impression it hadn't been Alejandro. Or maybe she was wrong. Maybe he'd instructed the men to only scare her. But her gut was telling her otherwise.

A knock at the door made her look up. "Come in," she said.

The door was pushed open, and in walked one of the guards tasked with patrolling the estate grounds.

"Leila's arrived," he said.

"Leila?" Anna looked at her watch. It was almost eleven at night. In less than ten minutes, she would have to leave for her meeting with Alejandro. What was Leila doing here? If this were any other day, Anna wouldn't mind. But with everything going on, she'd much prefer if both girls were at the Moon residence instead of here.

"Didn't you know she was coming over?" the guard asked, frowning.

Anna shook her head and got up from behind her desk. "Where is she?"

"They're in Sophia's bedroom."

———

Leila had operated under the assumption that she would need to convince Sophia to leave with her. She had been wrong. Leila wasn't even done stating her case against Anna, and Sophia was already packing her bag.

"You sure Chris won't mind if I stay at your place?" Sophia asked.

"I won't leave him the choice," Leila replied, determination ringing in her voice. "He takes you in, or we leave together."

Sophia looked at her. Tears were pooling in her eyes. "I hate my life."

"Don't say that," Leila said.

"No, it's true," Sophia said, her shoulders shaking out of control with each sob. "My father was a gangster, my mom died in a skiing accident, and my aunt is a drug dealer. What is there to love?"

"We'll get through this together." Leila wrapped her arms around her friend and pulled her close. "I promise."

She could feel Sophia's tears on her neck. Her own tears were flowing down her cheeks. They had to hurry up. They had to go.

"Are you ready?" Leila asked. "We need to go. Now. If Anna sees me here and figures out we know what she did, she'll kill us both."

Sophia slowly lifted her head. She wiped her eyes and nose with her hands. "Oh my God. You really think so? You really think she'd kill us?"

It seemed so unreal, so out of character. "I don't know," Leila replied after a moment. "But we'll be safer at my mom's place."

Sophia nodded. "I think so too."

Leila helped her friend close the suitcase. Sophia started to zip it but stopped halfway through.

"Why are—" started Leila, but Sophia placed a finger against her mouth, gesturing her to be quiet.

"Someone's coming," Sophia mouthed. "Hide."

Leila's heart began to thump uncontrollably in her chest. She tried to will the fear away, but it didn't budge.

Move. You have to move. Then she remembered the butcher knife. With trembling hands, she fumbled in her backpack for the knife. *There.*

The door to Sophia's bedroom swung open just as she removed the dishcloth from around the knife.

———

Anna entered Sophia's bedroom. She opened her mouth to speak, but the sight before her caused her to go mute. Leila was looking straight at her, brandishing a massive butcher knife. Behind Leila, Sophia was shaking like a leaf in a storm. On Sophia's bed was a suitcase.

"Please tell me what's going on," Anna managed to say, feeling weak at the knees. "What is this?"

"Let us through," warned Leila, waving the knife in front of her.

Anna was so confused by the whole scene that her brain wanted to shut down altogether. "What are you doing, Leila? I don't understand."

"Don't play stupid with me," growled Leila. "I know you killed Jack."

She gasped. The coldness of Leila's words froze Anna's insides. Darkness clawed at the edge of her vision. She placed her hand on the doorframe to steady herself. Now she understood. Somehow, Leila had gotten into her head the idea that she was responsible for Jack's death and that she had become a menace to Sophia.

Anna teared up. Leila was right.

———

Leila felt an unstoppable rage rising in her chest, a burning hatred as images of Jack flashed through her mind.

"You have stolen everything from me!" she yelled. "You took away my father. But that wasn't enough. Now you've taken Jack too!"

Anna whispered something that Leila didn't understand.

"What? What did you say?"

"I said I'm so sorry, Leila. I didn't mean for any of this to happen."

"How could you?" Leila asked, advancing toward Anna. "How could you betray my dad? How could you betray Sophia? And me? We trusted you!"

Leila was less than three feet away from her when Anna asked, "Are you gonna kill me? Was that your intention when you came here tonight, Leila? To kill me?"

The unexpected question shocked Leila back to her senses. "I'm here to save Sophia. She's suffered enough."

"I know. Trust me—I know."

Anna's honesty disarmed Leila. What was she doing with a knife? Who was she kidding? She wasn't going to kill anyone. Not tonight. Not ever. The mere thought of cutting Anna with Chris's butcher knife frightened her.

"Can we talk? Please," Anna pleaded.

Before Leila could reply, Sophia stepped forward and gently touched Leila's arm. "Yes. Let's talk."

CHAPTER TWENTY-FOUR

Miami, Florida

Anna patiently listened to Leila as she explained how she had come to the conclusion that Anna was responsible for Jack's death. Anna didn't interrupt her a single time. She didn't blame Leila for seeing her as public enemy number one. How could she? In a way, Anna knew that she deserved the designation. After all, it was under her nose that Alejandro had continued his drug operations.

"There's a lot of truth in what you said, Leila," Anna said once Leila was done. "But I swear to you that I had no idea this was going on. In fact, I only learned of one of my men's treachery today. Mauricio and I will soon leave to settle the issue once and for all."

"How?" Leila asked.

Anna looked at Sophia. Anna felt it was important that Sophia truly understood what she had tried to do since her dad's death.

"When Pierce safely brought you back from Mexico, I swore to him that I'd change the Garcia family's vocation. I was tired of all the violence. Like you, I've lost so much because of the bad choices our family made over the years. This life isn't what I want for you, Sophia. It's not what I want for myself. You deserve a shot at a normal life. You understand?"

Sophia nodded.

"I've worked extremely hard to begin transitioning our organization into something legitimate, away from the criminality it has been long associated with. But not everyone agrees with my decision. In fact, a lot of people are spending considerable time and money undermining my efforts to restructure."

"Why?" Sophia asked.

"Because these men, they don't want to change. Crime is all they know. That's their livelihood. That's how they make money, feed their families. They're afraid. They're afraid to change."

Anna switched her attention to Leila. "Your dad told me as much, but I didn't believe him. I thought that by leading by example, I could prove him wrong. I've failed."

"I'm sorry," Leila said, big tears rolling down her cheeks, one after the other.

"It's okay, Leila. How could you have known?"

"I should have trusted you. My dad trusts you. Why couldn't I do the same?"

"I'm gonna fix all of this," Anna said, placing her hands on Leila's shoulders. She didn't want to go into too much detail with the two teenagers, but she wanted them to know that everything would be all right.

"When?"

"Tonight. Tomorrow we start a new life, Sophia. Okay? We'll get away from all of this."

Sophia's face filled with panic. "Will I still be able to see Leila?"

"Yes, of course. But we'll talk more about it tomorrow. There are still a lot of things I need to figure out. Now I need to go."

Leila seemed relieved. Sophia too. "You girls will be okay?" Anna asked.

"I better get home," Leila said.

"I'll drop you off," Anna said.

CHAPTER TWENTY-FIVE

Venezuelan jungle

Godfrey estimated that they had traveled less than four miles when Papa-One raised his fist in the air. Seeing his escorts go down on one knee, Godfrey did the same and studied the ground in front of him. Darkness had fallen with an inky blackness that promised protection but also hindered their progress and heightened the risk of injury. The jungle canopy made it impracticable to use the small drone to conduct reconnaissance.

Godfrey remained immobile, firm and still as a statue, and listened to the jungle in perfect silence. More than anything, he wanted to ask Papa-One what had attracted his attention, but he remained quiet, his nerves tensing with every sound he didn't recognize.

The long day and the discomfort from staying in the same position for several long minutes made Godfrey fidget. The feeling of dampness and the frequent bustling of unknown insects over his body didn't help with his state of mind either.

A voice in his ear made him jump. "We have company. Get ready."

Get ready?

Godfrey tried to remember if he had chambered a round. He didn't think he had. Should he check? Maybe chamber another round, just to be sure? No, that would make too much noise. A sound froze him. He wasn't sure what it was, but it was a sound that didn't belong with the other sounds of the jungle. He wished he had a pair of night-vision goggles like Papa-One and Two had. At least he'd know where to shoot if it came to that.

An illumination flare popped high above their position. Then another, and another, their bright lights piercing through the jungle canopy. Godfrey heard Papa-Two swear as he flipped up his now-useless NVGs.

"American friends, I'm Colonel Carlos Arteaga of the National Army of the Bolivarian Republic of Venezuela," a lone voice pierced through the jungle. "We know where you are. We have you surrounded. I've ordered my men to hold fire. You have exactly two minutes to surrender. Any sudden movement will be considered an act of aggression."

Oh shit! They found us.

"If we surrender, we're dead," Papa-One said, steadfast. He clutched his weapon unyieldingly.

"Agreed," Papa-Two replied. "What do you think, Godfrey?"

Crude images of what General Peraza would do to him kept popping up in his mind. "We're dead one way or the other," Godfrey finally said. "They're all working for Peraza."

"Fuck this shit," Papa-One said. "I say we take a few of them with us." He dug into his pocket and placed the satellite phone into Godfrey's hand.

"Hold the number nine for two seconds," Papa-One said. "It will connect you to the tactical operations center in Virginia. Let them know what's going on. Call sign is Papa-One. Nimitz is the TOC."

Godfrey did what he was told. The call was picked up on the first ring.

"This is Nimitz, Papa-One. What's your situation?"

"Can you locate us using the GPS on our phone?" Godfrey asked.

"We have you on the map, Papa-One. You're still two miles south of your extract point."

"We won't make the extraction point," Godfrey said. "We're surrounded."

There was a brief pause, and then another voice came on the line. "Papa-One, this is Nimitz-Actual."

Nimitz-Actual was the call sign of either the administrator of the DEA or the director of the Intelligence Division. And since the director of the Intelligence Division was a woman, that meant that Godfrey was speaking directly to Tom Hauer.

"Papa-One and Two aren't available. My name is—"

Hauer cut him off. "I know who you are. What's the situation on the ground?"

"We're surrounded by the Venezuelan army."

"Peraza knows who you are?"

"Without a doubt."

"Goddamn it!"

"Sir, they have us left, right, and center. We have no way out. I need to tell you—"

"I want you to surrender."

Godfrey wasn't sure if he had heard the administrator correctly. "You want us to do what?"

"Surrender, and I'll get you guys out. I promise."

Godfrey had no idea how Hauer thought he could get them out of there. They weren't dealing with the regular armed forces of a legitimate country; they were dealing with what really amounted to General Peraza's private military. Godfrey wasn't optimistic about his chances of survival. He didn't believe Peraza would keep him alive long enough to be rescued. He told Hauer the same.

"I don't care what I have to do to bring you guys home," the administrator replied. "Our diplomatic ties with their government are shit anyway. I'll make as much noise as I can."

In the background, Colonel Arteaga was back on the PA. "You have thirty seconds left—then I'll order my troops to open fire."

A long sequence of white illumination flares popped above the jungle canopy. From his position, Godfrey could see dozens of soldiers moving like shadows through the jungle.

"With all due respect, sir, that won't work," Godfrey said. "Peraza is a different animal. And I know too much."

"So we were right?"

"There's definitely something going on. I've been able to put a few things together."

"What—"

"We're out of time. Mark my position, sir. I'll leave a flash drive behind. You can upload its contents remotely, but you'll need to get within five hundred feet to pick up the signal."

Before Hauer could reply, Godfrey powered off the satellite phone.

"What are we doing?" Papa-One asked him.

"Nimitz-Actual wants us to surrender," Godfrey replied.

"No way," Papa-Two retorted. "There's no fucking way I'm surrendering to these assholes."

Godfrey removed his left boot and flicked open a secret compartment in its heel.

"What are you doing?" Papa-One asked.

"I'm leaving a little something behind. Everything of importance I've learned in the last four years is on this," Godfrey said, palming a USB key.

CHAPTER TWENTY-SIX

Miami, Florida

Anna stared through the window of the Range Rover, high-rise hotels and condos crowding her vision against the night sky. Miami had grown so much in size and complexity over the last two decades that she sometimes felt like a tourist in her own hometown. The drama back at the house had shaken her, but now she felt better. Reenergized even. She was glad she had had the opportunity to talk with Sophia and Leila. Glad to have had the opportunity to deescalate the situation. Anna looked down at her lap, where her index finger hovered over the call button of her cell phone. She didn't dare press it. She wanted to speak with Sophia, to hear her voice, but at the same time, she didn't want her to worry. She was probably asleep by now. To call her would be selfish.

Everything is going to be all right, Anna told herself for the hundredth time. She placed her cell phone in the cup holder. She would talk to Sophia in the morning.

"How are you feeling?" Tasis asked from the driver's seat of the SUV.

"Fine."

Tasis looked at her in the rearview mirror. His eyes were caring. She'd known him for a long time, but it was the most tender she'd seen him.

"We're almost there," he said a minute later, turning the SUV into Wynwood Art District. Formerly part of an industrial district, previously abandoned warehouses were now occupied by trendy restaurants and cafés. Even at this time of night, pedestrians were roaming the streets, enjoying the breeze or the snappy music escaping from the lounges.

"This is it," Tasis announced. "To our left."

Anna's gaze stopped on a medium-size warehouse-type structure with bright pink neon lights. She didn't recognize the place. A long line of sharply dressed people was wrapped around the building.

"The warehouse is now a nightclub?" Anna asked.

"This is where Alejandro is running his business from," Tasis replied.

"Who owns it?"

"In theory, you own it through one of your subsidiaries."

"Why did my brother tell me he'd sold the place if he didn't?"

"I have no idea."

Anna let it go. She had more important things to worry about. Like the fact that she was about to sit down with a man who'd tried to have her killed.

How did it come to that?

Because this wasn't the kind of life she wanted for herself and for Sophia. For the past several months she'd tried to change it. Was there, too, a little part of her craving Pierce's approval? For some reason, she wanted him to be proud of her. Hunt wasn't the kind of man who would see a woman crime boss as a source of pride.

But was Hunt really the kind of man she and Sophia needed? Hunt's life wasn't rosy either. Violence seemed to follow him wherever he went. Would it continue even if they moved away together? She hoped not. But was hoping good enough? Could she take the chance?

With or without Hunt, it was time to get herself and Sophia out of this life while she still could.

Tasis parked the Range Rover in the closest spot he found, which was two blocks away from the warehouse. Anna stepped out of the SUV and onto the sidewalk. A warm breeze blew through her hair and tickled her face, carrying with it the salty scent of the ocean into the heart of the city. Tasis climbed out of the SUV and joined her on the sidewalk.

"Are you sure you don't want me to come in with you?"

"I'll call or text you when I'm done," Anna replied, looking him in the eyes, determined to convey a strength they both knew wasn't there. "Nothing's gonna happen to me."

Tasis sighed, giving up. "I'll be waiting right here, with the engine running. If you change your mind—"

Anna reached out and touched his arm. "I'll let you know, Mauricio. Thank you."

With one final nod, she turned around and headed toward the warehouse-turned-nightclub.

———

From a block away, Luis Ojeda watched Anna Garcia make her way toward the nightclub.

About time.

Ojeda had a plane to catch. If all went well—and he didn't see anything impeding his success—he'd be back in Caracas in time for lunch the next day. It was his father's seventieth birthday. Not something he wanted to miss.

Ojeda pulled on his unfiltered cigarette one last time before crushing it out under the sole of his shoe. From the inside breast pocket of his jacket, he removed a small plastic Ziploc bag. He unzipped the bag and carefully dropped the cigarette butt into it. He closed the bag and replaced it inside his jacket.

No point making it too easy for Miami's finest.

Since he had started working for General Peraza two years ago, Ojeda had killed sixteen men and three women. No children, though. It didn't mean he liked children, because he didn't. In fact, he wasn't afraid of calling his neighbors' kids all sorts of names if they woke him up on a Sunday morning. He was simply incapable of killing children. He never understood why. He saw it as a flaw, but that was fine by him, and General Peraza didn't seem to care either. The general had other people willing to do it when needed.

Ojeda peeked at his watch. Ten minutes had passed since Anna Garcia had entered the club. Ojeda took three deep breaths.

It was time to go to work.

A look in the direction of the Range Rover told him that Mauricio Tasis had climbed back into the SUV. Ojeda rose from the park bench he'd been sitting on for the last thirty minutes and nonchalantly used the sidewalk to approach the SUV by its passenger side. He pictured in his mind what was about to happen. It didn't matter how many times he played it in his head; it always ended the same way. And that made him smile.

As Ojeda closed the distance, a warm and familiar sensation flew through his body, and he took a moment to savor it. He'd always enjoyed the rush of adrenaline before a hit. He'd been trained to feel nothing for his targets, positive or negative.

Hate can be as dangerous a liability as sympathy.

Ojeda understood the meaning of these words, but as a diagnosed sociopath, it was easier for him to abide by them than it was for some of his colleagues. That was why his indisposition toward killing children bothered him so much. Wouldn't it be nice if he could find a shrink willing to help him understand *his flaw*?

Ojeda was less than five meters away from the Range Rover when his cell phone beeped twice in his pocket, signaling an incoming text message. He slipped his hand in his pocket and retrieved the phone.

Hold.

Ojeda smiled as if the message he had just received was funny and continued on the sidewalk past the parked Range Rover. He didn't know, or care about, the reason behind the sudden change of plan. He was an assassin, not a strategist. If his master wanted him to hold, he'd hold. He never understood people who questioned orders. Didn't make sense to him. Ojeda always carried out his orders without ever questioning their content. He didn't obey them out of any sense of inherent rightness, but simply because they were orders. He had to thank his father for that. His father had drilled into him at an early age the principle that the authorities must always be obeyed, no matter their requests. A principle he had followed through his military career with the Ninety-Ninth Army Special Forces Brigade.

His phone beeped again.

Contract postponed. Assume holding pattern until further instructions.

Well now, *that* was a problem. How was he supposed to make it to lunch tomorrow?

CHAPTER TWENTY-SEVEN

Helmand Province, Afghanistan

The refueling stop went without a hitch. Hunt felt the floor of the Super Huey shudder as it lifted off the ground once more.

Following the quick layover at the Kandahar Airfield, his original plan had been to land at Camp Dwyer—a Marine Corps installation and airfield located in the Gamir district of the Helmand River Valley—and drive to Marjah from there. He'd had to amend his plan when Pike had informed him during their refueling stop that a bomb-laden vehicle had gone off in Gamir, and everything was on lockdown. Instead of risking the drive across thirty miles of scorching desert to Marjah, Hunt had decided they'd land right in Azfaar's backyard.

The flight to Marjah was peaceful, and Hunt marveled at the green valley below and the mountains off in the distance. With all the blood spilled in the last two decades of warfare, he'd forgotten about the striking beauty of Afghanistan's soaring mountains, majestic lakes, and vast expanses of rolling hills of flower-covered terrain.

Hunt must have dozed off because when he opened his eyes, the crew chief was tapping him on the shoulder.

"We're ten minutes out," the crew chief said.

Hunt passed along the message to Abigail and Dante, who had both fallen asleep, and ordered everyone to check their gear one last time. They were five minutes out when Carter announced, "I have two military-aged men riding a motorcycle. They're riding west toward our target location. They're armed."

"Don't engage unless they fire at us."

Hunt grabbed the nearest headset, flipped it over his head, and instructed the pilot to stay well clear of the motorcycle.

"They'll see us land," the copilot said.

"That's fine," Hunt replied. "The crew chief can open up if they get too close, but for now we don't engage."

"Do you want us to remain on the ground?" the copilot asked.

Hunt weighed his options. Keeping the chopper on the ground would provide a faster extraction if things got hairy but would limit the amount of overwatch. As good as the Super Huey was, it wasn't a quiet bird. Hunt feared that keeping the helicopter on overwatch might actually attract more attention than they wanted.

"Keep it on the ground, but be ready to take off at a moment's notice."

"Will do."

Hunt wasn't overly worried about the men on the motorcycle. They'd keep an eye on them, but there could be a multitude of reasons for their presence.

The helicopter banked and dropped altitude as the pilot took a wide-arcing approach around the field where Hunt had instructed them to touch down. Its screaming blades kicked up sand and dust all around. The copilot cut the helicopter's engines, and the rotor whooshed slowly to a stop.

Hunt was the first to jump out of the chopper. Carter, Dante, and Abigail were next, and they all fanned out to set up a perimeter around the Super Huey. Azfaar's house was five hundred feet from the helicopter. When the dust and dirt cleared away, Hunt took a minute to scan the area, knowing the rest of his team was doing the same.

The rectangular bungalow, set in the middle of a large wheat field, was made of sun-dried bricks covered with mud and straw plaster. With only one door and four windows, it was smaller and more washed out than Hunt remembered. The last couple of years didn't seem to have been good for Azfaar. The wheat field had been hit hard by the dry weather and was in poor condition.

Movement at one of the windows caught his attention. A face appeared.

Hunt recognized the man instantly. *Azfaar.*

"I've got movement in the right front window," Hunt informed the rest of the team. "It's Azfaar."

Like most Afghan males, Azfaar had learned how to hold an AK-47 before he had learned how to do basic math, so Hunt made sure to let his team know that Azfaar was armed.

"I don't think he'll engage us, but don't let your guard down," he said. "Victor-Two, follow my lead. Three and Four, stay by the chopper, and cover our flanks and rear."

In a combat crouch, with his M4 at the ready, Hunt approached Azfaar's house while Carter took position behind him. They were still one hundred feet away from the door when Azfaar came out. Azfaar, a tall and proud man in his fifties, had an AK-47 slung over his shoulder, its muzzle pointing down at the ground. He was dressed in a loose-fitting white shirt, shapeless white pants, and a white kufi—a round brimless cap worn by some Afghan men to symbolize their status as family patriarch. Azfaar looked more curious than concerned and made no attempt to bring his rifle to bear. He smiled uncertainly, no doubt a tad uncomfortable with the helicopter standing in the middle of his field and armed men advancing toward him. It was impossible that he'd recognized Hunt or Carter from this distance, but he waved at them nonetheless.

Hunt, who now had his M4 at the low ready, waved back. Azfaar greeted them in Pashto with an expansive arm gesture. Then, as Hunt got closer, Azfaar froze, his eyes squinting as he concentrated on Hunt's face. The older man was studying him. Hunt's Pashto was basic at best, so he switched to English, knowing Azfaar had a good understanding of the language.

"We apologize for the disruption—" Hunt started.

"I know who you are," Azfaar interrupted in heavily accented English. His face suddenly grew sad, and his eyes clouded. "You were the Americans who were supposed to protect my family."

There was no point lying, so Hunt said, "We are. And I'm very sorry." Since it wouldn't bring any comfort to Azfaar, Hunt didn't try to justify his previous actions. He had followed his orders, and Azfaar probably knew that. Still, Hunt felt as if he had betrayed the man's trust. Not a good feeling, especially when one's actions were in part responsible for the extermination of a man's family. Azfaar looked much unhappier than he had the last time Hunt had seen him, and from the way he eyed Hunt, Hunt supposed a sizeable portion of that unhappiness was directed at him.

"Victor-One from Victor-Three," Dante said through Hunt's earbud.

"Go ahead, Victor-Three."

"I got two military-aged men about five hundred feet due east of my position. They're approaching on foot using the small ditch on the side of the road."

"Copy that, Victor-Three. The same we saw earlier?"

"Hard to say."

"Stand by," Hunt said, turning toward the new threat. He brought the M4 up to his shoulder.

Here they are. Sneaky bastards.

The men were both wearing typical Afghan outfits. They were advancing slowly through the small bushes, and their stealthy movement indicated they didn't want to be seen. Dante had done a good job spotting them.

"What do you think, Victor-Two?"

"I don't see any weapons, but one of them is holding something in his right hand," Carter replied.

Hunt focused his sights on the man who was closest to him. Carter was right. The man was holding what looked like a communication device. Hunt placed his cheek on the buttstock of his M4 and sighted on the man. At this distance, there would be very little wind to disturb a bullet's trajectory. What Hunt needed to see before he could pull the trigger was a weapon of some sort. A cell phone didn't cut it.

Azfaar mumbled something in Pashto.

"You know these guys?" Hunt asked.

Azfaar spat. "Thieves."

"Not good," Carter said. "They might see our helo as a big payday."

Hunt wasn't concerned about the two men. What concerned him was whom they could call. The region was swamped with insurgents, and there were more than a few warlords who'd pay handsomely to get their hands on a helicopter. Or a few dead Americans.

"You're trouble," Azfaar said, clearly upset. "They saw me with you. The Taliban will try to kill me now."

"All right, let's get inside," Hunt suggested. "Anyone else in the house?"

A glare of pure hatred shot from Azfaar's eyes. "Everyone's dead."

Hunt sympathized with the man. Azfaar had voluntarily stopped growing poppies, believing what the Americans had told him about making more money and receiving protection from coalition forces. What did he have to show for his misplaced trust in the US government? Now that he was here, Hunt regretted coming. This man had no reason to help them.

Hunt signaled Carter to move in. Weapon at the ready, Hunt followed Carter through the door. Entering, it took less than five seconds to determine that Azfaar had told them the truth. There was no one else present, nor was there any sign of anyone recently there other than Azfaar.

"Victor-Three, from One," Hunt said.

"Go for Victor-Three."

"We've moved inside the house. Keep an eye on these two guys, and let me know if they get any closer, will you?"

"Copy that, One. Will advise."

The inside of the house hadn't changed much since the last time Hunt had been there. It consisted of two bedrooms, a bathroom, and a kitchen, with a large living area in the center. As in most simple Afghan homes, Azfaar had almost no furniture. Mattresses and cushions were placed on the floor around the walls.

Azfaar gently unslung his AK-47 from his shoulder and rested it against the wall. "Tea," he said simply.

Hunt nodded. Declining wasn't an option. Afghan hospitality was legendary, and Hunt fondly remembered how generous and gracious Afghans really were. Hunt wanted more than anything to ask Azfaar to hurry up, but that would have been counterproductive. Instead he took the time to check in with Dante.

"Victor-Three from One."

"Go for Three."

"Give me a sitrep."

"The men haven't moved. They're still bunched together and lying low about five hundred feet east of our position."

"Copy that, Victor-Three."

Carter had taken position at the side of a frameless window, keeping watch. Azfaar walked back into the room and placed a wooden board on one of the cushions, on which he left a bowl of sugar before returning to the kitchen to get the teapot. He deposited the teapot on the wooden board with two small glasses and a small dish of sweets. With a broad gesture Azfaar invited Hunt to sit. Once the two men were facing each other, Azfaar poured Hunt a glass of hot black tea. Azfaar lodged a sugar cube between his teeth and took a sip.

Hunt raised his glass to his lips but immediately pulled it away. The tea was beyond hot. It was scalding. How Azfaar had been able to swallow the hot liquid, Hunt had no idea.

"Why have you come?" Azfaar asked, pouring himself a second glass.

"I need your help."

Azfaar fixed Hunt with a hard stare, a vein pulsing in his head. "I gave everything I had," he said. "Look around you. This is all I have left. Everyone is gone."

Hunt closed his eyes, feeling the man's agony. Hunt had nearly lost his daughter. He knew exactly how excruciating the pain could be.

"I wish what was torn away from you wasn't. I would do anything to bring back your loved ones, Azfaar. If I could go back in time and change the past, I would. But you know as well as I do that this isn't something I can do. I'm sorry."

"Then finish your tea, and leave me alone," Azfaar said, getting up.

From the pocket of his khaki pants, Hunt retrieved a brown envelope. He gently placed it on the wooden board next to the teapot.

"Here's five thousand dollars. Just to hear me out."

Azfaar didn't even look at the envelope. "What I want, you cannot give," he said.

"I know, but I'm afraid that without your help more people will die."

"Don't you Americans understand? I've lost everyone I cared for. Why would I care if your friends die?"

"I'm not talking about soldiers like me, but about young kids like Azzami and Farzaad," Hunt replied, naming Azfaar's two youngest children.

Hunt's words struck a chord. The resentment and the suffering pouring from Azfaar's face were soul crushing. It seemed as if one part of him demanded just revenge while the other part wanted to help. Hunt had no idea which side would win.

Finally, Azfaar poured himself another glass of tea.

"What is it that you want to know?" Azfaar asked, pocketing the brown envelope.

Hunt nodded his thanks. "We know that someone's developing a new drug, and we're looking for the lab. I was hoping you'd heard about it."

Azfaar stared at Hunt over the rim of his glass. Setting it down, he reached into his jacket and drew out a silver cigarette case with a box of matches. He took out a thinly rolled cigarette, then offered one to Hunt, who refused.

He waited while Azfaar smoked, slowly, as if he had all the time in the world.

Hunt was growing anxious. They had already spent too much time on location, and Azfaar's dark eyes looked as though they were miles away. Hunt was about to prod him when Azfaar said, "I'd like to go to America."

If Azfaar had wanted to take Hunt by surprise, he had succeeded. "What are you talking about? I thought you hated America. And what does it have to do with anything?"

Azfaar took a hard pull from his cigarette and deliberately blew a thick cloud in Hunt's direction. "It has everything to do, my American friend."

Hunt fanned the smoke away. Maybe they were getting somewhere after all. "You've heard about a lab, haven't you?"

"Maybe."

"Look, Azfaar, if you want me to take you with us back to the United States, you better start opening up a little."

"So you'll take me?" Azfaar asked, extinguishing the rest of his cigarette in his tea.

"If that lab really exists, and you can take me to them, then yes, I'll take you to the United States."

Carter twisted his head from the window and gave Hunt a look of glaring disapproval. They both knew it would be almost impossible to take an Afghan national to the United States. But that was a bridge Hunt would cross later. The priority was to establish if Azfaar was telling the truth or if he was playing them.

"What do you know about the lab?" Hunt asked.

"A lot," Azfaar said, lighting another cigarette.

"All right," Hunt replied, taking out his notepad. "You've got my full and undivided attention."

Azfaar tapped his cigarette with his finger, dropping the ashes into the tiny tea glass. "They first came to me six months ago," he said. "They knew who I was and what I had done."

"About the poppy fields, you mean?"

Azfaar nodded slowly, as if he was establishing something in his mind. "I was sure they were here to kill me, and know that I would have gladly welcomed death, but they didn't. They had something else in mind."

"Who's *they*?"

Azfaar chuckled, something Hunt had never seen him do. "You really don't know anything, do you?"

"Who's *they*, Azfaar?" Hunt repeated. He was forcing himself to keep his tone friendly and nonconfrontational, but he was losing the battle.

"Hezbollah."

Hezbollah? That doesn't make sense. It was common knowledge that Hezbollah had very little direct involvement in Afghanistan.

"You'll have to explain—"

The distinctive and mechanical spitting of at least half a dozen AK-47s firing several short bursts interrupted Hunt. Before Hunt could ask for a sitrep, the familiar sound of the Super Huey's door-mounted M240 machine gun joined in the ruckus.

"Contact! Contact!" broke in Dante. "Engaging multiple insurgents east and west of our location."

"Copy that, Victor-Three," Hunt replied, adjusting the sling of his M4. "Get on the second M240, and cover our exit. We're getting out."

Hunt turned to Azfaar, who was in the process of lighting another cigarette. "Did you call them?"

"You see any phone around here?" Azfaar replied, looking around his house.

"You're coming with us," Hunt said, grabbing him by the elbow.

The Afghan jerked his arm away. "I can stand on my own."

"You stay close to me," Hunt instructed. "And Victor-Two here, he'll be right behind you. Understood?"

Azfaar nodded and puffed once more on his cigarette. A burst of gunfire hit the outside of the house, reminding Hunt of a severe hailstorm.

"We need to go now," Carter said.

Hunt heard the Super Huey's engines whining as the pilot started them up.

"Victor-One from Victor-Four." That was Abigail. "Enemy fire is effective."

Abigail was trying to keep her voice neutral, but Hunt could hear the undercurrent of distress rearing its ugly head.

"Copy that, Victor-Three. We're coming out now with a plus-one."

Hunt wasn't crazy about the idea of crossing the five hundred feet of wide-open terrain between the house and the Super Huey, but there was no other way. Another volley hit the house. This time bullets shattered the window where Carter had been standing only seconds before. More bullets thumped against the outside walls. Adrenaline coursed through Hunt's veins.

"Ready?" he asked Carter.

"Ready."

Hunt opened the door, grabbed one of his two smoke grenades, and pulled the pin before realizing that with the Super Huey's blade already in rotation, his smoke would be pretty useless. With nothing else to do with it, Hunt hurled the smoke grenade into the no-man's-land between the house and the helicopter. A thick grayish smoke filled the air, at least for the moment.

"Follow me," Hunt reminded Azfaar before dashing toward the partial smoke screen.

"Victor-Three, we're coming in!" Carter called.

Hunt had traveled less than one hundred feet when the smoke dissipated, swirled away by the Super Huey's main rotor. Pushed by the chopper's blades, a wall of dust, grass, and small rocks smashed into Hunt's chest, almost bowling him over, but he pushed through. To his left, something caught his attention. Two hundred feet away, an insurgent was shouldering a rocket-propelled grenade.

"Keep going!" Hunt yelled at Carter and Azfaar as he dropped to one knee.

Hunt shouldered his M4, but before he could pull the trigger, the insurgent was cut down by one of Dante's M240 bursts. The RPG raced aimlessly into the air and exploded in the distance.

Automatic fire from two positions tore the earth all around him. Hunt hit the ground and rolled to his right. With his stomach pressed flat, he drew a bead on the first shooter and squeezed off two shots. The man collapsed headfirst into the field. The second shooter tried to retreat but was killed by one of the crew chief's well-aimed bursts from his door-mounted M240. In the distance, another AK-47 opened up, and Hunt heard the metallic ping of bullets striking the Super Huey's fuselage. An M4 responded, and the AK-47 fell silent.

"You're clear, Victor-One," Abigail came in with a ragged voice.

Hunt jumped back to his feet and raced the last four hundred feet to the Super Huey. The wash from the still-whirling rotor caused him to duck as he ran to the open door of the helicopter. The moment Hunt was in, the helicopter lifted off in a deafening roar. He cranked his neck to look for potential targets, but he had such poor visibility from his seat that he left the task to the crew chief and Dante. Both men were firing short controlled bursts of their machine guns to keep any unseen insurgents pinned down.

"You okay, boss?" Carter asked him.

"Yeah," Hunt said, slightly out of breath. "Anyone hit?"

"We're good," the crew chief replied.

Hunt looked at Azfaar. Even though he had lost his cigarette during the ordeal, the Afghan appeared completely unfazed by what had just happened. Abigail, though, was shaking like a leaf. She had the dazed look of someone who'd just been in combat for the first time.

"You okay, Abi?"

She looked wildly around, hyperventilating.

"I feel wobbly all around," she said between two quick breaths. "My hands are shaking so hard I'm terrified I'll squeeze the trigger accidentally."

Hunt gently angled her rifle to confirm she had put the M4 to safe. She had.

"You'll be fine," Hunt told her. "Now, close your eyes."

"Why?"

"Just close your eyes."

She did. "I killed one of them, I think," she said.

"They were firing at us. You protected yourself and the rest of the team. You did great."

At his words she opened her eyes and diverted them to the floor. Hunt had never been good with words of comfort. His daughter would certainly attest to that.

Doing great was probably not what she needed to hear.

"Listen, Abi," Hunt said, "the realization that someone you've never met wants to kill you is a hard thing to wrap your mind around. I get that. But you know what? This is what combat is. It ain't pretty, and it doesn't get easier. But you handle it, and you do what you can to survive and kill the enemy before he kills you. And today, that's what you did."

For now, that was all the relief Hunt could give her. Dante would have to take care of the rest.

"Switch places with me, Victor-Three," Hunt said.

Dante glanced at him, and Hunt signaled he wanted him seated next to Abigail. Once Dante was in front of him, Hunt took his place manning the door-mounted M240. It had been a while since Hunt had last operated an M240, but this was exactly like riding a bike; once you knew how, you never forgot.

"Boss," the crew chief said to Hunt. "Not sure we'll make it to Kandahar."

"How so?"

The crew chief pointed to a trail of smoke that had started billowing out of the tail section of the helicopter.

"How bad is it?" Hunt asked.

"No idea," the crew chief replied. "I'm not the one flying it, but the copilot has already advised the tower."

"Not much else we can do," Hunt conceded. Even though the mountains were sublime in the distance, Hunt was worried about the rugged terrain below. It offered little hope of a safe landing in case of emergency.

Seconds later, the crew chief's words made Hunt nostalgic for a mere engine-failure landing.

"RPG, two o'clock!" the crew chief screamed.

Hunt was thrust hard against his harness as the pilot banked sharply left. Hunt thought of Leila.

Please, God, let me live through this so I can see my daughter again.

Seconds later, he felt a bone-shattering jolt. White lights burst behind his eyes. And then nothing.

CHAPTER TWENTY-EIGHT

Venezuelan jungle

Peter Godfrey stealthily dug a small hole in the ground with his hands. It wasn't deep, maybe three or four inches, but it was enough to hide the USB key in. He swept dirt and vegetation over the hole in an effort to hide it from all but the closest scrutiny.

"We're out of time," Papa-One whispered.

Godfrey's heart was pounding. His mind was careening through the many different ways this situation could end. None of them was good. He could hear Papa-One and Two talking to each other in hushed tones, but his mind couldn't process what they were saying. He felt almost paralyzed by terror.

Venezuelan soldiers wearing jungle camouflage uniforms were slowly marching toward their position, their weapons raised and aimed at them.

"Drop your weapons, and stand up," Colonel Arteaga ordered, talking through his loudspeaker. "Put your hands on your head, and interlock your fingers. Do it now."

"Last chance to surrender," Papa-One told them.

Papa-Two spat on the ground. "Fuck 'em."

"Godfrey?" Papa-One asked.

"What Two said," he replied, resigned to the fact that he was going to die in the jungle.

"I can drop at least three of these bastards," Papa-Two said. "I'm about ready to go loud."

"Yeah, me too," Papa-One replied. "Sorry we couldn't get you out of here, Godfrey."

"That's okay," Godfrey replied, not really knowing why he had said that. He should have joined a real accounting firm, not the damn DEA. He had done it to impress a girl. In the end, she had left him for a lawyer.

Godfrey's hands were shaking, but he checked his rifle to make sure the safety was off.

The distinctive spit of bullets leaving the end of Papa-Two's suppressor at a high rate caught Godfrey by surprise. It was quickly followed by the loud crack of a sniper rifle. Papa-Two flew forward, as if kicked between the shoulder blades. The sniper's bullet cut through the contents of Papa-Two's backpack before entering his back and ripping through his abdomen.

To Godfrey's left, Papa-One was on the move and firing round after round at the silhouettes of the Venezuelan soldiers. Godfrey saw at least two of them fall before another loud crack reverberated through the jungle. The bullet must have hit Papa-One in the shoulder because Godfrey saw him spin in almost a full circle before he hit the ground.

It's over.

The entire firefight had lasted less than five seconds. Two DEA agents had been killed trying to save him, and here he was, the last man standing. He hadn't even fired a single shot.

I'm such a coward.

Shame overtook him, then rage. If he could only find the courage to raise his rifle, maybe the sniper could kill him too. That would be a relief. But cold, raw fear skittered through him, making his arms so heavy he couldn't lift his AK-103.

Godfrey chuckled to himself. *I can't even do that.*

He dropped the rifle at his side and fell to his knees. An immense sadness overwhelmed him.

A figure in uniform approached.

Arteaga. Godfrey had met the colonel on many occasions. He had always felt that there was something different about him, something Godfrey had never been able to quite figure out.

"Thank you for your cooperation, Mr. Godfrey," Colonel Arteaga said, this time without the help of his loudspeaker. "General Peraza will be pleased you've chosen to stay among the living."

All around Godfrey Venezuelan soldiers were turning on their flashlights. Something must have caught Arteaga's attention because he stopped midstride, looked to his right, and pulled a pistol from a drop holster on his leg.

"Your friend's alive, Mr. Godfrey," Arteaga said. The colonel sounded genuinely happy about his discovery. "Come and say goodbye."

Someone grabbed Godfrey under the armpits and jerked him to his feet. Godfrey tried to pull away. For his effort, he received a vicious punch in the kidney that dropped him back to his knees. The pain was immediate and severe, but he was yanked to his feet again. A huge hand encircled his neck from behind with a hold so powerful he felt his neck was about to be crushed.

"Walk," said the man to whom the hand belonged.

Godfrey obeyed. As he got closer to Colonel Arteaga, he heard Papa-One grunt and moan in pain.

"Come, come," Arteaga said, inviting him to look at his fallen comrade. "If he had simply surrendered like you, he wouldn't be in such pain right now."

Papa-One was lying on his back; blood welled from a bullet hole in his shoulder. With his functioning arm, Papa-One was clutching his stomach, where another round had hit. His fingers weren't enough to keep the blood from pouring out onto the muddy jungle floor.

"Would you like to help your friend, Mr. Godfrey?" Arteaga inquired.

"What?"

"Here, take this," Arteaga said, offering him his pistol. "Your friend can't be saved. That's a fact. So we can let him die here, alone in the jungle, or you can kill him now. Your choice, Mr. Godfrey. Personally, I'd much prefer to die from a gunshot than being eaten alive by an animal. But that's just me."

Godfrey started to shake. It began with his knees and crept up to his hands. His brain was working overtime as he desperately tried to find a solution to this mess. There was no way he was going to kill Papa-One.

A long whine of anguish sprang from Papa-One's mouth.

"Take the gun, Mr. Godfrey, and end your friend's misery."

Papa-One's eyes bored through him. He was hyperventilating now. "Do it," he said, through clenched teeth. "Do it."

Arteaga gently took Godfrey's forearm and placed the pistol in his trembling hand. He then closed Godfrey's fist around the grip and moved his arm until the pistol was aimed at Papa-One.

"Don't get any ideas, Mr. Godfrey. You'll be dead before you can turn the weapon on me."

"Do it," repeated Papa-One, almost pleading this time. His voice was so weak, so despairing, that Godfrey started to pull the trigger.

"Listen to your friend, Mr. Godfrey. Stop being a coward, and squeeze that trigger."

Godfrey lined up the pistol's sight on Papa-One's head. At least this way he was sure to kill him rapidly.

What the fuck am I doing?

Something snapped in Godfrey's mind, and suddenly, he didn't care anymore. Didn't care if he lived or died, didn't care if the DEA actually sent someone to retrieve the USB key or not. The only thing he knew for sure was that he wasn't going to kill his fellow agent.

With a speed and power that surprised even him, Godfrey spun on his heels, aimed the pistol straight at Arteaga's chest, and pulled the trigger.

Nothing happened.

Again he pulled the trigger. Again nothing.

Then something hit the back of his head, and for a moment, it felt as if his brain actually slammed against the inside of his skull. Then everything went black.

CHAPTER TWENTY-NINE

Miami, Florida

Anna walked purposefully down the street in the direction of *her* nightclub. She would have given the nightclub away if it meant she could spend the night watching chick flicks with Sophia. She continued past the long line of clubbers still waiting impatiently for the God of the Velvet Rope to allow them entry. As Anna approached the entrance, the front door opened. She recognized the man who held it open.

Santiago Mayo. Alejandro's brother. She had never quite figured out why—maybe it was just her instinctive antennae—but she had never liked the man.

She swallowed hard. She didn't want Santiago to think she was a scared little girl. A couple of male clubbers tried to sneak through the opened door, but Santiago shot his right hand forward and seized one of them by the wrist.

The man yelled in pain, and his knees buckled.

"Ladies first," Santiago said, turning his attention to Anna.

Santiago held the door ajar, and Anna slipped inside. Unbearably loud Latin music assaulted her ears. She cringed, unconsciously reeling back.

"Not your kind of music?" Santiago asked with the slightest hint of contempt.

"Where are they?" Anna replied, ignoring him. "I don't have all night."

He led her across the dimly lit nightclub. The decor was impressive, the space elegant. Dozens of crystal chandeliers dangled from the high ceiling. The gray marble floors and the classy white loungers suggested that Alejandro had spared no expense renovating the place.

With my money.

The crowd inside the club was thick, and the driving beat of salsa music pumped through high-end speakers as they walked through the mass of sweaty bodies. The scene was much as she had expected. There were two jam-packed bars where men were slouched, their eyes fixed on the dance floor, where women wearing tight, revealing clothes were gyrating their hips and pouting their lips. Six large birdcages hung above the dance floor, in which semiclad dancers were either dancing the salsa or pretending to have sex together. Anna couldn't tell which.

"This way," Santiago said, steering her toward a stairway leading to the basement. "They're waiting for you."

When she reached the foot of the stairs, two men wearing dark business suits had their eyes locked on her. She didn't know their names, but she had seen their faces before.

"Please follow us, Miss Garcia," the shorter of the two said. "Alejandro and his guests are expecting you."

Despite the tailor's best efforts—the cut of his jacket and the extra padding—there was still a slight bulge under his left arm where the shoulder holster was hanging. If he was armed, no doubt the other man was too. That was fine with her. She was carrying too. Concealed under her shirt and tucked snugly in a leather holster at the small of her back, her SIG Sauer P238 had a round chambered and was ready to go.

The basement was well lit. It ran the entire length of the club and was fitted with a multitude of elegantly furnished rooms, one billiard room, and a large kitchen area from which came the wonderful warm and rich aromas of meat and spices.

Whatever they're cooking, it's a far cry from the cheese-laden, fat-drenched Mexican food they're serving upstairs.

In the next room, a large wine cooler sat against the far wall. Two more men she'd never seen before, these armed with mini-Uzis, were standing beside it.

"You guys aren't kidding around. Must have some expensive wines in there," Anna said.

One of the Uzi guys gave her a forced smile.

The wine cooler suddenly swung away from the wall, exposing a reinforced steel door.

"Please wait here," the shorter man said while his partner punched a code into the keypad.

Anna was tempted to remind him that she owned the place but bit her tongue. A small light flashed green, and the man who had entered the code pressed his thumb on the biometric reader. The green light blinked twice, and the door clicked open, revealing another stairwell.

"This way, Miss Garcia," the man said, beckoning her toward the steps.

"You're not coming?"

"We'll be here when you get back," he replied.

Anna proceeded down the steps and noticed how narrow they were and how many there were. She had never seen that staircase before, and she gathered Alejandro had added it during his renovations. She grabbed the handrail at her side. She was halfway down when a man appeared at the bottom of the stairs. He was thick through the arms and barrel chested.

Alejandro.

He offered his hand as she came off the last two steps, but she slapped it away. A flash of anger crossed his face, and he wagged his finger at her.

"You bitch," he said.

"Alejandro, please be a gentleman," a man called from behind him. The voice was deep and rich, clearly belonging to someone used to wielding authority.

Anna tried to walk around Alejandro, but he stepped in front of her. For a long moment, they stared at each other in silent challenge. She fought the urge to strike him between the legs.

"That's enough, Alejandro." This time there was no mistaking the steel in the man's voice.

Alejandro stepped aside and let her through. A dozen feet behind him, in the middle of what looked like a modern conference room, stood a thirtysomething, smartly dressed, medium-height, well-built man. But it was the man's eyes that struck Anna. They were remarkable. They were the greenest eyes she had ever seen. They were such a unique shade of green that it was almost impossible not to stare at them. They reminded Anna of the purest of emerald stones. For a second, she lost her concentration.

"Hello, Miss Garcia," the man said, walking toward her with a slight limp. "My name is Jorge Ramirez."

Ramirez extended his hand. Something in the back of Anna's mind told her she'd better shake it.

"These men are my colleagues," Ramirez added, directing her toward a large round conference table, where half a dozen men were eating a late dinner.

Anna had dealt with enough narco-traffickers to recognize that two of the six men at the table belonged to that group. The other four, though, sent chills down her spine. They looked at her with scorn, as if it was beneath them to be in the same room as her. Their greasy black hair was in sharp contrast to the well-groomed narcos.

"Who are you? And who are they?" Anna asked.

"All in due time, Miss Garcia. Please have a seat."

There were two seats open at the table. She chose the one farthest from the unkempt males. Ramirez seemed to notice, and the trace of an amused smile appeared on his lips.

A waiter came down the stairs and placed a generous plate of meat and vegetables in front of her. He left without saying a word.

"I'm glad you could join us this evening," Ramirez said.

"I didn't have much choice, did I?"

Ramirez grinned, and Anna had to admit the man had a great smile.

And perfect teeth too.

"Would you like something to drink? A glass of water perhaps?"

"Why am I here, Mr. Ramirez?"

"Flat or sparkling? I'm drinking Perrier," Ramirez said, holding his glass.

She sighed. "Sparkling."

"Alejandro, please pour Miss Garcia a glass of Perrier."

Alejandro, who had been standing a few feet behind Ramirez, threw her a glance of such acute dislike that she almost reached for her pistol. Anna had no idea what was going on. Was Alejandro working for Ramirez? Alejandro wasn't the kind of man to be bossed around by a stranger. And what about the four men who looked like terrorists?

Terrorists?

Could that be it? She hoped not. She looked in their direction. The dark narrow eyes appeared menacing one moment and devoid of emotion the next, malevolence oozing from every pore; she could almost smell their misogyny from across the table. Her throat tightened. They looked exactly like the pictures Hunt had shown her of the insurgents he had once fought in Iraq. Or was it Afghanistan?

Shit! How had these men entered the country? Had her family facilitated their arrival in any way?

Stupid questions! Of course we did. Dad and Tony had been doing it for years. Drugs. Weapons. Cheap laborers. And now terrorists. Fuck!

"Are you okay, Miss Garcia?" Ramirez asked, bringing her back to reality. "It looked like you were somewhere else. Aren't you hungry?"

"I'd like to know what I'm doing here," Anna said. She picked up a fork and proceeded to move the food around her plate before continuing. "I was under the impression I'd meet with Alejandro to discuss issues related to my organization. It's clear to me that Alejandro isn't in charge here, and you have me surrounded. So let's cut to the chase, and you tell me what the hell is going on."

Ramirez leaned back in his chair and crossed his hands behind his head.

"I'd like to offer you a job, Miss Garcia," Ramirez said, as Alejandro came back with Anna's Perrier.

"A job?"

"Alejandro told me that when your father and brother were in charge, you were responsible for keeping the books straight. Isn't that right?"

Anna had always been a willing participant in the family business. She had never known the operational details, but it would be a lie to say she hadn't known the family money came from the drug trade.

"Why does it matter to you?" Anna asked him.

"And isn't it true that you graduated with a master's degree in computer science from the Florida Institute of Technology?"

"Again, why does this matter?"

"I'd like you to do for me the same things you did for your father."

"And why would I do that?"

"Because, Miss Garcia, as of this morning, I've taken over the Garcia crime syndicate, and I'm killing everyone who isn't pulling their weight."

Ramirez's words shocked her, and she stared at him openmouthed. Had Ramirez ordered the morning hit on her men? Emotionally shaken by the cold-blooded way Ramirez had stated his case, Anna wondered if he would have the guts to murder her in her own nightclub if she refused. Or was it *his* nightclub now?

"Why did you target us?" Anna asked, tightening her grip around her fork.

"Because you're weak," Ramirez said bluntly. "The Garcia crime syndicate is only a shadow of what it was mere months ago. But even with a divided leadership, you still possess the greatest distribution network in Florida."

"If you know me as well as you think you do, Mr. Ramirez, you're aware that I'm trying to steer my business in another direction."

"And how successful have you been?"

Until today's events, she had believed that progress had been made. Maybe not as fast as she had hoped, but progress nonetheless. Now, she wasn't sure. For how long had Ramirez been stalking them?

"How about I let you and Alejandro play together? I'll walk out if this is what you want," Anna offered. She was tired of this life. She wanted out. She had tried her best, and her best had failed.

"Not an option, I'm afraid," Ramirez said. "You see, my employer is in a rush. He fears that if you or Alejandro were to leave, half of the syndicate would follow. And that, Miss Garcia, would be quite problematic to my employer, as it would delay the distribution schedule he has established."

"As far as I'm concerned, you and your *colleagues* are responsible for the death of all the young athletes who overdosed on your shit. In my book, that makes the lot of you a bunch of terrorists. I'll never work for you."

Anna saw by Ramirez's expression that her words didn't have their intended effect. On the contrary, Ramirez genuinely looked regretful. The same thing couldn't be said of the four unkempt men at the other end of the table. They had stopped eating, and hot colors flooded their cheeks.

"For reasons outside of my control," Ramirez said, his eyes cold and menacing, glancing over at the *terrorists*, "I was forced to begin the distribution of our new product before the final testing results came back. Obviously, this was a grave mistake. One I vow not to repeat."

"Screw you! Your rush to market cost the lives—"

"Oh, get off your high horse, Miss Garcia," Ramirez interrupted her. "You and your family have been in the drug business for decades. Don't play the victim card at this table."

As much as she hated to admit it, she was guilty as charged. And it revolted her.

"Anyway," Ramirez continued, waving a dismissive hand, "we've addressed the chemical imbalance that caused our product to malfunction. We're fixing it as we speak, and we'll resume distribution very soon."

Malfunction. Ramirez made it sound so mechanical.

"So, Miss Garcia, what should I tell my employer?"

"Why don't you share with me who he is? I'd like to know who I'll be working for."

Ramirez smiled. "Very well. I work for the Spider, Miss Garcia. And if you value your life, I suggest you accept his offer."

CHAPTER THIRTY

Near Turgua, Venezuela

The Spider stared at the unconscious man lying on the ground at the edge of his flashlight's beam. The man's wrists were cuffed behind his back, and his legs were tied together at the ankles. The black hood over the man's head billowed in and out with his quickening breath. Maybe Peter Godfrey was awake after all.

Peraza took a moment to set aside the turmoil that was within him and looked up to the sky. There were no stars. Only clouds he couldn't see. He closed his eyes and let the warm wind wash over his face. It was soon going to rain. From where he stood, he had an excellent view of Caracas ten miles away. At night, it was impossible to discern the new Caracas from the old. Once a thriving city, his country's capital had lost its glamour years ago and was now buckling under hyperinflation and poverty. Decades ago, Peraza used to come to the same spot to admire the vibrant city Caracas once was. Now, he was here to kill a man.

"General Peraza?"

Peraza turned to face Colonel Arteaga. Arteaga had proven himself to Peraza over and over again. Within the government of President Capriles, Colonel Arteaga was known for his uncanny spy-catching ability. He was the best there was.

"We're ready?" Peraza asked.

"Yes, sir. We are."

Peraza nodded. "Any losses?"

"Three men."

Peraza bowed his head and took a moment to reflect on how lucky he was to be at the top of the food chain. While most of his fellow countrymen couldn't afford to feed their families, he had millions of American dollars tucked away in an offshore account. In Venezuela one never knew when the tide would change, so he needed to be ready.

Hero one day. Villain the next.

With great power came even greater responsibility. Peraza saw it as his personal mission in life to bring back prosperity to his country. Venezuela should be one of the world's richest countries. While the Saudis, Russians, and even the Americans and Canadians continued to make headlines as petroleum giants, it was Venezuela that had the largest reserves of crude.

Last time Peraza had talked to President Capriles about it, Capriles had been adamant.

"Can't you see what's going on, General? The Americans are engaged in destructive economic sabotage. We must stop them by any means necessary."

Not lost on Peraza was that Capriles hadn't mentioned his own mismanagement of government funds—since Capriles had already sold off the country's gold reserves and used the oil infrastructure as collateral for loans, there was no easy way out of the financial mess.

But Capriles was also correct that the Americans and others had sabotaged Venezuela and then refused to provide help for the crisis they'd perpetuated. And that was something Peraza could take action about. But first he needed to ensure the Americans didn't know enough of the plan to stop him.

"Once we're done here, Colonel," he said to Arteaga, "see that their families are taken care of."

"Yes, sir."

Peraza knelt down next to Godfrey and rested a hand on his shoulder. Godfrey's body jumped at the touch, confirming to Peraza that his former accountant was awake.

"Relax, Peter," Peraza said, chuckling. "This will be over soon. I just have a few questions I'd like you to answer."

Peraza slowly lifted the hood from Godfrey's head. A set of terrified eyes stared back at him, glinting in the beam of his light.

———

Godfrey blinked several times, the sharp beam of the flashlight blinding him. He had a splitting headache and terrific thirst. No doubt he had a concussion from the hit he'd taken on the back of the head.

Was Papa-One okay? Was he still alive? He wished he knew the man's real name. A growing sense of panic filled his chest. His heart pounded wildly. His worst nightmare was now reality. Even though he couldn't see the general, it was his voice and the smell of his cologne. Godfrey knew what was about to happen to him. There was no cavalry coming to stop whatever Peraza had in mind for him. The best thing he could hope for was a quick death.

"I'm disappointed, Peter. You know that, right?" Peraza asked him.

Staying silent wasn't an option with Peraza, so he said, "What you're doing is wrong."

"I see," Peraza said, helping Godfrey up to his feet. "How long have you been working for me, Peter?"

"Four years."

"Four years, yes. And in those four years, my dear Peter, haven't you seen what has happened to our once-great country?"

"People like you and Capriles are running it into the ground, that's what I see. You've pocketed—"

The punch came in fast and hard. Peraza's fist caught him under the chin, thrusting his head up and back and sending a huge jolt of pain and disorientation through him. The strike sent him reeling back and into the arms of Colonel Arteaga.

"Can't you see I'm fighting to make Venezuela great again?" Peraza growled.

"What do you want from me?" Godfrey asked, spitting out a mouthful of blood.

Peraza looked at Godfrey as if he were a strange animal. After a few seconds, he switched his attention to Colonel Arteaga. "Tie him up, and let's begin."

Two soldiers materialized next to him and pushed him forward. Godfrey stumbled sluggishly and nearly fell because his legs didn't respond as they normally did. Something wet hit his face. He looked up at the night sky, and huge rain pellets started to come down. Lightning bolts split the night, and thunder soon followed. There was a short reprieve, and then the rain began to fall even harder, bands of it coming faster and closer together. In no time at all, Godfrey was drenched from head to toe. His hiking boots were soaked, and his muddy pants stuck to his legs, like wax to a candlewick.

Four powerful beams of light suddenly stabbed through the darkness. Engines rumbled to life, and through the thick rain, Godfrey saw two SUVs parked facing each other. The distance between their respective front bumpers was about twenty feet. He didn't fully grasp the horror of what was about to happen until Colonel Arteaga tied Godfrey's already-handcuffed wrists to the chain attached to one SUV's bumper.

"Please don't," Godfrey pleaded as Arteaga tied his ankle shackles to the other SUV.

They were going to use the SUVs to dismember him.

"The first minute will be the most painful, Peter," explained Peraza. "Since your hands are tied behind your back, your shoulders will pop out of their sockets when your ligaments and tendons are stretched. Don't fight it. You can't win against V-8 engines."

"Don't do this, General," Godfrey begged, tearing up. "Please."

Oh my God! Why didn't I die in that damn jungle?

"It's entirely up to you, Peter."

"What do you want?" Godfrey asked as his bladder released. Despite the torrential rain, he smelled his own urine as the warm liquid poured down both his legs.

"What does the DEA know about Butterfly?"

Butterfly? What the fuck's Butterfly?

Everything Godfrey had learned about Afghanistan, along with the data he'd been able to download and photograph from Peraza's office, was on the USB key he had buried in the ground back in the jungle. The only details he had sent his handler about Afghanistan were a few notes he had included in his last report. In Godfrey's opinion, his notes were enough to warrant further investigation, but he had no way of knowing if the DEA had been able to corroborate the intelligence he had sent their way or if they had acted upon it. But Butterfly? He had never seen or read anything about that name. Or had he? Had he missed something?

Dread welled up in his chest. Godfrey forced himself to speak. "Nothing. They know nothing. I know nothing."

Peraza must have seen the confusion in Godfrey's face because he smiled thinly.

"I'm not sure I believe you, Peter. You're a good liar. You tricked me once. Who's to say you're not doing it again?"

"I don't know anything about Butterfly. I swear." Godfrey's whole body shook with terror.

"Would you like to know what Butterfly is?" Peraza asked. Then he paused before adding, "I'm tempted to keep you alive, Peter. Would you like to witness the slow destruction of the next generation of Americans?"

At that moment, Godfrey couldn't care less about what might happen to other people, even if they were Americans. His only concern was himself.

"What . . . what is it?"

"You have to tell me something first, Peter," Peraza said. "Who else is working with you? How many cockroaches like you have infiltrated my circle?"

That was yet another question he didn't have an answer to. How was he supposed to know? To the best of his knowledge, he was the only one. Had Peraza discovered another mole?

"I don't know," Godfrey replied.

Peraza raised his right hand in the air and made a circular motion with his index finger.

The two SUVs slowly started to back up in opposite directions. The next thing Godfrey knew, his feet were pulled from under him, and he was violently hurled backward at the same time. His arms snapped to the rear, and his shoulders dislocated with loud popping sounds. Godfrey was flat on his back, floating half a foot above the ground with his arms stretched above his head and his legs pulling him in another direction. The pain, piercing and unrelenting, was like nothing he could have imagined.

Next to him Peraza was talking, but Godfrey was in such agony he couldn't understand a word. A visceral scream came out of his mouth, Godfrey's desperation echoing through the valley, and then all the air seemed to escape his lungs. His mouth remained opened wide in agony, but no additional sounds came out. To make the pain stop, he'd do or say anything.

There was a sudden release of tension, and Peraza's voice broke through the fog of pain.

"How many, Peter? How many other American agents are there in my ranks?"

"I don't know! There's no one else! There's no one else!" Godfrey yelled back.

Rain slapped against Godfrey's face. He blinked the water from his eyes and tried to focus. Peraza's mouth was drawn into a line.

"What about my distribution schedule in Florida? Have you told the DEA?"

"No! I don't know!" Godfrey shouted. "Please let me go! I don't know anything!"

"That's not good enough, Peter. Not good enough."

Godfrey's throat knotted in anticipation of more pain to come. The SUVs' engines revved, but they didn't move.

"What did you tell them about Butterfly?"

"Nothing. I swear to God!"

"Stop lying to me, Peter, because I'm about to rip you apart. Do you understand?" Peraza hissed in his ear. "Tell me everything you know about Butterfly. Everything!"

How could he make Peraza believe him? How could he prove he didn't know anything about Butterfly? He couldn't think straight. The pain. The fucking pain. His brain was shutting down, and a blackness overwhelmed him. For a second, he felt the hands of death caress him.

Yes. Please. Take me.

Then he was awake again. *The USB key.*

He needed to tell Peraza about the USB key he had buried in the jungle. That was the ultimate proof. If he could only tell Peraza about it, everything would be okay. He was sure of it.

But Godfrey didn't have the strength to speak. He didn't have the strength to open his eyes. He didn't have the strength to do anything. A frosty numbness overtook his body down to his bones. He was so cold.

Why am I so damn cold?

From far away, he heard Colonel Arteaga's voice. "Maybe he doesn't know."

"Oh, I know he doesn't. He would have said something if he knew."

"What now?"

"We proceed as planned. We fix the product in house; then we ship to Ramirez in Florida."

"Maybe we shouldn't have used the Afghans," Arteaga said.

"We had no other choice," Peraza said. "We had to outsource it to protect Capriles. I tried to set up production to Mexico, but the Black Tosca cartel couldn't guarantee adequate protection and secrecy."

"Very well, General. What about him?"

"I'll finish him myself. He's my mistake."

Godfrey felt a tug at his ankles, followed by one at his wrists. His body dropped to the sodden ground, and a piece of fabric was forced into his mouth. He drifted in and out of consciousness. In the background, metal hit dirt—*shovels, digging,* a part of his brain said—and conversations were being carried on in low voices with occasional laughter.

"You're a pitiful sight, Peter," Peraza said. "Usually I'd put a bullet in your head and be done with it, but not today. Not for you."

The first kick to his head nearly knocked him out. He felt himself being dragged across the muddy ground, and then he was falling, but only a short distance. For a few moments, there was silence, and all he could see when he opened his eyes in the darkness was the blur of rain. A flicker of hope kicked in—maybe whoever Hauer had sent would find him here, save him—but then the first shovelful of dirt filled his nose and mouth, and the flicker of hope he was holding on to disappeared.

CHAPTER THIRTY-ONE

Miami, Florida

Anna was in an untenable situation. The only two options in front of her were bad. If she accepted Jorge Ramirez's offer, she'd be going against everything she wanted for her future. But if she refused, she was pretty sure Ramirez would kill her. Or would he give Alejandro the task? She couldn't tell. Behind his quaint facade, there was a darker side to Ramirez. Anna could sense it. He was a dangerous man and obviously capable of extreme violence. Why else would the Spider employ him?

The Spider.

She wondered how General Peraza had earned his nickname. And who the hell had started giving nicknames to narcos? Last year, her family had had to deal with the Black Tosca, and now the Spider?

"Miss Garcia? What would you like to do?" Ramirez asked, bringing her out of her reverie.

"How long will this arrangement last?" she asked, drinking the last of her Perrier.

"For as long as the Spider says it does," Ramirez replied.

"And what is the product you'd like us to distribute for you?"

"Continue to distribute, Miss Garcia," Ramirez corrected her. "Our chemists came up with a new synthetic amphetamine that can block pain at its source, improve muscular strength and performance, and remain completely undetectable by drug tests."

"What's so novel about that?"

"We can mass-produce it for less than ten cents a pill, and we made it approximately three times more addictive than heroin."

That last bit terrified her, considering that heroin was one of the most addictive drugs on the market. If what Ramirez was saying was true, an entire generation could be at risk. The amphetamine epidemic that had started eight weeks ago was far from over. In fact, it would continue to expand. She forced a smile. "And how much would we be selling these pills for?"

"Two dollars a pop."

Anna's eyes went wide with shock. Her mouth opened, but no sound came out.

"Yes, I know," Ramirez said. "A profit margin so high it's almost unheard of. So what will it be? Are you in or out, Miss Garcia?"

Funny how Ramirez made it sound as if she had a choice. *Live or die.*

"Maybe I was foolish in wanting to steer my organization into something we're clearly not," she conceded, doing her very best to sound sincere. "Your proposition makes financial sense for all parties. Alejandro was correct in his assessment."

"See? I told you," Ramirez said, turning to Alejandro.

Alejandro didn't look convinced, but he didn't argue. Maybe Ramirez had threatened him too. She would have to find out who had made first contact with the other, Ramirez or Alejandro.

"I'm glad we've figured this thing out," Ramirez continued, pulling a cell phone from the breast pocket of his suit jacket. "Excuse me a moment. I have a quick text to send."

Alejandro's features remained impassive. The same couldn't be said about the four terrorists. They weren't shy about openly displaying their disdain for her.

"Thanks for coming, Miss Garcia," Ramirez said, putting down his phone on the white tablecloth. "I'll be in touch."

Anna swallowed her indignation at being dismissed and smiled. She nodded at Ramirez as she pushed back her chair and stood up. But as soon as she took a step toward the stairwell, her stomach contracted. This had been way too easy. It was inconceivable that Ramirez would believe she had caved without a fight.

What could she do? What would Hunt do?

With one swift, economical movement—just as Hunt had shown her—she pulled her pistol from its holster and swung it around until her sights were on Ramirez.

Ramirez stood there, his hands in the air, staring at her with a huge smile on his face.

"I was getting worried, Miss Garcia. I was getting *very* worried."

"What the fuck are you talking about?"

"You're wondering who ordered the hit on your men this morning, aren't you?" Ramirez said, slowly getting up.

"Sit your ass down!"

"As you wish. But you must know that if you shoot me, you'll die here, right?"

Anna looked around her. The four terrorists and the two narcos were still eating, not even bothering to look at her. Alejandro had his pistol in one hand, but it was pointed toward the ground. Behind her, though, the two men she had seen upstairs less than ten minutes ago were pointing their Uzis at her back.

"And tell me, Miss Garcia—who's going to take care of poor little Sophia if you're dead?"

"Did you do it? Did you kill my men?" Anna asked.

"Alejandro killed those men. I barely suggested it."

Anna briefly wondered if she'd be quick enough to shoot both men dead before the guards killed her. She had killed before, but it had been in self-defense. She'd never fired a weapon in anger before. And she wasn't about to now.

She lowered her pistol. "Why? Why did you have to kill those men? What did they do to you?"

"You see, Miss Garcia, that's not how the game is played," Ramirez retorted. "You don't ask questions, and you do what I say."

"You son of a bitch," she said through locked teeth.

"That being said," Ramirez continued with a disarming smile that pissed her off even more, "I'm glad you confronted me about it. It would have been very upsetting to me if you had walked out of here without tackling the issue. In fact, it would have been hard for me to trust you."

"I won't forget this," she said, holstering her pistol.

"Oh, but you will, Miss Garcia. You absolutely will. Sophia's life depends on it. Betray me—and she dies."

CHAPTER THIRTY-TWO

Jalalabad, Nangarhar Province, Afghanistan

Barry Pike was doing everything he could to reestablish contact with Hunt and his team, including placing numerous calls to Hunt's satellite phone. Fifteen minutes had elapsed since the pilot had sent his Mayday.

"Victor-One, this is Echo-One, do you copy?" Pike repeated for the hundredth time. "I say again, do you copy?"

Colleen Crawford, seated next to him, was on a conference call with Tom Hauer and US Army General Karl Montgomery, commanding officer of the American contingent at the Kandahar Airfield. General Montgomery was the only one with the authority to approve the deployment of the QRF, a platoon-size unit capable of quickly assisting another unit in need. And right now, it wasn't looking good. The only saving grace was that Pike had been able to pinpoint the exact location of the crash site.

The call was encrypted at the highest level, but Crawford had put the conversation on speaker so she could continue to work while Hauer and Montgomery argued about what to do with the QRF.

"I won't order the QRF and search and rescue birds to take off until we know if the mission is rescue or recovery, Mr. Hauer," General Montgomery said. "I have units presently engaged in combat. They have the priority. Your office should have coordinated with mine prior to sending your agents."

"How long till the Reaper gets there?" Hauer asked.

"Stand by."

The MQ-9 Reaper was an unmanned aerial vehicle—a drone—capable of remotely controlled flight operations. In this instance, the Reaper's pilot was based in Las Vegas. Designed both as a high-altitude surveillance aircraft and a hunter-killer, the Reaper was fitted with approximately 4,600 pounds of ordnance, including air-to-air missiles and laser-guided bombs.

"Another five minutes and we should have eyes on the crash site," General Montgomery said.

"Can you link the Reaper pilot to my TOC in Jalalabad, General?" Hauer asked. "That would make it easier for everybody."

That would be great, Pike thought.

"If there are survivors," General Montgomery said, "I'll authorize the feed transfer with the understanding that the officer in charge of the QRF will have authority."

"Agreed," Hauer was quick to say. "Thank you. You got that, Echo-One?"

"Yes, sir," Pike replied. "We're ready to receive the video feed."

Pike wasn't a pious man, but he bowed his head and made a silent prayer for the safety of Hunt's team. The next few minutes seemed the longest in Pike's life as he continued to attempt to communicate with Victor-One. Again, he had no success.

"Mr. Hauer," General Montgomery said, "I've authorized the QRF—call sign Romeo—to respond to the crash site."

"Thank you, General," Hauer replied.

"Echo-One, this is Avenger-Five. Infrared transmission is now available," the Reaper pilot said from his ground control station in Las Vegas.

That was great news. If Montgomery had authorized the deployment of the QRF, it meant there were survivors. Pike and Crawford raised their fists in victory.

"Please route IR to channel Charlie-Four," Pike requested, his pulse skyrocketing.

"Copy that, Echo-One. Sending to Charlie-Four . . . now!"

A few seconds later, the IR video feed transmitted from the Reaper appeared on Pike's screen, the transmission having bounced from a satellite orbiting well above Earth.

"Avenger-Five from Echo-One, I have a good feed."

Crawford had joined Pike, and they were both looking at the screen, trying to figure out what they were actually seeing. Crawford, Pike, and Hauer were now on the same net as Avenger-Five, the Reaper pilot.

"What are you seeing?" Hauer asked. From his Virginia office, the DEA administrator didn't have access to the Reaper's feed.

"We have four, possibly five or six survivors," Pike replied. "They seem to be pinned down by a large enemy force coming from both sides of the crash site."

"How long until the QRF gets there?" Hauer asked.

"About twenty minutes," Crawford replied, tracking the progress of the V-22 Osprey.

The Osprey, a tilt-rotor aircraft capable of vertical and short takeoffs and landings, had been developed to provide long-range insertion and extraction capabilities to special operations personnel.

"They're on the move," Pike called out.

"Echo-One from Avenger-Five. I have what looks like a small farmhouse about a quarter of a mile south of the crash site."

"That's where they're going," Crawford said, looking over a map of the area.

Pike's eyes were glued to his screen. There were two groups of two moving away slowly from the crash site. One member of each group was carrying an injured person while the other was returning fire. Unfortunately, the insurgents were quickly gaining ground.

"They'll never make it," Pike said, his jaw hurting from clenching it so hard.

"Avenger-Five from Echo-Two. What kind of ordnance does the Reaper have?"

"I have four Hellfires and two Sidewinders, Echo-One," the pilot replied. "But I have to get clearance from Romeo-One before I can engage targets on the ground. Copy?"

"Echo-One, copy. Please let us know."

Pike and Crawford looked at each other, concerned. Pike understood he wasn't in the chain of command and had no say in the matter, but he willed Romeo-One to give his blessing. Without the Reaper's support, Hunt's team would be quickly overrun.

"Echo-One, Avenger-Four," the Reaper pilot finally said. "I've been cleared to engage."

Pike was grateful, but there was little time to celebrate. One of the two-man teams he was following had just stopped moving.

"Someone's been hit," Crawford said, stating the obvious.

"Avenger-Four from Echo-One," Pike said, "I have four enemy combatants four hundred or so meters east of our guys. Can you engage with a Hellfire?"

There was a slight delay, and then the Reaper pilot said, "Affirmative. Friendlies are outside the blast radius. I can put a missile on target with minimal risk to Victor elements."

The "minimal risk" assessment didn't give Pike a warm and fuzzy feeling, but it was either that or do nothing, in which case the rescue mission would become a recovery mission.

"Copy that, Avenger-Four. Engage."

C'mon, c'mon, c'mon. Pike's fingers drummed impatiently on the desk as he waited for the pilot to confirm the missile launch.

"Echo-One, target acquired. Ten seconds to missile launch."

Pike knew there was an approximately two-second lag in control input between the ground control station in Las Vegas and the drone 7,500 miles away. Keeping the laser-targeting reticule locked in wasn't as simple as it sounded.

"Echo-One, missile launch," the pilot said. Then, a second later, he added, "Good launch. Splash in ten seconds."

In his mind's eye, Pike visualized the Hellfire going supersonic. Since the hundred-pound air-to-ground Hellfire was traveling faster than sound, its sonic boom would reach the insurgents *after* the missile had hit them. The insurgents wouldn't hear their killer coming.

Exactly ten seconds after the launch, Pike's IR feed bloomed white. He heard Crawford's sharp intake of breath next to him and realized he was holding his own.

When the white glare dissipated, Pike started breathing again. The Hellfire had done its job.

"Good shooting, Avenger-Four," Pike said.

Now it was up to the Osprey to bring their team home.

CHAPTER THIRTY-THREE

Helmand Province, Afghanistan

The moment Hunt had opened his eyes, his vision had blurred, and he'd found himself lying motionless on the crisp, thinly frosted grass. He'd tried to understand what had happened and where he was. The faint smell of burnt goat dung wafting from a nearby field reminded him he was in Afghanistan.

The RPG. Oh fuck!

Chaos had ensued after that. The pilot was dead, and the copilot was critical, but seeing how badly damaged the Super Huey was, it was a small miracle they weren't all dead.

Azfaar had been tossed out of the chopper prior to impact—Carter had seen him unbuckle himself when they were going down—and they'd lost sat comms, so no one had been able to make contact with Echo-One back at the TOC to determine if they had a fix on their location for a rescue operation.

The crew chief was in poor shape—the end of his tibia protruded through a laceration on the inside of his right leg. Within minutes Abigail had done a recce and discovered an abandoned farmhouse about a quarter of a mile away. Rather than remain in the open where they were sitting ducks, they'd decided to head to the farmhouse to regroup.

Hunt had been about to give the order to move out when an M4 had shattered the silence with six quick shots.

"Contact! Contact!" had come through their earpieces from Carter, who had been maintaining a perimeter. "We have multiple targets approaching our position on foot."

———

Abigail had been hauling the crew chief in a fireman's carry, trying to move him to safety, when she fell forward in a spray of blood. A second later, Hunt heard the unmistakable crack of a sniper's high-powered rifle.

"Abi!" Hunt yelled, crawling toward her. "Abigail?"

"What the fuck's going on, Pierce?" Dante called out in a panicked voice. "Abi's hit?"

"Stand by, Victor-Three. Stand by!"

"Fuck this, I'm coming over—"

Another loud crack echoed in the distance. "Stay down, Dante! We're taking sniper fire."

"For Christ's sake, Pierce, is she okay?"

As Hunt got closer, he saw that Abigail was still moving. The crew chief, though, wasn't. The sniper's bullet had taken off the top half of his head. The force of the impact had simply thrown Abigail off balance.

"You okay, Abi?" Hunt asked.

"Yeah, I think so," she replied. Where was the scared woman from before the crash? Gone was the frightened ex-DEA special agent. She had been replaced by a warrior. That was what they all needed to be if they wanted to survive this.

"Victor-Four's fine," Hunt said, keying his mic. "We need to find a way to take out that sniper. The insurgents are using him to cover their advance."

Next to him, Abigail gagged and started vomiting. Hunt figured she'd just realized that the crew chief had lost half his head and that she was covered with his blood.

Hunt gave her a few seconds, then said, "Don't look at him, Abi. Make your way toward me, okay? And keep low. Hug the dirt."

She had just reached him when the sniper fired again. A bullet ricocheted off a huge flat rock five feet to his right. He heard the crack of another bullet as it broke the sound barrier over his head. But this time, Hunt saw the muzzle flash. He knew where the sniper was firing from. He trained his M4 in that direction. Hunt couldn't see if he was hitting his target, but at least the sniper would have no choice but to take cover.

Then a huge explosion rocked the ground, and a ball of flame and smoke billowed skyward from the enemy position Hunt had been pumping rounds into.

What the hell was that?

"Victor-One, you okay?" Carter said. "Did you blow something up?"

Even though he couldn't hear it, Hunt was confident a drone was circling overhead. The insurgents had just been taken out by a drone strike.

"I think someone has eyes on us, gentlemen," Hunt said. "That was either a Predator or a Reaper."

Carter let out a whoop. "That got our guys scared, too, Victor-One," Carter said. "They're withdrawing."

"Then it's time to move," Hunt ordered. "Victor-Four's taking the lead."

Hunt reached down and grabbed the crew chief's lifeless body. He must have weighed close to 170 pounds.

How did Abigail manage to carry him that far?

Hunt carried the crew chief on his shoulder and followed Abigail, who had her M4 up and was scanning for threats. Another explosion sounded in the distance behind them.

"I think they got the other ones too," Dante said over the comms.

Hunt didn't bother looking over his shoulder. He was too focused on making sure they weren't getting into an ambush of some sort. The farmhouse was in the middle of a clearing the size of about two football fields. The clearing was fairly flat and more than large enough to accommodate a couple of helicopters or a V-22 Osprey sent to extract them. That was good. What wasn't so good was that they had to cross the open field to get to the house.

Hunt carefully rested the crew chief's body on the ground, then waited for Dante and Carter to join them at the edge of the orchard. From one of his pockets, he retrieved a miniature spotting scope and searched for anything out of the ordinary. The farmhouse looked unoccupied, but that would need to be confirmed. Hunt focused his attention on the edge of the tree line surrounding the farmhouse.

There. Azfaar.

On the other side of the clearing, about ten feet into the tree line, the Afghan farmer was limping away. Hunt almost ran after him, but it would have been careless. He first needed to ensure the safety of his team.

Hunt turned to Abi. She was speaking in a low, urgent tone to Dante, who'd arrived with Carter and the limping copilot. Her head was close to his, and it was clear to Hunt that Dante was troubled about the whole situation. For a moment, Hunt had mistakenly led him to believe his wife had been shot.

"You guys are good?" Hunt asked. As much as he'd like to give them some alone time, they needed to get moving.

"We're good," Dante replied for both of them. His voice betrayed a lack of confidence in his own assessment, but he was a soldier, and Hunt knew he'd push through.

"Abi, you stay here and cover our rear while the three of us clear the farmhouse. Understood?"

"Yeah, I got it."

Hunt caught the copilot's eyes. The man gave him a twisted grin.

"Hang on, buddy. We'll get you some help," Hunt told him with a smile. "And you're pretty cool for an air force guy, you know that? On me," Hunt said to the others, breaking the tree line.

Hunched over in a combat crouch, his rifle held up and ready to fire, he dogtrotted across the clearing toward the farmhouse, knowing that Dante and Carter were doing the same behind him and covering their respective arcs of fire.

That's not a farmhouse. More of a medium-size shed.

The building was made of dried mud bricks and had a roof, which would at least offer some protection against small arms fire. The design wasn't very elaborate. There were two windows and one entry door that Hunt could see. He kept his M4 trained on the window on the left of the entry door and instructed Carter to cover the right one as they approached.

The door was half-open, and beyond the obvious sounds of four-legged critters, there was no sign of life inside. Hunt was the first in, his M4 ready in case he had missed something, and he took the right corner while Carter took the left.

"Clear," Hunt said for the benefit of Dante, who had stayed outside.

"Go help Abi with the casualties," Hunt ordered Carter and Dante once they were all inside. "Then I want you to continue trying to get the comms back with our TOC. Understood?"

"Got it, boss," Carter replied. "Where are you going?"

"I'm going after Azfaar."

CHAPTER THIRTY-FOUR

Helmand Province, Afghanistan

Hunt raced toward the tree line, half expecting to get shot at any moment by an unseen attacker. A big explosion echoed in the distance.

Another drone strike. That was good—it meant the team back at the TOC had eyes on the situation. It also meant there were more insurgents out there than he'd hoped. They'd be making their way toward the farmhouse at any moment, which meant his team wouldn't have much reprieve. He hoped the QRF was on its way, but he knew that if it arrived, it wouldn't wait for him for long. He needed to get Azfaar and get him back to the farmhouse—now.

Azfaar had heard the explosion too. He turned around and looked directly at Hunt, but he didn't stop. Instead, Azfaar quickened his pace and moved deeper into the orchard.

"Azfaar!" Hunt shouted after him.

Didn't the man want to come to America? Why was he running away? Hunt reached the tree line and swore under his breath. Aware that an insurgent could be hidden behind the next tree, Hunt didn't like the idea of venturing deeper into the orchard. He had no choice but to slow down. Still, he wasn't ready to let Azfaar get away. The Afghan farmer had information Hunt desperately needed.

Hunt's eyes darted quickly from left to right, boosted by the fear of losing Azfaar's trail. As Hunt progressed farther away from the farmhouse, he also left the orchard behind. It abruptly transitioned into a much thicker-wooded area. In front of him were four trails, each heading in a different direction. If he took the wrong trail, he might never catch up to Azfaar. He was about to start down the second trail from the right when he noticed a series of tiny blood drops to his left. With a newfound energy, Hunt lowered himself into a combat crouch and followed the edge of the trail. He had traveled less than fifty meters when he came around a bend and found Azfaar. He was sitting down, his back against a big rock, looking into the distance.

Hunt followed his gaze. There was a large opening between the trees through which he could see the valley spread out below, with more mountains in the background. A small lake glittered in the distance.

"Isn't it beautiful?" Azfaar asked, his voice hoarse with pain. "That's my Afghanistan. The one I want to remember."

Hunt approached, his M4 aimed in front of him, his eyes on its lethal red dot as he swept the wooded area.

Once he was sure the immediate vicinity was secured, Hunt put a knee down next to Azfaar. "Why did you run away?"

Azfaar coughed, blood coming out in faint specks. "I didn't want them to catch me with you."

"You hurt?" Hunt let his M4 fall against its sling and frisked Azfaar for injuries. His hand came back covered in blood.

"I miraculously escaped from the crash unscathed," Azfaar said. "I thanked Allah for sparing my life."

"Then you got shot," Hunt said matter-of-factly.

Azfaar laughed, but his chuckles turned into a major coughing fit. More blood came out.

"A stray bullet is my guess," Azfaar said, wincing in pain.

With his index finger, Hunt found what he was looking for—the entry wound. Had the bullet gone all the way through?

"Stop, my friend," Azfaar said, placing a hand on Hunt's forearm. "Please."

Hunt ignored him and continued to look for the exit wound he hoped was there. "You'll bleed out if I don't fix this," Hunt said.

"That's okay," the Afghan said. "Please."

Hunt was doing his best to keep pressure on the entry wound, but he was getting nowhere with the exit wound. The bullet was still inside Azfaar. There was no point in trying to get it out. Azfaar didn't have the time or the blood pressure to withstand field surgery. Truth be told, Hunt doubted he could pull through.

"Did you know that Kabul was once called the Paris of Central Asia?" Azfaar asked through gritted teeth.

The question surprised Hunt. "What?"

"It was once easy to fall in love with my country," Azfaar continued, his voice barely above a whisper. "The natural beauty of the landscape, the rugged mountains, its valleys and gorges with the passes that linked them. I wish you could have seen that."

Azfaar had tears in his eyes. The man was dying, and he knew it.

"I'm sorry, Azfaar. I can't find the exit wound."

"Don't be sorry. These aren't tears of sadness. They're tears of joy. Allah is taking me with him this time."

A branch snapped to Hunt's right. He knew the forest could get noisy. Trees got knocked over by hard winds. Dead branches blew off and fell down. Sometimes a jackal, a wolf, or even a wild sheep would move through dry timber and sound like an eighteen-wheeler. But there was a distinctive sound to a dry branch breaking under a man's foot. It was a deep and subdued crack, a sound that Hunt often associated with a silenced gunshot from his pistol.

Hunt brought his M4 to the ready, all his senses straining to determine exactly where the sound had come from. His peripheral vision caught movement about fifty meters down the trail. A couple of meters from the edge of the trail, two insurgents were walking, one behind the other. They were both wearing checkered head wraps and *perahan tunban*—the traditional long shirt and pants, or man jammies, as

US soldiers called them. There was no way they could miss Hunt and Azfaar. And they didn't. Surprise flashed across the first insurgent's face. His body tensed, and he fumbled with his weapon.

He didn't look even twenty. *He's just a kid.*

Hunt hesitated, but only for a moment. His training took over, and he pulled the trigger twice in less than half a second, striking his target square in the chest. The muzzle of his M4 moved slightly to the left, and Hunt pulled the trigger the moment his sights were on the second insurgent.

Pop!

For a second, Hunt had no clue what had just happened, except that he'd missed his target. The insurgent had hit the deck and disappeared into the foliage.

Hunt angled his M4 to the left and saw a round wedged between the bolt and the ejection port's opening. His rifle had jammed.

You've got to be kidding me. Hunt was about to clear the jam when the insurgent opened up with his AK-47. Bullets smacked against the tree trunk to his right. Hunt let go of his M4 and dove toward Azfaar. He pinned the older Afghan to the ground.

"You stay here. You don't die."

"You're a fool if you think I can move."

Hunt rolled off Azfaar, cleared his jam, and inserted a fresh magazine. He then pulled his pistol from its holster and handed it to Azfaar.

"Every five seconds, I want you to fire two shots in the air. Make sure to hide your muzzle flash. Got it?"

Alert from the adrenaline rush despite his severe condition, Azfaar nodded.

Staying low, Hunt used the terrain to his advantage. He didn't want to leave the insurgent time to think.

Two quick pistol shots sounded from behind him. Half a second later, the crack of bullets firing in that direction told Hunt the insurgent had taken Azfaar's bait. Hunt now had a good idea where the insurgent was. He broke into a full sprint, jerking left and right and using trees as cover as he made his approach.

Two more pistol shots. This time, the insurgent returned fire with a long burst of his AK-47 that lasted just under three seconds.

He's empty. Hunt launched forward, his feet barely making any noise as they moved over the soft debris of the forest floor. Hunt expected to hear two more shots, but they didn't come. He didn't have the time to worry about Azfaar's fate, not until he had neutralized the threat.

Hunt spotted the insurgent. The man was crouched behind a large tree twenty meters away and completely exposed to Hunt's approach. The insurgent was fumbling with his weapon, trying to ram a new magazine home. Hunt fired twice.

"Victor-One, from Two. Sitrep, over," came Carter's voice in his earpiece.

The rest of his team had probably heard the gunfire.

"Two, this is One. I engaged two tangos. Both are down. I'm with our asset. He's not ambulatory."

"You need assistance, One?"

"Negative. Stay put."

"Copy that. Staying put. Two out."

Hunt ran back to Azfaar. "It's me coming in. Don't shoot!"

But Azfaar was in no position to shoot. He was lying on his back, immobile, eyes closed with his right arm limp at his side. Hunt's pistol had slipped from his hand.

"Azfaar? Azfaar? You hear me?"

The Afghan slowly opened his eyes, but they weren't focusing on anything. Azfaar looked very weak, but at least he was alive.

"You got—" Azfaar started to say, but the words disappeared in a violent coughing fit.

There was nothing Hunt could do for him. Azfaar was too far gone. He had minutes to live. At most.

"Yeah, I got both of them," Hunt said. "We're safe. For now."

"Butterfly," Azfaar said, barely loud enough for Hunt to hear. "Re . . . remember Butterfly."

"Butterfly? Did you say Butterfly?"

"Water. I need . . . ," Azfaar said, running his dry tongue over his parched lips.

From one of his plate carrier pockets, Hunt retrieved one of his two emergency water pouches. He tore it open and lifted Azfaar's head. He tilted the water pouch until it rested against Azfaar's lips. Azfaar drank long and deep, water dripping off his chin and into the hollow of his neck.

"Thank you."

"What's Butterfly, Azfaar? Tell me."

"It's . . . the name of the Spider's operation."

General Peraza. "What's the Spider's endgame?"

Azfaar sighed, clearly exasperated with the conversation.

"Manufacturing a . . . new drug. Cheap pills. Dangerous."

"Are you sure, Azfaar? How do you know this?"

Azfaar looked tired, exhausted. His dark eyes were pits of shadow.

"They used my house . . . there's a hidden entrance in my bedroom that leads . . . that leads to a laboratory. They . . . they left. In a hurry. Weeks ago. Rumors of . . . an American team looking for them. Scared. They were."

"They knew we were looking for them? How?"

Azfaar shook his head. "Don't know. But they were still watching me. Who do you think fired on us at my place?"

"I can't believe you were part of this," Hunt said, chastising himself for not thinking about Azfaar before today.

"Not given . . . a choice. There's . . . there was another lab in the Nangarhar Province. I . . . I don't know where."

So at least the intelligence they had pulled from the laptop they had seized in Paraguay had been valid. They had simply been unable to locate the laboratory. He wondered if it was because that lab had been shut down, too, due to the *American team* searching for them.

"Those drugs killed a lot of American children, Azfaar. Why didn't you tell me this when we were at your house? We could have searched the laboratory," Hunt asked softly. There was no point losing his temper with a dying man.

"Something must . . . have gone wrong. The pills were supposed to be highly addictive. Not supposed to kill."

"You should have told me," Hunt repeated.

"I wanted to get out," Azfaar replied, a weak smile appearing on his otherwise stern countenance. "Now that they were done with me . . ."

"They would have killed you," Hunt finished his sentence for him.

Azfaar closed his eyes and nodded. "I knew you wouldn't take me to the United States. I—"

"I would have tried," Hunt said, meaning it.

"There's another man," Azfaar said, opening his eyes and grabbing Hunt's arm. "Jorge Ramirez. Jorge—"

"Ramirez, I got it," Hunt said.

Carter's voice came in through Hunt's earpiece. "One, this is Two. I just established contact with call sign Romeo-One. Romeo-One is QRF. ETA is less than one mike."

Hunt stood still, trying to hear the incoming aircraft beyond the sounds of the forest, but he heard nothing, his hearing still impaired due to the recent firefight.

"Roger your last transmission, Victor-Two. I'm on my way."

"Copy that, One."

Hunt turned his attention back to Azfaar. He was panting, and a new coughing fit left him wheezing. Hunt picked up his pistol, changed the magazine, and holstered it.

"All right, my friend," Hunt said, lifting the injured man on his shoulder. "Let's get you some help."

Azfaar yelped in pain, but Hunt ignored him. He started to trot down the trail, looking left and right for any sign of danger. Then he heard it. There was no mistaking it for anything else. The faint thrumming of a plane's engines. A few seconds later, Hunt reached the orchard and saw the flat-bottomed, rounded nose cone of a V-22 Osprey flying overhead.

Thank God.

"Hang on, Azfaar," Hunt said, panting. "We're almost there."

That was when an AK-47 rattled behind him. Then another one. Bullets zipped past to his right and left, rustling through the bushes and snapping branches in two. Hunt didn't flinch. He ran harder through the orchard. His legs ached, his lungs were burning, but he didn't dare stop and look behind him. He wished he could call for help, but he was holding his M4 in his right hand and using his left arm to keep Azfaar from falling off his shoulder. More rounds thudded into the trees around him.

He still had two or three hundred meters to go, and he was starting to believe he wouldn't make it. It was like being in a dream, or a nightmare in this case. His legs were pumping, but the farmhouse remained distant, somehow unreachable. And then a bullet, fired from somewhere behind him, grazed his leg, throwing Hunt off balance. Another bullet glanced off the edge of Hunt's helmet, jerking his head to the side and knocking him down, both Azfaar and his M4 slipping from his grasp.

Fuuuck!

Hunt had no time to reflect. He scrambled behind a nearby rock, dragging Azfaar and the rifle with him. He glanced at his injured leg. The injury was superficial. The bullet had cut through his trousers but had barely broken the skin. Hunt glanced over the rock to see how many enemy combatants were making their way toward his position.

Shit. Shit. Shit.

There were way too many of them—and those were just the ones he could see. This damn rock was going to be his Alamo.

Hunt never saw or heard the Hellfire missile traveling at just under one thousand miles per hour, but what he did see and hear was the ear-shattering explosion. The blast struck him like an invisible hand, whacking him behind the shoulder blades. He was showered with burning debris. Hunt felt as if he had been run over by a school bus. He had a throbbing sensation in the back of his neck and head. The numbness slowly released its grasp on him, allowing Hunt to rise sluggishly from the ground. Slightly dazed, he looked around. Many of the trees around him were on fire, and there was a crater the size of a family-size hot tub where the insurgents had been standing less than thirty seconds ago.

Drone strike.

The strike gave Hunt an opportunity to withdraw. He looked at Azfaar. The Afghan was still breathing, but he had lost consciousness.

"Pierce! Pierce! We're coming in!" shouted Carter.

Hunt raised his eyes and saw Carter and Dante approaching in combat crouch.

"You okay, brother? We've been trying to reach you over the comms," Carter asked.

"I'm fine," Hunt replied, glad to see his friends. He'd have to check his radio. The explosion had probably damaged it.

"Is he alive?" Carter asked, nodding toward Azfaar.

"Barely," Hunt replied. "He needs a surgeon."

"The Osprey is in a holding pattern a couple miles from here," Dante explained. "The QRF is waiting for our word."

"I got him," Carter said, picking up the wounded man. Carter threw him over his shoulder in a fireman's carry as if Azfaar were a mere ten-pound bag of potatoes.

Hunt led the way out of the orchard, and not a moment too soon. He had had enough of Afghanistan for a lifetime. He needed to provide Hauer with the intel he had gathered from his discussion with Azfaar and get back to Leila and Anna.

Behind him, Dante was asking Abigail to pop some smokes to help the QRF locate their exact position. Sixty seconds later, when they finally crossed the tree line into the open field, Hunt looked up to see the V-22 Osprey floating one hundred feet over the farmhouse, its heavy twin rotors swirling smoke and grit all around. As soon as the aircraft touched down, the rear ramp lowered with a mechanical whine, and marines poured out of the cargo area. They quickly set up a defensive perimeter around the aircraft.

A corpsman sprinted in their direction.

"Do you need assistance, sir?" he asked.

Hunt pointed to Azfaar. "He needs medical attention, and we have two more inside the farmhouse."

Two more corpsmen joined the first. They were carrying a stretcher. Hunt wiped his hand across his face, doing his best to clear the dirt from his eyes. When he could see again, he noticed a marine officer jogging toward him.

"Mr. Hunt?"

"Yeah, that's me," Hunt yelled back.

"I'm Romeo-One," the officer informed him. "I've been in communication with your TOC, so they know exactly what's going on. They expect you to call them from Kandahar once we land."

"Will do," Hunt replied, sure Pike and Crawford had played an important role in the rescue operation. "What about my pilot? We couldn't extract him from the Super Huey. He's still at the crash site."

"We know, and there's another QRF on its way. They have two A-10s acting as support and will stop by the crash site to retrieve your man."

"Can't we go now?" Hunt asked. "It's not even half a mile away."

"Negative," the marine said. "The enemy is fast approaching our position, and we've lost our drone support. We need to get this bird out of here ASAP."

Hunt understood. Without air support, it would be too dangerous to attempt the recovery. "Got it. Thanks."

The marine officer nodded. "Sorry for your losses, Mr. Hunt."

Hunt's stomach turned when he saw the corpsmen loading the crew chief into the V-22. At least the copilot was able to get in on his own two feet.

"We have to go, Pierce," Carter shouted. "Let's go."

Hunt followed Carter and Dante into the V-22, ducking as he passed under the huge blades rotating above his head. Inside the cargo hold, he took a seat next to Abigail. Her face was a mask of dirt and blood. She'd never be the same, but at least she was holding it together.

She wasn't the only kick-ass woman he knew. He wondered how long it would take for him to get back to Florida. Every time he thought about Anna and Leila, a knot tightened in his chest as if it were being squeezed by a vise. He didn't want to lose Anna, but he couldn't bear living without his daughter. Leila, whose love was everything to him, had told him in no uncertain terms that she blamed Anna for Jack's death. Hunt was in an impossible position, and he was powerless to do anything about it until he was back in the United States.

The ramp closed, and the aircraft lifted off. In the faint light of the cargo compartment, Azfaar's skin looked colorless. His breathing was increasingly erratic, and Hunt feared he wouldn't make it to Kandahar.

As if God—or Allah in this case—had read his mind, Azfaar began convulsing on the stretcher. The two corpsmen taking care of him started chest compressions. They tried for ten minutes to save him. When they stopped, Hunt's heart sank. Azfaar was dead.

CHAPTER THIRTY-FIVE

Miami, Florida

Anna exited the nightclub and walked to the Range Rover. Even though the inside of the club was still packed, outside the queue had dwindled. Anna was in way over her head, and she knew it. Jorge Ramirez was bad news. Maybe a united Garcia crime syndicate led by Tony could have fought him off, but not anymore. Ramirez had said so himself: the Garcia family was weak.

Anna had never heard of Ramirez before, but she was well aware of the Spider. Since the death of the Black Tosca, the Spider—who had previously kept his bidding mostly in South America—had quickly climbed the ladder of success in the underworld. Buoyed by a sudden, and what seemed to her almost unlimited, supply of cash, the Spider had his fingers in many pies. But never in a million years had Anna thought the Spider would take over her organization and use it to poison young Americans. Maybe she'd been too naive. Wasn't it true that for years the Garcias had been the obvious choice for anyone trying to get into the US distribution network?

An image of Leila's boyfriend flashed in her mind. A sudden wave of nausea ripped through her gut, compelling her to stop and lean over. She forced the bitter taste back down her throat and wiped the moisture from her forehead. The nausea persisted and was now complemented by an overwhelming dizziness. A second wave of nausea rose from her stomach, and this time there was no forcing it down. She doubled over and vomited all over the sidewalk until there was nothing left.

She lifted her head and saw Tasis jogging toward her.

"Anna, are you all right?"

Deeply embarrassed, she wiped her mouth with her forearm.

"Oh my God, that was terrible," she said weakly. She could feel the bile rising in her throat again, the acidic saliva accumulating at the back of her mouth.

"What happened in there?" Tasis asked.

"Not now, Mauricio," she replied. "I need to think."

"Okay, let's get you out of here." He led the way to the Range Rover.

As she followed him, she couldn't shake the feeling that someone was watching her.

Anna hated the feeling of being trapped in a corner. There was one thing she could do to get out, but she wasn't sure she had the courage to do it.

———

From the back seat of his black Mercedes SUV, Luis Ojeda had a great view of the scene unfolding two blocks away. Through his powerful night-vision spotting scope, he could see everyone as if it were daytime. He watched the green image of Anna Garcia emptying her stomach on the sidewalk. A weak grin touched his mouth. In her defense, she wasn't the first criminal leader to get sick after meeting with Jorge Ramirez. Ramirez had a special way of making people feel either extremely comfortable in his presence or in fear for their lives. It was clear which of the two he had served to Anna Garcia.

Following Ramirez's last text, Ojeda had returned to his car to observe the aftermath of the meeting. He already knew pretty much all there was to know about Garcia and her organization. Of course, it was impossible to plan for every possibility, but as a professional assassin, it was his duty to be as well prepared as possible. The more intelligence he could gather on a target, the better. He wanted to know who all the players were, their favorite restaurants, where they had their gym membership, where their friends lived, and especially where their children went to school. Over the years, Ojeda had found that children were a great bargaining chip—just the threat of harm allowed him to manipulate his targets.

He was about to replace the thermal scope in its case and get some sleep for the night when his phone beeped twice.

Full surveillance package for thirty-six hours. Report back any useful intelligence.

No way he'd be able to get a decent night's sleep now. Ramirez wanted him to monitor Garcia for the next day or so. It looked as though his boss wasn't entirely satisfied with Garcia's performance at the meeting. What Garcia did and who she contacted in the next thirty-six hours might determine if she lived or died.

Ojeda didn't care. The only thing bugging him was that he needed to pick up a gift for his father's birthday.

A knock on the back window made him jump. Two police officers were standing on the sidewalk.

Ojeda chastised himself for being caught off guard, but he wasn't overly worried about his predicament. His backstop, prepared by the SEBIN—the national intelligence service of Venezuela—was bulletproof. It identified him as a military attaché of the Bolivarian Republic of Venezuela to the United States.

He gently opened the back door. "Good evening, Officers," he said, smiling.

"Good evening, sir," the shorter of the two officers said. "Would you please step out?" The officer took a step back, giving himself some extra space.

Ojeda could see a marine corps tattoo on his oversize forearm. The second officer—the taller one—removed his handheld flashlight from his duty belt and proceeded to walk around the SUV.

"Can I help you with something, gentlemen?" Ojeda asked, keeping an eye on the second officer, who had now reached the rear of the SUV.

"Anyone else in the vehicle, sir?" the second officer asked, shining his flashlight inside.

"I'm by myself, Officer. Is there a problem?"

"Not at all," the first officer replied. "We saw movement in your vehicle, and we simply wondered if you needed assistance."

Ojeda forced a chuckle. "Well, that's very nice of you. I was just chilling until I felt comfortable to drive."

"Why's that? You had a few drinks?"

"Maybe one or two too many, I have to admit." Ojeda angled his body to allow him to keep watch on the second officer, who had now stopped next to the front passenger-side window.

"Please look at me, sir," the first officer said.

"I'm sorry, Officer. What was your question?"

"Why were you in the back seat of your vehicle?"

"I know the law. Can't be behind the wheel if my blood alcohol concentration is above the limit."

"We certainly appreciate you putting safety first, sir."

"I was actually thinking about calling a cab. Do you mind?" Ojeda asked, making a show of pulling his cell phone from his pocket.

"Excuse me, sir?" That was from the second officer, the one with the flashlight. "What's in the case?"

"The case?"

"Yeah, there's a Pelican case on the back seat."

"It's an expensive camera," Ojeda replied nonchalantly. "I used it to photograph yachts at Haulover."

Baker's Haulover Inlet was a man-made channel connecting the northern end of Biscayne Bay with the Atlantic Ocean. Since Haulover was the only inlet between Miami's Government Cut and Port Everglades in Fort Lauderdale, it was popular with boaters even though it had a reputation for difficult tidal conditions.

"You used it today?" the short officer asked.

"I certainly did."

"Anything interesting? I'm a big boating fan too. I have my own center console. Twenty-four footer," the officer explained.

Ojeda didn't like the direction in which the conversation was heading. He knew next to nothing about boats.

"I think I'm gonna call that cab now, if you don't mind."

"Sure," the officer replied. "But let's see some ID first."

Behind him, the taller officer was radioing in the license plate. The Mercedes belonged to a small rental agency owned by a shell company managed by the Venezuelan government. The officer wouldn't find anything suspicious.

Ojeda fetched his wallet from his back pocket and handed his Louisiana driver's license to the officer. The officer frowned.

"Louisiana? What brings you to Miami?"

"Work, I'm afraid."

"What kind of work?"

"I work at the Venezuelan Consulate General in New Orleans," Ojeda replied.

"You're a diplomat?"

"I'm one of the military attachés."

"No kidding? What branch of service?"

"Army," Ojeda answered. Pointing a finger at the officer's tattoo, he continued, "And I see you were with the marines."

"Semper fi," the officer replied.

A quick glance to his left revealed that the tall officer was in the process of using his cell phone to take a picture of the vehicle.

"Excuse me, what are you doing?" Ojeda asked him. Alarm bells rang in his head. There was more to these officers than he had initially given them credit for.

"Don't worry about it, sir."

"Listen, I'm playing it cool with you guys, but I have diplomatic immunity," Ojeda warned. "Don't take pictures of the vehicle, please."

The tall officer backed off. "My apologies, sir. Nice wheels you have there. I'll delete the pic."

Ojeda doubted he'd do so but didn't want to push the issue. He'd have to find new transportation for the rest of his operation, which was a shame. He actually liked the SUV. Same went for his credentials. He'd need a new set of those too.

"There you go, sir," the short officer said, handing back his driver's license. "Enjoy the rest of your evening."

Two miles away, Anna's phone vibrated. She entered her six-digit personal identification number. The message was from Officer Davis, one of the cops the Garcia family had on the take. She read the text. A photo of a black late-model Mercedes SUV was also attached.

"You were right, Mauricio," Anna said from the back seat. "They had someone outside the club."

"Venezuelan?"

"Seems like it," Anna replied. "The guy's name is Ernesto Sadel. Believe it or not, he's a military attaché from Louisiana."

"I thought the embassy was in Washington."

"Officer Davis's text says that Sadel works out of the Venezuelan Consulate General in New Orleans."

"That means Ramirez wasn't lying. He has the full support of the Venezuelan government. That's not good, Anna."

"I know."

"Was Davis able to put the tracker in play?"

"He did."

"What are you gonna do?"

"I'm gonna call Tom Hauer and ask for his help," Anna said, her mind set. "I have no other choice. Whatever he wants in exchange, I'll give."

CHAPTER THIRTY-SIX

DEA Headquarters
Arlington, Virginia

Tom Hauer had just returned to his office. Hunt and the surviving members of his team were safely aboard the V-22 Osprey that would bring them back to Kandahar Airfield. Hauer poured himself two fingers of single malt from the expensive bottle his wife had gifted him for his fifty-fifth birthday four years ago. Hauer didn't drink much, but when he did, he enjoyed the good stuff.

Tonight's drink wasn't a celebration or because he deserved it. He needed it to take the edge off. Truth be told, this had been one of the worst days in DEA history. Hauer had lost a long-serving undercover agent and two special operators, and that was just in Venezuela. In Afghanistan, Pierce Hunt's helicopter had been shot down by insurgents and had cost the lives of its pilot and crew chief. It was a miracle there weren't more casualties.

What a mess!

And what should he do about Anna Garcia? Goddamn Hunt had put him in a terrible position by encouraging him to trust Anna's plan to transition her late father's crime syndicate into something more legitimate. He'd known how tiny the chances were that she would succeed, but he'd found the idea of an unconventional solution appealing. Wasn't it better to have the Garcia syndicate dismantled from the inside, all of those traffickers and dealers gone legit, than to pursue years of attempted arrests and prosecutions that would result in only a fraction of those criminals being punished and probably no reduction in the flow of drugs?

But the chance he'd taken on Anna had opened the door to a whole new drug epidemic coming from seemingly out of nowhere. Children were dead. Was that Hauer's fault? He knew the attorney general—and maybe even the president—would be grilling him at the meeting in the morning.

Hauer didn't blame them. He wanted answers, too, but he was at a loss. Despite the threat he'd made to Anna in their last conversation, he hadn't yet had a chance to task his deputy with launching a fresh investigation into her culpability in the athletes' deaths. Was it too late to even put the genie back in the bottle now that the drug was out there? Hauer used to be a big believer in preventive strategies—going to schools and talking to students about the negative effects different types of drug had on the human brain. But how did you convince a generation that thought chewing Tide PODS was cool?

He hoped that the recent deaths wouldn't be in vain and that the media's coverage of this tragedy would convince at least some potential customers of the dangers associated with these synthetic drugs.

And meanwhile, Hauer would keep trying to cut off the sources of the drugs entering the country. A task made even harder now with Godfrey's death. He only hoped the team he'd dispatched could recover the data from the USB drive.

Hauer took a sip from his drink and looked at his watch. He still had a few hours before his meeting with the president. It was too late for him to drive home. Good thing he always kept a fresh suit in his office. He finished his drink in one large gulp, took half a second to enjoy it, then walked to his private bathroom—one of the few privileges of his position—to shave and shower. Then he'd write his report and at least try to prepare for his meeting at the White House.

Hauer was halfway to the bathroom when his personal cell phone vibrated on his desk. He thought about letting it go to voicemail, but at this hour of the night, it could only be his wife.

Poor Julia. Alone in her big house, again. Hauer's schedule didn't allow for much quality time with his wife. They had talked about it before he'd accepted the position, but neither of them could have known how taxing his work would become. They were way overdue for a vacation, and he had promised to take her someplace nice the moment his workload slackened just a bit. She had shown him pictures of a beautiful beach house in Palm Cay, a small gated community in the Bahamas. He even remembered the name of the place.

Blue Horizon Villa. A perfect name for a perfect place, but after today's events in Florida, Afghanistan, and Venezuela, Hauer feared long walks on the beach with his wife were still months away.

He picked up the phone without looking at the display.

"Hey, honey—"

"Is this Tom Hauer?" a woman asked, interrupting him. The voice had a soft Spanish accent slipping through it.

Hauer looked at the display. The number was blocked.

"Who's this, and how did you get this number?" he growled.

"It's Anna Garcia, Mr. Hauer."

Anna Garcia calling his personal line wasn't good news. The proper thing to do would be to ask her to call his office the next morning. His personal cell phone was secured, but not to the same level as his office line. And he'd love to record the conversation. He didn't trust Anna anymore.

"I'm sorry, Miss Garcia, but I'm gonna hang up now. Goodbye—"

"Please, Mr. Hauer, don't. I want to turn myself in."

That was a surprise. Hauer's mouth opened, but no sound came out. Anna calling him and offering to turn herself in was the last thing he had expected a minute ago when he was on his way to the bathroom.

"Mr. Hauer, I believe my life's in danger."

The next words came out of his mouth fast and hard. "You believe your life's in danger? What about that? Aren't you the new head of the Garcia crime syndicate? Wouldn't you say that comes with the territory?"

Surprising him for the second time in the same minute, Anna's reply was controlled, her voice measured.

"I completely understand, Mr. Hauer, and frankly, I'd feel the same way if I was in your shoes. But I need your help."

Hauer sighed heavily. He wasn't going to apologize to Anna, but he had to admit he was curious.

"Pierce told me I could trust you," Anna added.

Hauer was beginning to think that Hunt was more trouble than he was worth. But he knew that to be false. Should he share with Anna what had happened to Hunt in Afghanistan?

God, no! She isn't cleared to hear that.

Hauer would need to be careful. He'd had a single two-ounce drink, but he wasn't thinking clearly. *Maybe the lack of sleep is getting to me.*

"Okay, Miss Garcia, you have thirty seconds."

Anna didn't waste any time. "I know who's responsible for producing and distributing the amphetamine pills that killed so many. I believe rogue elements within my organization played a major role in the drug-related deaths of—"

"Stop right there, Miss Garcia," Hauer said, his heart rate picking up. "Not on the phone. Where are you right now?"

"In my car, driving back to the family estate."

Hauer's mind was racing. It wasn't every day that the head of one of the biggest crime syndicates in Florida called you to admit to a felony offense. There was definitely more to this, but Hauer couldn't continue this exchange over his personal phone. Like it or not, there were procedures to follow. In a case as big as this, he didn't want to shoulder all the blame if the case ended up being tossed out of court because he hadn't respected the rules.

"Don't go to your estate, Miss Garcia. Find a coffee shop, a mall parking lot, or just stop safely on the side of the road, and I'll have a special agent meet you within the hour."

"Are you recording this conversation?" Anna asked. "Please tell me you are."

Hauer knew how to record conversations on his DEA cell phone and on his office landline, but not on his personal phone. His predecessor had asked that all his calls, even the incoming and outgoing calls on his personal device, be recorded, but Hauer valued his privacy and didn't believe the DEA—or the analysts listening in—needed to know how his son was doing and what his wife had prepared for dinner.

"I'm not, but as I said, I'll have a special—"

"Listen to me, Tom, and take notes," Anna said, her voice turning authoritative. "I might not have an hour."

Hauer let Anna's familiarity slip by. There was something she needed to say, and his gut told him he'd better listen *and take notes*. He opened his drawer and fetched a pad of writing paper and a pen. He put on his reading glasses, put the phone on speaker mode.

"What is it that can't wait?"

For the next five minutes, Hauer listened, took notes, and interrupted Anna only a few times to ask clarifying questions. When she finished, Hauer thanked her and told her he'd be in touch shortly. After he hung up, he sat back in his chair, his eyes closed, ruminating on what the head of the Garcia family had just told him.

Was it the truth? Or was she playing an angle he just couldn't see? Hauer couldn't keep this newly acquired intelligence to himself—he would need help to verify Anna's claim. What she had told him was so big that Hauer had no choice but to call his boss, Gerard Mackey, the attorney general of the United States.

The AG would decide who else to invite to the White House meeting. If this went the way Hauer thought it was going, there would be a whole lot more people in the Oval Office than the president had bargained for.

There was one other call he needed to make first.

CHAPTER THIRTY-SEVEN

Kandahar Airfield
Afghanistan

Throughout the Osprey ride, Hunt kept his eyes on Azfaar's body. One of the corpsmen had the decency to cover his body with an emergency blanket. That didn't help with the blood pouring out from under the stretcher, but at least Hunt didn't have to face his failure. Azfaar's death was on him.

Hunt spent the rest of the trip thinking about Leila, Anna, and all the bad decisions he'd made over the last sixteen years. Was his decision to get involved with Anna a mistake? It certainly looked like it, but damn if he didn't love this woman with all of his heart. As much as the evidence was stacked up against her, deep down Hunt knew Anna was a woman of her word. No way she would have betrayed him or Leila. For Hunt, loving someone meant working yourself threadbare for her if necessary, and that was exactly what he would do for Anna. No, falling for her hadn't been a mistake. He'd be right by her side, and together they would prove her innocence to Hauer.

And to Leila.

The landing gear locking into place brought him back from his reverie. Hunt could almost feel the engines rotating upward, stabilizing the V-22 before slowly lowering it to the tarmac below. The wheels touched down with a definite thud. They were still taxiing when the Osprey crew chief approached him, a satellite phone in his hand.

"Mr. Hunt," the crew chief said, handing him the phone, "it's for you."

"Is the line secured?" Hunt asked.

"Yes, sir."

Hunt pressed the satellite phone against his ear and said, "This is Hunt."

"Glad you're safe, Pierce," Tom Hauer said. "We were all very worried about you and your team."

"Yes, sir, but we lost an asset and two good men," Hunt reminded him.

"Did you get anything from your asset?"

Hauer wasn't known to be a sensitive man, but he was respectful, and Hunt knew how much he cared about his subordinates. For him to forgo saying anything about the loss of two men under his command meant that his reason for calling Hunt troubled him immensely.

"I did, but I'll need to corroborate the intel and do some research before sending you my report."

"Does it confirm our suspicions about Venezuela?" Hauer asked.

"As a matter of fact, it does. But we were too late to stop the drugs from being moved out from the labs."

"Yeah, I know. And Anna Garcia just called me."

"She what?" Hunt was baffled.

Why would Anna do something like that? Was it her way of fighting back? Of defending herself? Hunt hoped Leila hadn't escalated her claim that Anna was behind the drugs that killed Jack.

Hauer seemed to hesitate, but only for a second. "Her organization played a major role in the distribution of the amphetamine pills that killed the football players."

Hunt's heart dropped to the pit of his stomach and twisted in a knot. *Oh shit.*

"Pierce, you still there?" Hauer asked. "Pierce?"

"Yeah, I'm here. Please tell me Anna didn't have personal knowledge of this," Hunt said, holding his breath.

"She didn't."

Hunt gusted a huge sigh of relief. *Thank God.*

"That's a huge weight off my shoulders," Hunt admitted.

"We'll know more soon enough," Hauer said. "Anna's turning herself in. And she asked for our protection."

"How did it come to this?" Hunt murmured. "What a shit show."

"And there's more," continued Hauer. "I lost three assets in Venezuela today. It's all linked together, I think."

"Sir, what are you saying?" Hunt asked, suddenly tired.

"I'm saying that I need you and the rest of the team back stateside as soon as you can. Let Crawford and Pike dismantle the TOC while you get your ass back here pronto."

"Okay."

"DOJ's sending a private charter to pick you up. It will land at Jalalabad Airport in twelve hours. Be ready."

"We will," Hunt managed to say, but Hauer had already hung up.

Hunt handed the satellite phone back to the crew chief and thanked him. He took a moment to gather his thoughts and to prioritize what he had to do. At the top of his list was to call Leila. He had to let her know that Anna was innocent.

"What was that all about?" Carter asked, bringing him back to the present.

"I'm not sure," Hunt admitted. "But did you get your typhoid vaccine?"

"What? Why?"

"Because you'll need it. I have a feeling we're going to Venezuela."

CHAPTER THIRTY-EIGHT

The White House
Washington, DC

Tom Hauer was tired, irritated, and pissed off. It had been a long night. He was the last person to walk into the Oval Office. It was only his second visit to the White House and his first to the most prestigious office in the world, where so much history had been made. The office was tastefully decorated and airy but a tad smaller than he had pictured it, though the view out the large window toward the Washington Monument was nothing less than spectacular.

There were two armchairs in front of the fireplace. President Joshua Reilly was seated in the one to the right while Attorney General Gerard Mackey occupied the left one. Two long sofas stretched parallel to each other, between which was a large glass coffee table. Hauer sat on the first couch, with Secretary of Defense James Flynn seated directly to his right. Dorothy Triggs was the only occupant of the second sofa. Hauer had met Triggs on numerous occasions, and they had a solid working relationship. Even surrounded by the most influential men in America, she wasn't a shrinking violet. As the deputy director of the Directorate of Operations, she wielded a lot of power within the intelligence community, and Hauer knew she had President Reilly's ear.

And rightly so, thought Hauer. In his opinion, Dorothy Triggs had the brightest mind of the entire intelligence community. He would be surprised if she didn't end up the next director of the Central Intelligence Agency.

There was a gentle knock at the door; then a White House staffer appeared with a coffee service and set it in the middle of the glass table.

Once they'd taken their drinks and exchanged some congenial chit-chat, Reilly dove into the matter at hand. "Originally, this meeting was supposed to be a quick get-together between Tom, Gerard, and I to discuss an operation the DEA is conducting in Afghanistan. Early this morning, Gerard called me with some additional information regarding the mission in Afghanistan but also about the animals that might be responsible for the production and distribution of the amphetamine pills that have wreaked havoc on our youth. We're here to discuss our options as a nation and to learn what we can do to punish those responsible. Any questions?"

There were none.

"All right then," Reilly continued, moving on. "I'd like to make sure everyone is on the same page here, so why don't we give the floor to Tom so he can bring us up to date?"

Hauer's eyes automatically darted to Attorney General Mackey for his approval. Mackey shot him back a look that meant, *When the president of the United States asks you something, you don't need anyone else's permission.*

Hauer took a deep breath, glanced at his notes, and looked directly at his president.

"Thank you, Mr. President. About ten weeks ago, I received a tip indicating that Pascual Andrade, a high-ranking member of the Black Tosca cartel, was in New Orleans. Following a short foot chase, we were able to neutralize Andrade, only to learn that we had inadvertently interrupted a CIA operation."

The president looked at Triggs. "A CIA operation in New Orleans?" he asked.

"Totally legal, Mr. President. I assure you," Triggs replied. "We were simply trying to recruit a foreign national—"

"You wanted to recruit Andrade?" Reilly asked.

"We almost did, sir."

The president held Triggs's gaze for a few moments, and then he turned his attention back to Hauer. "Please continue."

"Thank you, Mr. President," Hauer said. "Following a thorough interrogation, Andrade admitted that the senior leadership of the Black Tosca cartel was scheduled to meet a representative of General Euclides Peraza, a.k.a. the Spider, in Paraguay."

"The Spider?" President Reilly asked.

"That's correct," Hauer said. "In the underworld, General Peraza is known as the Spider due to his network of spies. He's also the commanding officer of the Operational Strategic Command of the Venezuelan armed forces. He's a powerful military figure in Venezuela and a trusted aide to President Capriles."

"The Defense Intelligence Agency has a complete file on him," added the secretary of defense.

"What can you tell us about him, General Flynn?" the president asked.

"He's a dedicated man, loyal to his country, and has the respect of his troops. But we know he's heavily involved in the drug trade."

"And that's your assessment, too, Dorothy?" Reilly asked.

"It is," Triggs confirmed, brushing a strand of blonde hair behind her ear. "We've had our eyes on General Peraza for a little while now, and we were curious about that meeting in Paraguay. Because of the Black Tosca angle, one of Tom's consultants was attached to the team I sent to Paraguay. At some point during the operation, the team stumbled upon a laptop. We were able to break the encryption. Based on the contents, I concluded that the DEA should have first crack at the file."

Meaning you didn't want to waste precious resources on what could be a wild and expensive goose chase. But Hauer had been playing the DC game long enough to know it never hurt to be nice with the other kids playing in the same sandbox. "What the DDO sends my way is always quite valuable."

"I've found the same thing," Reilly replied. "So you sent a team to investigate, Tom?"

Again, Hauer shot a quick look at Mackey, who gave him a furtive shake of the head.

That's interesting. Mackey had yet to tell President Reilly about Pierce Hunt's team. Hunt's team was the first DEA squad to be entirely black—which meant that its funding came from a budget that was hidden from the public and from most congressional oversight. Attorney General Mackey had verbally given Hauer the green light, but it was apparent he hadn't yet informed President Reilly. So unless the president asked him a specific question about the resources he had sent to Afghanistan, Hauer wouldn't volunteer information.

"Yes, sir, I did. For almost two months, nothing came of it. The memo DDO Triggs sent me indicated that a clandestine lab had been set up in Afghanistan, more precisely in the Nangarhar Province, to produce a cheap synthetic drug destined for the American market."

"Who ordered that lab to be set up? The Black Tosca cartel?" Reilly asked.

"At the time we weren't sure, but now we know it was the Spider," Hauer answered.

"I'll be damned," Reilly said. "Do we know how the Spider was planning on importing the drugs?"

"By using the distribution network of the Garcia crime syndicate in Florida."

"The Garcia crime syndicate? Their leader, Vicente Garcia, was killed last year in an ambush, right?"

"You're correct, sir. And it was his granddaughter, Sophia, that was kidnapped by the Black Tosca and taken to Mexico to be killed live on social media."

"That's the operation we talked about earlier," Triggs said. "The DEA sent a low-signature team to rescue her—"

"That low-signature team left a fucking mess behind them," Reilly said, but for the first time that morning, a smile appeared on his lips. It didn't last long, but it told Hauer the president was pleased with the results. Yes, Hunt had gone ballistic when he'd learned his daughter had been kidnapped too. Yes, he had left a bloodbath behind him, and the president had had to personally call the Mexican president to explain the situation. But in Hauer's mind, it was a small price to pay for rescuing the girls and taking down the Black Tosca.

"I believe the DEA sent the same team to Afghanistan, didn't you, Tom?" Secretary of Defense James Flynn asked.

Well, the cat's out of the bag now, Hauer thought.

From the corner of his eye, he saw Mackey's face flush with anger. Hauer wondered what angle Flynn was playing. He'd have to tread carefully.

"I did," Hauer said.

President Reilly turned his attention to him. "I was under the impression that in exchange for not being prosecuted for their crimes in Mexico, the men and women involved with the San Miguel de Allende operation were to be fired from the DEA. Am I to understand that they weren't? We're talking about Pierce Hunt, aren't we?"

"Yes, sir. The task force leader was indeed Pierce Hunt. And yes, I fired them all personally," Hauer said, wondering if he was about to get the same treatment.

"What were they doing in Afghanistan then?"

"It appears to me that the DEA was running its own black team in Afghanistan," the secretary of defense said.

Everyone's eyes were on Hauer. Except for President Reilly, they all knew that the DEA had fielded a black team in Afghanistan. Until now, Hauer hadn't thought it was a problem. But somehow, he had pissed off Flynn.

"Following DDO Triggs's memo, it's true that I took the decision to outsource the investigation—"

"Why is that?" Reilly asked.

"Hunt was the consultant attached to the team the CIA sent to Paraguay. Moreover, he's a decorated Army Ranger. I felt Hunt was the perfect guy to operate in Afghanistan because he—"

"You haven't answered my question, Tom," Reilly said. "Let me rephrase it for you. Why couldn't you send one of your regular teams?"

"The thought of having plausible deniability crossed my mind, sir," Hauer replied honestly.

"Why would you need that?" Reilly asked. "What kind of operation were you running?"

The sofa had suddenly become very uncomfortable, and Hauer shifted his weight around the edge of it.

"We aren't getting the same kind of cooperation from tribal leaders we used to," Hauer said. "To get to the bottom of this, I needed a team that wasn't afraid of ruffling a few feathers if need be."

"You certainly accomplished that," the secretary of defense said snidely. "Mr. President, I had to deploy two QRFs to pull his team out when their chopper was shot down by enemy fire."

That's what this is all about. Flynn's pissed off I didn't inform him personally about my team being in theater.

"I'm grateful for your assistance, General," Hauer said. "And so are Hunt and his team."

"You still lost two army special operations aviators," Flynn barked. "If you had cared to let me know you had a team on the ground, I could have prevented this."

"How?" Hauer asked him, about to lose his temper.

"By throwing your team out of my theater of operations," Flynn snapped back. "Since your little adventure, Taliban activities have picked up significantly, increasing the risk to my troops."

"Mr. President," Hauer said, trying to regain control of the narrative, "before their chopper was shot down by insurgents, Hunt's team was able to get in contact with a local asset they had developed. This asset provided valuable intelligence regarding Operation Butterfly."

"Butterfly? You certainly have my undivided attention," the president said.

"To make a long story short, Hunt's asset was approached by Hezbollah to provide space for a secret laboratory that would be used to produce a cheap, highly addictive amphetamine pill that could be sold with an enormous profit margin in the United States."

"Hezbollah?" President Reilly asked. "Since when is Hezbollah active in Afghanistan?"

"Since General Peraza asked them to be," Hauer explained. "It is now my understanding, Mr. President, that Hezbollah was serving as a proxy for the Spider. We're not sure yet what the financial arrangement was, but we're confident Hezbollah was given a blueprint of the drug they were to manufacture. There's no way they could have come up with this themselves. They aren't sophisticated enough."

It was as if a curse had fallen upon the Oval Office. A heavy silence filled the room. That was definitely not the reaction Hauer had expected. He had anticipated some pushback and the need to defend his assessment, but even President Reilly's face was grim.

Flynn was the first to break the silence. "I'll be damned."

"Tom, are you absolutely sure that General Peraza is behind this?" President Reilly asked.

"I am," Hauer replied without hesitation. "Not only did we already know that remnants of the Black Tosca cartel were meeting with representatives of the Venezuelan government in Paraguay, but I also received a call from Anna Garcia."

"The head of a crime family contacted you? That's a bit weird, isn't it?" asked Triggs. "What did she want?"

"Since her father's and brother's deaths at the hand of the Black Tosca, Anna Garcia has decided to transform the Garcia crime syndicate into something more legitimate."

Flynn chuckled. "Oh, I'm sure that's gone well."

"Of course it hasn't," Hauer said. "Elements within her own ranks defected to other criminal organizations while others tried to torpedo her efforts—"

"By killing three of the men still loyal to her," Triggs said, finishing the sentence for him.

That gave Hauer pause. The ambush that had killed the three men had made the local newspapers, but their identities were yet to be released. He didn't think the incident had a big enough national security implication to make it to Triggs's desk. Had someone in his office been keeping her apprised?

"You're right, Dorothy," Hauer said. "That's exactly what they did, and by doing so, they forced her into a corner. She admitted that the Garcia crime family is responsible for the distribution of the amphetamine pills that killed so many, although she had no personal knowledge of it."

"What's Garcia's connection with Venezuela?" President Reilly asked.

"Last night, Anna Garcia met a man named Jorge Ramirez at a club in Miami."

"Are you kidding me?" Triggs said, agitated. "Jorge Ramirez is in the US?"

"At least as of last night he was. Why?" Hauer asked.

"We've been tracking his movements recently. He's a person of interest," Triggs said, at the same time typing a message on her mobile device. "I had no idea he was in the United States."

"Actually, based on what Garcia told me, he's the Spider's right-hand man," Hauer said. "Ramirez told Garcia that the deaths were tragic accidents caused by the pills being distributed before they were properly vetted."

Hauer didn't think it was necessary to mention that Hezbollah had had to rush the drug out of Afghanistan due to Hunt's team breathing down their collective neck. Whoever had left the laptop behind must have known there was a risk of it leading to their labs.

"Anything else to confirm General Peraza's involvement other than a phone call from a known criminal?" Flynn asked.

Hauer cleared his throat. He understood General Flynn's reticence. "A long-established DEA asset confirmed as much yesterday."

"What asset? The DEA has someone in Venezuela?" Triggs asked.

Hauer nodded. "We had an asset deep within General Peraza's close circle. This was the asset who provided the initial intel on the where-abouts of Pascual Andrade. *Had* being the operative word here, I'm afraid. My asset was killed yesterday."

"You had an asset in Venezuela, and you didn't bother letting me know?" Flynn exploded. "Mr. President, this is unacceptable. First Afghanistan, and now Venezuela? What kind of outfit is he running?"

In situations like these, Hauer had learned that to remain calm was the best way to go.

"Again, Mr. President, I understand General Flynn's annoyance, but the DEA isn't in the habit of openly discussing its intelligence-gathering capabilities with other agencies, as I'm sure the CIA and DIA aren't either."

Reilly turned to Flynn. "I was fully briefed on the DEA asset two months ago. This is a nonissue. Can we move on, Mr. Secretary?"

"My apologies, sir."

"Thank you, Mr. Secretary," Reilly replied, clearly annoyed. The president's eyes moved to Hauer. "Go on, Tom."

"During the last four years, our asset's work allowed us to make several arrests within the United States and to seize numerous small- and medium-size quantities of cocaine and heroin. All signs pointed to an increase in the Venezuelan government's commitment to penetrating the US drug market and their willingness to partner with other organizations to do so—hence the meeting with the Black Tosca cartel. General Peraza had another meeting yesterday at one of his secret camps in the Venezuelan jungle, but we don't know with who. Our asset was ambushed and killed by Peraza's men on his way to the meeting."

"Why was he ambushed? Did Peraza break his cover?" Triggs asked, taking notes.

"We believe so," Hauer replied.

"So we lost whatever intelligence your asset had collected," President Reilly concluded.

"That's the thing, sir," Hauer said. "I'm confident that our asset was able to bury an encrypted thumb drive at the ambush site before his death. It's my opinion that whatever is on that drive would reveal not only General Peraza as the drug lord he really is but could also expose weaknesses in President Capriles's government—"

"Weaknesses we could exploit to our advantage," Triggs said. "With the stunt Capriles pulled this morning, we'll need the international community's help if we want to oust him. With the Russians now involved, it complicates things."

"What stunt are we talking about here?" Mackey asked.

As the junior official in the room, Hauer wouldn't have asked the question, but he was glad his boss had. Flynn's eyes moved to the president, who nodded.

"It's gonna be all over the news channels within the hour," the president said.

Now Hauer's curiosity was piqued even more.

"At zero six hundred hours this morning, two Russian bomber aircrafts capable of carrying nuclear weapons landed at Maiquetía airport," Flynn said. "The two bombers were accompanied by a heavy-lift cargo plane and a passenger plane."

"As I'm sure you can appreciate, Tom, Russia's involvement in Venezuela muddies the water quite a bit for us," the president said. "We have to tread very, very carefully."

"I wasn't aware the Russians had a play in Venezuela," Hauer admitted.

"The countries were always close," Triggs explained. "But since Capriles's visit to Moscow last October, the Russians have become a key lender of last resort for them. As their economy implodes, the Venezuelans need the Russians to invest heavily in their oil industry and to support their military."

Two corrupt governments squandering public funds and suppressing the liberty and freedom of their people by joining forces together. That's just great.

"One thing is sure, though," President Reilly said. "If the Venezuelan government is directly responsible for the deaths of our athletes, we won't let them get away with it. We just have to be smart about how we play it."

"I can have military options available to you before noon, Mr. President," Flynn said.

"I'm not sure that's the best course of action," Triggs said. "Until we have definite proof of their involvement, we won't get the international community's support."

President Reilly mulled that over for a moment, then said, "Let me be clear about this, folks. I want you to find a way to get us international support, but I don't want an international incident in Venezuela that's going to make us look like we're the aggressors. I want no military personnel within Venezuela's borders. Is that understood?"

"Yes, Mr. President," everyone said almost in unison.

"If this thumb drive delivers us the proof we need, maybe this is the key to getting rid of Leopoldo Capriles once and for all. Why don't you take point on this, Tom?"

The reason President Reilly wanted him to take the lead wasn't lost on Hauer. He was the junior guy. If for some reason things didn't work out, Hauer was expendable.

"Of course, Mr. President," Hauer said, placing his political neck on the chopping block.

Hauer was under no illusion: to keep his head, he'd have to rely on Pierce Hunt.

CHAPTER THIRTY-NINE

MacDill Air Force Base
Tampa, Florida

Hunt rolled off the hood of the Mercedes G-Class he had used as a bed for the last six hours and sleepwalked to his assigned seat along the side of the cargo bay of the C-17 Globemaster. They had just been told to strap in for landing at MacDill.

Before settling for the hood of the vehicle as a makeshift bed, Hunt had tried to open its doors so he could lie down on the back seat, but the doors were locked. Filling the plane's cargo bay behind the G-Class were two armored black S-Class Mercedes and a multitude of large pallets of supplies. In addition to him and Carter, the air force C-17 was transporting another team of three operators, and they had appropriated the only hammocks available. Like Hunt and Carter, they kept to themselves and slept for most of the flight.

The plane touched down smoothly and taxied to its assigned spot. The three operators who had spent the night in the hammocks climbed into the vehicles in the cargo hold. Before closing the door, the operator driving the G-Class waved at Hunt, a big smile on his face.

"You guys slept well?" he asked.

Hunt gave him the finger, and the man laughed. A moment later, the tail end of the C-17 lowered, letting sunshine into the darkened cargo area of the plane. Three forklifts worked in unison, unloading the supply pallets in less than ten minutes. The fresh air was a welcome but short relief—the three operators all started their vehicles, then drove down the ramp. A minute later, they were gone too.

"What now?" Carter asked him.

Hunt used the fabric ties attached to the frame of the plane to pull himself upright from the seat. Back in Kandahar, a corpsman had cleaned and disinfected his leg wound before patching it up, but it still stung where the bullet had caressed his skin.

"Not sure," Hunt admitted. "Let's get out of this thing before it leaves again."

They picked up their duffel bags and the rest of their gear and made their way down the ramp. The late-afternoon sun felt good on his face, and Hunt took a deep breath to clear his mind. He had managed four solid hours of sleep on the flight. It was the best he was going to get. With a cold shower and a gallon of coffee, he was confident he could function toward whatever the day—or Tom Hauer—would bring.

"Mr. Hunt and Mr. Carter?" a voice called from Hunt's right.

A man dressed in blue jeans, white sneakers, and a black polo shirt was leaning against a dark-colored Ford Explorer. A gold DEA badge was clipped to his belt next to a pancake-style holster, which held his DEA-issued Glock 22.

"That's us," Hunt replied, making his way to the man.

"I'm Special Agent Kleiner," he said, introducing himself. "Tom Hauer sent me to greet you."

Hunt and Carter shook Kleiner's hand. "I was under the impression he'd be here."

"Something came up, I'm afraid," Kleiner replied. "Don't ask me what it is, 'cause I don't know. My job is to bring you guys to the comms room and keep my mouth shut."

Hunt and Carter stowed their gear in the back of the SUV and climbed aboard.

"I didn't know the DEA had an office at MacDill," Carter said.

"And I thought you two were fired," Kleiner countered, but he was smiling. He must have seen the surprised look on Hunt's face because he added, "Rumors about what happened in San Miguel de Allende are still flying around the office."

"That file is supposed to be sealed," grunted Hunt. "Part of the deal."

Kleiner chuckled. "Ah, c'mon, you know how it is. Guys like to talk shit. Especially when one of us gets to kick the ass of a major drug cartel."

Hunt understood. He'd been there too. The DEA, like all federal agencies, could become one big rumor mill as every special agent tried to figure out how the ass-kicking had actually gone down. Someone always knew someone who had talked to someone who'd been there. But instead of feeling proud, Hunt felt sad. His heart broke every time he thought about his brief conversation with Leila and how she'd assumed he wouldn't take her side. Didn't she know yet that she was the reason he did what he did? He hoped that one day she'd see him for the hardworking and dedicated man he was. Not just as some kind of gun-toting former federal agent looking for his adrenaline rush.

Kleiner made a left toward the building housing the 290th Joint Communications Support Squadron. Hunt and Carter climbed out of the Explorer and grabbed their gear from the back. Kleiner arranged for them to sign in, then waited with them while a security forces senior airman used his magnetic card to unlock the elevator.

"This is as far as I go," Kleiner said. "I'll be here when you're done."

Hunt and Carter rode the elevator down to the second basement, where they were greeted by an air force captain.

"Good morning, gentlemen. I'm with the 290th."

"Nice to meet you," Hunt said, accepting the man's hand.

"While you were on your way, I received instructions to provide you with a secure link to the White House. I'll escort you to one of our bubble rooms."

They followed the captain to a door a few steps away. He entered an eight-digit code into a wall-mounted touch pad located next to the door. A fingerprint reader lowered, and Hunt watched him press his index finger onto the glass. An orange light pulsed around his finger, and then a second later, the orange light turned blue, and a faint pneumatic hiss came from the door. The captain pushed the door open. Inside the comms room, air force personnel were seated behind a bank of computers and other electronic instruments. Each person on duty appeared to be totally immersed in their work, making sporadic entries on their keyboards or talking into headsets. The air force captain handed Hunt a device similar to an iPad and led him across the floor to another room.

"This is one of our bubbles. It's totally soundproof, and the walls are designed to block electronic signals. Whatever you say or hear can't be recorded."

"Thank you," Hunt said.

The captain left the room and closed the door behind him with a heavy thunk, sealing them in. Hunt took a seat at the table, and Carter did the same.

"What are we supposed to do?" Carter asked.

Hunt examined the device the captain had given him. There was no button to push and no switch to turn the power on. Hunt shrugged and placed the device on the table. He closed his eyes and stretched his arms in front of him.

"You okay, Pierce?"

"I can't stop thinking about Leila, brother. I miss her like crazy."

Carter gave him an understanding look. "I haven't spoken to Emma since we left Jalalabad to talk to Azfaar."

"Are you gonna tell her what happened?"

"Are you nuts?" Carter replied. "You think she'd let me go out with you again if she knew we were shot down?"

Carter had a point. Hunt would have to think long and hard about what he would and wouldn't share with Leila. And what about Anna? What should he tell her?

Hey, Anna! While I was in Afghanistan, the helicopter I was in was shot down. The crash killed the pilot instantly, and the crew chief caught a round at the back of the head while we were trying to exfil.

Hunt didn't think that would work very well. Anna was trying to extricate herself and Sophia from a life of violence. Would it really be in her and Sophia's best interest to move in with him? His homelife wasn't stable. Not nearly enough. Uncomfortable? Certainly not as grand as what they were accustomed to. Unpredictable? Most definitely. Yet Anna had made it clear she wanted to be with him. What was he supposed to do? Feeling a headache coming, Hunt massaged his temples with his fingers.

Suddenly, Tom Hauer's face appeared in high definition on the device.

"You're all set, sir," someone said next to Hauer.

The administrator of the DEA thanked him, and Hunt knew Hauer was waiting for whoever had been with him to leave before starting the conversation.

"Nice to see you two," Hauer said once he was alone. "And thanks for taking my call. Sorry I couldn't meet you at MacDill."

"No worries, sir," Hunt replied. "How's Anna?"

"I have agents on their way to her now. She'll be brought in and questioned, Pierce. Just as she requested."

"What about Sophia?"

"I see you haven't spoken to Jasmine."

"No, I haven't," Hunt snapped back. "And it's not because I didn't want to."

"I know that," Hauer said. "Sophia will be staying with Jasmine and Chris."

Hunt had to give it to Anna for having the courage to solicit Jasmine's help. His ex-wife wasn't Anna's biggest fan. But the fact that Jasmine had agreed to care for Sophia proved Hunt's long-held opinion that he had never deserved a woman like Jasmine DeGray. Leila might have picked the short straw when it came to having him as a father, but she'd definitely won the jackpot with Jasmine as her mom.

"She'll need protection," Hunt said.

"Already done. Sophia will be protected round the clock. And so will Anna, of course. If all goes well, Anna will be on her way to Weston in a little less than a couple of hours."

"What do you mean 'if all goes well'?"

"I promise I'll answer your question, but please allow me to put everything into context."

Hunt sighed but nodded. He was dying to hear the whole picture anyway.

"Late last night, Anna came in contact with Jorge Ramirez."

Hunt and Carter looked at each other.

"Yeah, I know. I read your after-action report," Hauer continued. "It's the same guy your asset Azfaar mentioned."

"What did he say to Anna?"

"He told her the Spider was moving production of the amphetamine pills back to Venezuela so that they could be tested before going to market."

"Please tell me you have a lead on this," Hunt said.

"Maybe," Hauer said, scratching his head. "I don't want to get too deep into the details of the operation, but for the last four years the DEA had an asset within General Peraza's close circle. Our asset, along with two DEA special agents, was killed trying to exfil after being ambushed by Peraza's men. And by Peraza's men, I mean the Venezuelan armed forces."

That was a bombshell. And a disaster. Hunt understood better than most the sacrifices needed to stay undercover for such a long period of time.

"Please tell me there's a SEAL team on its way to kill the motherfuckers," Carter said.

"I wish," Hauer replied. "Not sure how well versed you are in today's international headlines, but the Russians just flew two aircrafts capable of carrying nuclear weapons to Maiquetía airport. President Reilly was very clear about what we can and can't do about this situation."

"For God's sake, sir, we know—" Hunt started, but Hauer cut him off.

"The president understands the situation, but we can't risk an open conflict with the Russians. Before he orders the military to act against Venezuela, he wants the support of the international community. He believes that if we can get that support, the Russians will back off."

"I understand the Russian presence complicates things, sir," Hunt said, his voice sounding more composed than he felt. "But we can't let Peraza get away with this simply because the Russians are playing hardball."

"Oh, but we're not," Hauer replied. "Before he passed, our asset hid a thumb drive in the Venezuelan jungle. We believe it contains proof of Peraza's misdeeds."

Hunt smiled. "And since you can't send regular forces to Venezuela, you thought about us."

"I won't lie to you, gents," Hauer said, looking straight at the camera. "It won't be an easy one. We'll prepare you the best way we can by arranging for backstops and providing transportation to South America, but once you're there, you're on your own. Well, almost."

Hunt frowned. "Almost?"

"In Colombia, you'll link with two CIA officers who will help you cross into Venezuela."

The CIA? "Does the name Queen Bee ring a bell?" Hunt asked.

"Queen who?"

Hunt conveyed to Hauer what Ms. Red had told him in Paraguay. "So I'm wondering if one of these two officers is Queen Bee," Hunt concluded.

"I have no idea," Hauer responded. "What I can tell you is that these two CIA officers report directly to Dorothy Triggs."

"Isn't Triggs the head of the Directorate of Operations?" Carter asked.

"Yep, that's her," Hunt said.

"What do you guys think? You're willing to give it a shot?" Hauer asked.

Hunt looked at Carter. Carter didn't need to say anything for Hunt to know what was in his friend's head. Carter was a warrior too. He'd go where he was needed for the greater good of his country.

"When do we leave?" Hunt asked.

"Depends on you," Hauer replied. "The sooner the better, but I thought you'd want to stop by Miami to see your daughter, Pierce. And Anna, too, maybe? A couple hours won't change the mission profile.

"And same goes with you, Simon," Hauer continued. "I'm sure Emma wouldn't mind if you were to stop by. Special Agent Kleiner just confirmed there's a plane ready to take you to Miami Executive Airport if you wish."

Hunt very much appreciated Hauer's offer. Usually, these short layovers with loved ones were the hardest, especially when you hadn't seen them for months. They often led to heartbreaks, frustrations, and additional stress for everyone involved. But in this particular situation, Hunt couldn't afford not to go. There were a lot of issues that needed to be ironed out. Chief among them was the feud between Leila and Anna.

"What do you say?" Hunt asked Carter.

"Just for a few hours? I don't know, brother," Carter replied. "I have a feeling that if Emma ever learned I had the opportunity to see her and didn't, she'll cut my balls off."

"All right, sir. We'll stop by Miami. Thanks for doing this," Hunt said.

"Absolutely," Hauer said, smiling. "I'll let the pilots know. While you two are in Miami, I'll have a mission brief prepared for you." His face disappeared from the device.

"Why do I think this trip to Miami will give us more grief than we've bargained for?" Carter asked, getting up from his chair.

Hunt didn't even bother to reply to his friend. Except for a few tears from Leila, and maybe a slap in the face from Anna, what could go wrong?

CHAPTER FORTY

Coral Gables, Florida

Anna Garcia's estate was an eight-thousand-square-foot Spanish-style waterfront mansion located in Coral Gables. Ojeda knew it had previously belonged to her brother, Tony, but when he'd passed, she had inherited it. Security was tight within the property lines, but he had no issues installing his two sticky cameras on nearby utility poles to keep watch on the main gate of the estate, the only street access to the long driveway leading to the house.

Using a new alias, Ojeda had gotten a Toyota Sequoia SUV from the rental company and booked himself into a four-star hotel a few blocks away from the Garcia residence. A couple of hours ago, the niece, Sophia, had returned home, accompanied by her driver and at least two bodyguards in an armored Suburban. The cameras' angles weren't perfect, but the live feed appeared clear of static on his laptop.

Ojeda wasn't hungry, but he had to eat. He ordered a veggie omelet and coffee from the room-service menu. Just when he was about to hang up, he decided to splurge and added a side of hash browns. The concierge who took his order let him know it would be ready in forty-five minutes.

Forty-five minutes for an omelet? Ojeda never understood why room service always took so long. It didn't matter where he was in the world or what the star rating of the hotel was: room service was always slow and usually not that tasty either. Good thing he wasn't hungry.

Fifteen minutes later, he was surprised by a gentle knock at his door.

"Room service," a voice called from the hallway.

Ojeda was instantly suspicious. His left hand shot out and wrapped around the cool plastic grip of his Glock 19. He closed his laptop with the other. Ten seconds later, there was another knock.

"Room service," the voice called again. He looked through the peephole and saw a woman in a hotel uniform standing next to a room-service table.

Ojeda unlocked the bolt and flipped the latch, hiding his Glock behind his back as he opened the door to greet the hotel employee.

"I'll take it from here," Ojeda said, sliding his Glock into the back of his waistband.

She handed him the check, and he signed it.

Ojeda watched her until she disappeared from sight. Once she was gone, he lifted the lid covering the plate and felt suddenly hungry at the sight of the nicely rolled veggie omelet. The hash browns, though, were another story. They didn't look or smell appetizing.

He carried the omelet to the small work desk on which he had left his laptop. He flipped the device open and waited for the laptop to pick up the wireless cameras' signals. While the laptop loaded the data, he started on the omelet, which was bursting with cheese, mushrooms, onions, and green peppers. Ojeda chewed thoughtfully, wondering what his dad was doing at the moment and how pissed he must have been receiving the note letting him know that his only child wouldn't be joining him for his seventieth birthday.

Movements on his screen made Ojeda stop midbite. Two sedans had stopped in front of Anna Garcia's gate. A man dressed in a dark suit climbed out of the lead vehicle and pressed a button on the intercom. Ojeda had no sound, so he couldn't hear what the man said, but the gate opened, and the man returned to his car. Ojeda wasn't able to read the license plate off the lead car because the second vehicle had stopped too close to its rear bumper, but he had no difficulty scribbling down the plate of the second car.

The vehicles headed up the driveway toward Anna Garcia's house. Ojeda pulled his cell phone from his pocket and sent a quick text to a contact at the consulate. Four minutes later he got his reply. It confirmed his suspicions.

Now, even if he could have chartered a plane back to Venezuela—not that he could afford to anyway—his last hope of making it back before his dad's bedtime had just evaporated. Ojeda couldn't unsee what he had seen, and he was duty bound to inform Ramirez. Not doing so could cost him a lot more than a lost birthday party. With some regret, he called Ramirez.

As usual, his boss picked up right away.

"Two unmarked police cars just entered the premises of Garcia's house," Ojeda said, playing with the omelet with his fork.

"They just drove in, or they broke in?" Ramirez asked.

"Looked to me like they were invited in. It wasn't obvious that the cars were unmarked police vehicles. I think they were trying to keep it low key."

"The bitch," Ramirez spat. "The fucking traitorous bitch!"

"What do you want me to do?"

"For this I'll have to ask the Spider directly. This will affect his schedule," Ramirez replied, his voice strained. "For now, stay put. I'll call you back with further instructions."

Ojeda placed his cell phone next to his laptop. He walked to the double bed, where he had placed his suitcase. He unzipped it and flipped the top open. Ojeda took off his black sweater and, over his white T-shirt, put on the soft body armor he kept in the suitcase. He covered the bulletproof vest with his sweater, then took two fragmentation grenades from the suitcase and placed them in front of him on the bed. Next came the modified drone. He attached the two grenades to the specially built clips under the belly of the drone but left the safety pins attached. He switched on the drone and the remote control and tested their batteries. Satisfied that all was in working order, he replaced the drone in the suitcase. His phone vibrated on the desk.

"Yes?"

"He wants you to take her out."

"What about the child?"

"Her, too, and anyone else you want. I don't care."

"Very well," Ojeda replied, his mind already prepping for what was to come.

"For your exfil, we'll have a plane ready for you at the Miami Executive Airport."

Ojeda smiled. He'd be traveling aboard a private jet after all.

CHAPTER FORTY-ONE

Coral Gables, Florida

Anna Garcia opened the door and let the four DEA agents in.

"Thank you for coming, gentlemen."

"I'm Special Agent Irvine Kahn," one of them said, extending his hand. "Here are my colleagues, Special Agents Salas, Patterson, and McCarthy."

Anna shook their hands and introduced them to Sophia, who was standing next to her.

"Why don't you go into the living room, Sophia?" Anna asked her niece. "I'll join you in a bit."

Sophia nodded and waved goodbye to the four agents.

"I appreciate you being here more than you know," Anna said, once Sophia was out of earshot.

"It's an unusual request, that's for damn sure," Kahn said. "Not that I'm complaining, but we were working on major files when we were instructed to drop everything and take care of this."

"I'm sure you were," Anna said. "But this is bigger than all of us, I assure you."

"Are you ready to go? Do you need help packing your bags?"

"I'm all set," Anna said, pointing to the small carry-on luggage at her side.

"You travel light," Kahn said.

"I'm not as high maintenance as I look," Anna said with a smile.

"I knew that," Kahn replied. "Pierce Hunt doesn't do high maintenance." At her surprised look, he added, "The DEA office in Weston isn't that big, Miss Garcia. Everyone knows who Hunt is."

This wasn't a surprise to Anna. Hunt had a reputation. Some loved him; others hated him. Most law enforcement officers thought he was a hero for taking a stand against that anticop reporter Luke Moore the year before. Moore's recklessness had spoiled a raid against a Black Tosca–run safe house in Chicago and cost a dozen enslaved women, and a DEA agent, their lives. Hunt's response, though, had almost cost him his career.

"So what do you know about the guy who was waiting for me outside the nightclub?" Anna asked.

"We know that his real name isn't Ernesto Sadel," replied Special Agent McCarthy, the only female of the four. "That being said, there's an Ernesto Sadel who matches the physical description of the man your contact encountered last night who indeed works out of the Venezuelan Consulate General in New Orleans. That tells us that the Venezuelan government is involved in covering for this guy."

"Okay, so who is he?"

"We think he might be Luis Ojeda, but we're not sure yet," Kahn answered. "We've forwarded his picture to our Intelligence Division. We should get a confirmation on his identity by the end of the day."

"That's fine, but that doesn't tell me much," Anna said. "What else do you know about him?"

"If he is in fact Luis Ojeda, we know he was once a Venezuelan armed forces officer with the Ninety-Ninth Army Special Forces Brigade. Now he works as an enforcer for the Spider," Kahn replied.

"And by that you mean he kills people for a living. He's an assassin." That wasn't a question. Anna was simply stating the obvious.

"Something like that, yes. But he won't be a problem for much longer," Kahn said, his bright blue eyes exuding confidence. He glanced at his watch. "We found his rental car in a hotel parking lot not far from here. Our agents are closing in on his room as we speak. He should be in custody within the next ten minutes."

That was great news and one less thing she needed to worry about. Her thoughts moved to Sophia. She was going to spend the next little while with Leila and the Moon family. That was a much better option than the alternative: turning her over to the Florida Department of Children and Families.

Tom Hauer was confident they would be able to find a good family for Sophia to live with until things cleared up. But Anna had argued that taking in Sophia would expose any family to a higher security risk. Hauer had countered by explaining that Sophia would undergo a name change, attend a new school, and wouldn't be allowed to contact her former friends—all of which would alleviate the risk. In Anna's opinion, after less than a year since her kidnapping, Sophia needed stability in her life and was still too fragile to go through such a process.

Jasmine DeGray and Chris Moon had been a godsend. Anna had felt weird asking a favor from Hunt's ex-wife—being the reason why their marriage hadn't worked out made Anna feel pretty shitty about herself, even though Hunt had insisted it was entirely his fault. One way or the other, Anna wouldn't have blamed Jasmine DeGray for despising her. But as awkward as the conversation had been, the woman had been nothing but kind to her. After a short consultation with her husband, Jasmine had readily agreed to take Sophia in. The only request she'd made was that Anna didn't send her security detail with Sophia. They didn't want to deal with anyone associated with the Garcia crime syndicate. To reassure Anna, Moon had promised he'd hire the best security contractors money could buy. Hauer had promised to provide additional teams for Sophia's protection.

"Anna?" Sophia shouted from the living room. "Chris is here. And Leila too!"

Anna made her way to the large living room patio doors and joined Sophia, who was waiting for her friend on the terrace. Mauricio Tasis and two of her men helped Moon tie his boat to the dock. Leila was already running toward Sophia. The bond between the two teenagers was deep and strong and had an intimacy reminiscent of family. Anna was glad Sophia had developed such a friendship. She wished she had a good friend like that, but her lifestyle had never allowed for one.

From the dock, Moon glanced in her direction. She waved at him. He didn't wave back. Moon was a great stepdad to Leila, and it was easy to see he loved her as he would his own daughter, but Anna had the feeling he didn't think much of her or her life choices.

Special Agent Kahn, who had followed her outside, said, "Chris Moon, star quarterback of the Miami Dolphins, in the flesh. I'll be damned."

"You know he's the husband of Pierce's ex-wife, right?"

"Of course, but I never thought I'd see him. The guy's a legend. Best quarterback the Dolphins ever had. Better than Marino."

"Well, he's here now. You'll have the chance to tell him how you feel."

Moon jogged toward the terrace, trying to catch up to Leila.

The weather outside was nice, and the waters were calm. Anna presumed Moon had decided to take the boat instead of driving to cheer Leila up. Anna couldn't even begin to imagine how she felt after losing Jack.

But that's not entirely true, is it? A picture of Leila holding the butcher knife flashed in her mind. Knowing that her family's resources had played a role in his death sickened her. That was one more reason why she needed to push through with her plan. Collaborating with the DEA ensured she and Sophia would receive the necessary protection against the Spider—which was really the most important thing. And it would give her a chance to redeem herself. It was the right thing to do.

Deep down, even if he would have never admitted it, she knew her dad would be proud of her. He hadn't had the same qualms about the family's criminal empire that she had, but he'd been a firm believer in sticking to one's convictions.

A movement in her field of vision caught her attention, but she lost it almost immediately. Anna remained fixed in place, only her eyes darting left and right, trying to figure out what she had seen. Her ears, not her eyes, found it first, through a gentle buzzing sound to her right. But when she scanned the sky, she saw nothing.

"What are you looking at?" Kahn asked.

"I thought . . . never mind." Anna shook her head as Moon made his way to the terrace.

Chris Moon was an imposing man. Tall and broad shouldered and tipping the scale at close to 210 pounds, he had sharp eyes that saw more than he let on. He was more than a pretty face gifted with a powerful and precise right arm.

"Thanks for coming, Chris," Anna said, offering her hand.

Moon shook his head. "I'm doing this for Sophia. She doesn't deserve any of this. You and Hunt make quite a pair. Trouble abounds around you two."

Anna wasn't surprised that he considered her the enemy. In a sense, she was. But it still stung coming from him.

Kahn introduced himself, though he seemed too shy to say anything more to Moon. Moon shook his hand. "Tom Hauer has already sent a two-man team to my residence. They're waiting for us to get back."

Tasis, who had just finished loading Sophia's suitcase into Moon's boat, joined them on the terrace.

"Sophia's all set," he said.

"Thanks, Mauricio," Anna said. "I'll say my goodbyes to Sophia—then I'll be leaving too."

Anna left the three men on the terrace and crossed the manicured lawn. Sophia and Leila were standing next to each other, playing with their phones. Sophia didn't notice her until she placed her hands on her shoulders.

"Hey," Anna said. "You okay?"

Sophia turned to face her. She was putting on a brave face, but her eyes were moist and red.

"I'm gonna miss you," Sophia said, sliding her arms around Anna's neck. "How long will I stay at Leila's?"

Anna wanted to reply, but the words caught in her throat. She wanted to comfort Sophia, to tell her how much she loved her, how much Sophia meant to her, but she felt so much guilt about the whole situation that only tears came out. She held on tight to her niece.

"You deserve so much better, my angel," Anna said. "So much better."

"But I love you," Sophia pleaded. "Why can't I stay with you? What have I done to you that you don't want me around anymore? Is it because I wanted to leave? Because I know you had nothing to do with Jack's death. I know it now. I'm sorry."

Sophia's words bit deep into Anna's heart. "It's not like that, Sophia. It's just—"

Sophia pulled back until Anna was forced to release the hug. "Whatever. I'll see you when I see you." Sophia turned on her heels and walked away with Leila, who waved a sheepish goodbye.

Anna stood there on the verge of tears, feeling all alone in the world. A minute later, Moon started the engines, and the Blackwater 43 SportFish roared to life. Tasis threw the line to Leila, and they were off. Anna stood motionless till the last echo of the motors faded away.

"I can't believe she's gone," Tasis said. "I can't shake the feeling that I've failed you."

"No, my loyal friend," she replied. "You never once failed me. We all make our choices in this life."

Everything her dad and brother had worked so hard for was crumbling down. As if she needed to remind herself, she repeated the words like a mantra:

And that's a good thing.

CHAPTER FORTY-TWO

Coral Gables, Florida

Luis Ojeda cursed out loud. He would kill with his bare hands the geek who had built the drone back in New Orleans. Diplomat or not, Ojeda would have the man's head. He had promised Ojeda there would be no interference between the drone and the controller as long as the distance remained within one and a half miles.

Mierda!

Ojeda cursed again as the large center-console boat left the dock behind Anna Garcia's house. If the drone had worked as advertised, Ojeda would have dropped the two grenades the drone carried right on the terrace. The explosion would have killed Anna Garcia, and Ojeda would have been on his way to the Miami Executive Airport and the jet Ramirez had promised. But seconds before he could push the release button on the remote control, radio interference messed with the controls. The drone, losing its link, automatically headed back to where it had started its flight.

Ojeda had just regained full control of the drone when a window on his laptop popped up. He glanced at the screen and smiled. The cops had found the decoy hotel he had checked into. A wireless sticky camera he had installed in the hallway leading to his room showed the officers' progress. By the way they moved, Ojeda could tell they weren't regular patrolmen in SWAT uniforms. DEA? FBI? It made no difference who they were or how well trained they were; nothing could prepare them for what would happen next.

Ojeda picked up his cell phone, waited for the facial recognition software to unlock the screen, and pressed the number two key for ten seconds. He strained to hear what he knew was coming. There it was—a muffled explosion off in the distance. When he looked at his laptop again, the image of the officers had been replaced by a blank screen. There was no way to know if the officers were dead or simply injured, but he was sure of one thing: he had slowed his pursuers down. And now, with the drone's batteries almost exhausted, it was time to move to plan B.

Ojeda stepped onto the large balcony and squinted, trying to locate the drone. It appeared moments later, and he expertly landed it on the balcony. He carefully removed the two grenades one by one, making sure to keep the charging handle pressed against the body of the gre-nade, and slid the safety pin back into place. He then replaced the drone and the remote control in his suitcase.

His suitcase zipped up, Ojeda dialed Alejandro Mayo's number.

"I was told you might call. Good news, then, yes?"

"Not what we were hoping for, but your boss—"

"The bitch ain't my boss!" Alejandro growled.

Ojeda held back a chuckle. That was exactly the reaction he'd been hoping for.

"My apologies. You're right, of course. Are you and your brother ready? Are you where you were told to be?"

"Yes, and we brought a few friends with us. By the way, did you have anything to do with that big boom we heard?"

Ojeda ignored the question, but Alejandro had just confirmed that he was indeed where he was supposed to be. The plan had called for a three-man assault on Anna Garcia's SUV—Ojeda and the Mayo brothers—but the arrival of the four DEA agents meant the extra men would be welcome.

"How many vehicles do you have?" Ojeda asked.

"We have three vehicles, two men per vehicle."

Perfect. Ojeda gave them the address of his hotel and asked them to be at the lobby door in exactly four minutes.

Ojeda felt energized. He had a woman to kill.

CHAPTER FORTY-THREE

Coral Gables, Florida

Anna was about to close the patio door when she heard the explosion. Even though she wasn't in immediate danger, she freaked out, fearing it was Chris Moon's boat that had just blown up. Before she could move, though, Special Agent Kahn grabbed her and took her inside the residence.

"What are you doing?" she yelled at him. "Let me go!"

"It's not safe out there," Kahn replied. "Until we know where the explosion came from, you're staying inside."

"My niece—"

"Don't worry—your niece is fine. It didn't come from the boat."

"How can you be so sure?"

Kahn let her go. She was about to repeat the question, but he held the palm of his hand up, stopping her. He was listening to something someone was saying in his earpiece.

"Oh my God," Kahn whispered.

For a second, Kahn looked as if he was about to vomit. Then he regained control and took charge of the situation.

"We need to take you to a secure location, Miss Garcia," he said. "Now."

"Something happened. It's the explosion, isn't it?"

Kahn nodded but didn't elaborate. He spent the next thirty seconds giving instructions to the three other agents. The two drivers got in their respective vehicles, and then Special Agent McCarthy led the way out of the main entrance, her pistol at the low ready, followed closely by Anna. Special Agent Kahn closed the rank, and he, too, had his pistol out.

In front of Anna, McCarthy opened the rear passenger door of one of the Ford sedans.

"Get in!" Kahn said.

Mauricio Tasis ran from the side of the house. "What's going on? Where are you taking her?" Tasis asked, his hand behind his back, where Anna knew he kept a small pistol.

"Get out of here!" Kahn screamed, aiming his service pistol at Tasis.

Anna stopped, one leg in the car. "Lower your goddamn weapon," she said, pressing down on Kahn's forearm.

Kahn took a sidestep, evading her reach. "I said get out of the way, or I'll take you down."

He was yelling now, spitting saliva, and clearly under immense stress. Tasis's eyes darted from Kahn to Anna, then back to Kahn. Anna had only to nod and Tasis would spring into action, taking his chances against the DEA agents. The situation was spiraling out of control.

"Stand down, Mauricio. Stand down," Anna said. "Please!"

Tasis took one last venomous look at Kahn, then slowly stepped back from the car, his hands at his side.

"Where are you taking her?" Tasis asked again.

"They're taking me to a secure location. I'll get in touch with you by the end of the day," Anna said. "I promise. Please open the gate, Mauricio."

That wasn't what Tasis wanted to hear, but, loyal till the end, he acquiesced to Anna's demand. Gently, so he wouldn't get shot by Kahn, who still had his pistol trained on him, Tasis reached in his jeans pocket and retrieved a remote gate opener. Anna felt McCarthy's hand on her back, guiding her inside the sedan. Kahn took the front passenger seat while McCarthy ran to the second vehicle.

"Let's go," Kahn said to the driver. "Let's get out of here."

CHAPTER FORTY-FOUR

Coral Gables, Florida

Hunt was getting used to traveling aboard private jets. Chris Moon had chartered one for the rescue mission in San Miguel de Allende, the DOJ had provided one from Kandahar Airfield to Ramstein in Germany before they caught the C-17 to MacDill, and now the deputy director of the Directorate of Operations, Dorothy Triggs, had given them access to a Cessna Citation X to travel to Miami. The flight took less than sixty minutes. Upon arrival, a GMC Yukon was waiting for them, compliments of Tom Hauer.

Special Agent Kleiner had traveled with them and had been on the phone nonstop during their flight, doing his best to get them the necessary gear for their mission in Venezuela. Prior to boarding the Citation X, Hunt had called Jasmine to reassure her he was fine and let her know that he was planning to see Leila. She'd mentioned that Leila and Moon were heading by boat to Anna's house to pick up Sophia. Since Hunt and Carter were on a tight schedule and Anna's house was closer to the airport, Hunt told Jasmine he'd stop by the Garcias' residence and catch Anna and Leila at the same time. Jasmine had assured him she'd contact Moon and let him know to wait for Hunt at Anna's house.

"Good news," Kleiner said from the driver's seat next to Hunt. "Your old boss Daniel McMaster has agreed to provide all the gear you'll need."

In the back seat, Carter was on the phone with his wife. "Does he know me and Simon are the recipients?" Hunt asked.

"Not sure. I didn't tell him, and he didn't ask any questions. I think Hauer briefed him."

"McMaster is one of the good guys," Hunt said.

His relationship with Daniel McMaster, the special agent in charge of the Miami Field Division, was somewhat complicated. McMaster had allowed Hunt's transfer to Miami after the incident in Chicago that had nearly cost him his career, and he had been supportive when Hunt started pursuing the Black Tosca to rescue his daughter and Sophia. But the Black Tosca's web had extended even into McMaster's own family— a discovery Hunt had kept secret from McMaster for many reasons.

"Emma happens to be on her way to see Jasmine," Carter said, ending his call. He reached for the cooler behind the second-row seat.

"That's perfect," Hunt replied. "We'll stop by Anna's first, and then we'll head over to Moon's house."

"Hauer wants you wheels up at nineteen hundred hours. By then, I'll have the brief ready, and we'll go through it together," Kleiner said.

"Are we flying the Cessna to South America?" Carter asked, handing a sandwich and a bottle of water to Hunt.

"We are. That's why they chose this plane. It has sufficient range to reach Colombia without the need to refuel."

The fact that the CIA had given them access to one of their jets meant that they were serious about this mission.

"How are you feeling, Pierce?" Carter asked between bites of a ham sandwich.

"I'm fine, brother. Just wish we had a bit more time with our families."

"True that."

Kleiner's phone rang, vibrating in the cup holder beside Hunt. Hunt watched Kleiner try to answer it by pushing the call button on the steering wheel, but the cell wasn't linked to the Yukon.

"Can you just pick it up for me, please?" Kleiner said, accelerating through a yellow light.

Hunt accepted the call. "This is Special Agent Kleiner's phone."

"Why are you answering Kleiner's phone, Pierce? Everything okay?" Hauer's voice sounded stressed.

"He's driving, sir. What's up?"

"Where are you exactly?"

Hunt craned his neck to look out the window, trying to catch the name of the street.

"We're at the corner of Old Cutler Road and . . . Pine Drive. Why?"

"Anna Garcia is being evacuated to one of our safe houses," Hauer said.

That grabbed Hunt's attention. "What happened?"

"The team tasked with the capture of Luis Ojeda, a man we believe has been hired to kill Anna, walked into a trap."

"Any casualties?" Hunt asked.

"We don't know yet. It just happened."

"Any leads on that asshole?"

"None, but we're working on it. His picture is going out to all law enforcement agencies within the next fifteen minutes. We'll catch him."

"What about Leila and Sophia?" Hunt asked, remembering that his daughter was supposed to pick up Sophia at Anna's house.

"The agent in charge of Anna's protective detail informed me that Leila and Sophia left on Chris Moon's boat a few minutes prior to the explosion."

Leila and Sophia are safe. At least there's that.

"What can we do to help, sir?" Hunt asked.

"Regular law enforcement will handle it here, Pierce," Hauer said. "There's not much you and Carter can contribute in your . . . uh, special capacity."

"I see."

"What I need you and Carter to do is to get your butts back onto the plane. The sooner we get the intel on that USB drive, the better. God forbid any officers died today, because the SecDef will try to use their deaths to force President Reilly into launching a missile strike against Venezuela."

"And what's wrong with the SecDef's plan? Missile strikes sound like a good plan to me," Hunt grunted.

"Goddamn it, Pierce—"

"I know," Hunt interrupted. "The Russians."

"Call me back once you're at the airport."

Hunt sighed deeply. There would be no time to see Leila after all. He ran a hand through his long hair. Maybe it was for the best. His daughter would probably have condemned him for his hair and unkempt beard anyway. Hunt smiled.

I can't help myself. Every time I think about her, I smile. No matter how screwed up or how dire the situation was, thinking about his daughter helped him cope.

She's my lifeline. And she probably doesn't even know it. There were so many things he wished he could tell her, but when it was time to say them, they always came out wrong.

Hunt replaced the phone in the cup holder and updated Carter and Kleiner. Carter was disappointed he wouldn't have the chance to see his wife, but he soldiered on.

"Emma is a tough woman," Carter said. "She'll get it."

Even though Hunt understood the overall situation, he wasn't happy with it.

Years ago, after a noteworthy and unsanctioned operation he had led in Iraq to save a man's life, Hunt had made a promise to himself that he'd never again use excessive violence to achieve an objective. He had broken that promise only once—with a guy named Pomar—in order to save Leila and Sophia. But for Luis Ojeda, he'd break his promise again in a heartbeat, and he'd do it with a big freaking smile on his face.

Hunt looked at his watch. At that time in the afternoon—rush hour was no joke in Miami—it would take them approximately forty minutes to get back to the airport. By then Leila would be back at Moon's house, and he would call her.

Kleiner was about to make a U-turn when two Ford sedans speeding in the opposite direction caught Hunt's eyes. The two-car convoy forced Kleiner to stop and to wait for the next break in traffic. Hunt couldn't be certain, but he thought he had recognized the man sitting in the front passenger seat of the lead vehicle.

Was that Irvine Kahn?

Hunt made the connection to the Miami field agent instantly: Anna was in one of the vehicles. *If they're following protocols, she's in the first car.* Not that it changed anything. He wasn't about to ask Kleiner to stop the motorcade so he could see Anna. He had his orders.

I'm so close. So close and yet so goddamn far.

The traffic light turned yellow, and Kleiner was about to accelerate through the intersection to initiate the U-turn when Hunt saw three black BMW X5s hasten to make the light.

"Careful!" Hunt shouted.

Somehow, Kleiner managed to stop the GMC Yukon mere inches from the first hard-charging BMW's driver's door. The three BMWs passed so close to the Yukon that it shook from side to side in the wind created by the SUVs. And for a fraction of a second, Hunt saw the driver's face.

Alejandro Mayo.

This was no coincidence. If Anna was in the DEA motorcade, Alejandro was after her. Alejandro had challenged Anna's leadership at every opportunity.

"Follow those three X5s," Hunt ordered Kleiner.

Kleiner didn't hesitate and made the U-turn the moment the light changed to red. By the time the Yukon made its turn, the BMWs were already two hundred meters away. Hunt once again grabbed Kleiner's phone and tried to dial Hauer's number.

"How do you unlock this phone?" Hunt asked.

"It's facial recognition only," Kleiner said, taking the phone away from Hunt and placing it in front of his face.

"It locks itself after ten seconds if you don't use it," Kleiner warned. "I don't want to put that phone in front of my face while I drive if I don't have to. Capisce?"

"What's going on, Pierce?" Carter asked from the back seat.

"I'm sure those two Ford sedans that passed were DEA cars, and I think Irvine Kahn was driving the lead vehicle," Hunt explained, while punching Hauer's numbers.

"They must be taking Anna to the safe house."

"My thoughts exactly, brother. Problem is, they're being followed by these three X5s, and I'm almost certain Alejandro Mayo was driving one of the vehicles."

"Remind me who that is?" Carter asked.

Hunt didn't have time to respond as Hauer answered. Hunt sketched out the situation. "Alejandro Mayo," he added for Carter and Kleiner's benefit, "is a top lieutenant in the Garcia crime syndicate. He and his brother, Santiago, strongly oppose Anna's leadership."

The Yukon swerved right at the last moment, almost rear-ending a car that wasn't moving fast enough for Kleiner's taste.

"Listen to me carefully, Pierce," Hauer said. "Internal struggles within the Garcia family are the least of our problems right now. Okay?"

"I'm listening," Hunt said, holding on for dear life as Kleiner navigated the heavy traffic at a high speed.

"Santiago Mayo is who the Carol City Chiefs coach told us he bought the amphetamines from, and we know the Mayos are working with Ramirez. We've been trying to locate Santiago for weeks, but the man is like a ghost. The point is, if they know Anna is turning herself in, that puts them in direct conflict. These guys aren't there to protect Anna—they want to kill her."

That made sense. Hunt considered the explosion earlier. Was it possible that Luis Ojeda was with them in one of the SUVs?

"There's a chance Ojeda is with them to supervise the operation, sir," Hunt said. "You need to advise Special Agent Kahn of the situation."

"Linda Ramer is on the phone with Special Agent Kahn," Hauer said. "I read her in regarding your team. Stand by a moment, Pierce. I think she wants to speak with you."

Hunt didn't know Ramer personally, but he had heard great things about the director of the DEA's Intelligence Division. She had a reputation as a straight shooter, though, so Hunt wondered how she'd react to Hunt and Carter working directly for Hauer.

"Can you take them out, Mr. Hunt?" Ramer asked, joining the conversation.

"Stand by," Hunt replied.

Hunt looked at Carter. His friend had been following the conversation as much as he could. Hunt took a moment to fill Carter and Kleiner in.

"I'm not sure if it's tactically possible," Carter said once Hunt was done. "I have my nine millimeter and two spare magazines but no body armor."

"Same here, Pierce. Sorry, but there's no way we can take out three vehicles with pistols only," Kleiner said.

As much as Hunt wanted to engage, it wasn't the right thing to do.

"Ma'am, I suggest you call the locals," Hunt said. "We're not equipped to engage three vehicles and an unknown number of bad guys in broad daylight. It's rush hour, and the odds of civilian casualties are too high. The protective detail should take evasive maneuvers until MDPD can intercept the BMWs. We'll do what we can from the rear."

Up ahead, Hunt could see that a red light had forced the two-car DEA motorcade to a stop. Heavy traffic prevented the sedans from continuing through the intersection, and stopped vehicles to their left and right impeded their exit. Unlike unmarked police vehicles, the DEA cars likely weren't equipped with emergency lights.

Damn it! They're boxed in. One hundred feet behind the two sedans, the three BMWs were niggling their way closer.

"Tell the locals to hurry up," Hunt said. "It's about to turn ugly."

Despite being outgunned and outnumbered, Hunt realized that if he wanted to save Anna, they had no choice but to engage with the three BMWs. It was going to be only a matter of seconds before Anna and her protective detail came under fire.

"Patch me through to Kahn, ma'am. Now!"

But it was too late. Someone from one of the BMWs opened up on the DEA motorcade while they were sitting ducks. Hunt watched helplessly as bullets tore through both vehicles.

Anna! No!

Hunt and Carter climbed out of the Yukon at the same time. Armed only with their pistols, they advanced to make contact.

CHAPTER FORTY-FIVE

Coral Gables, Florida

Anna first realized that something was wrong when Kahn started looking almost nonstop in the rearview mirror. As they sped through the next intersection, Anna started to turn around to see what he was looking at, but Kahn caught her first.

"Don't turn around!"

"Are we being followed?"

Before he could answer, his phone rang. Less than ten seconds into the conversation, his body became rigid. If she hadn't been sure something was wrong before, she was now.

"Shit!" Kahn exclaimed.

"Please tell me what's going on," Anna said.

"Can you see those three BMWs behind us?"

"I can look now? Because a minute ago you didn't want me to."

"Stop being a prick, and tell me if the three BMWs following us belong to you."

Anna unbuckled her seat belt and turned around. It was difficult to see far since the second DEA vehicle was right behind them, obstructing her view. Past it, she could see a black BMW, aggressively swerving in and out of traffic.

"It's hard to say. It could be one of ours."

"We think Alejandro Mayo could be in one of the BMWs."

Anna's heart skipped a beat. Fear took hold of her. *He knows. Ramirez knows I betrayed him. Oh my God! Sophia. Please, God. Not again.*

"Get us out of here," Kahn said to the driver.

Kahn bent forward and reached for a bag at his feet. Inside the bag was an MP5 submachine gun. Things were getting serious. Anna realized she was shaking. She wasn't afraid for her life per se; she was terrified that if something happened to her, Sophia would be left alone.

And who knows with these animals? Even if they kill me, who says they won't go after Sophia anyway?

The traffic light at the intersection ahead switched from yellow to red, and the driver had no choice but to stop. He tried to move forward and even used the horn, but there was no way through the heavy traffic. They were boxed in. Anna took another look. She could now see three BMWs approaching their position from different angles.

She turned back to the front, praying for the traffic light to turn green.

Why is it taking so long? C'mon!

When she looked back toward the BMWs, she saw that one of them had its front passenger window down with the ominous barrel of a gun pointed in her direction. Before she could warn anyone, bullets tore into the car, shattering glass and ripping into the back seat. Anna ducked instinctively. One round caught the driver in the back of the head while another passed through the driver's seat and slammed into his back. He slumped forward on the steering wheel, dead. With the transmission still in drive, the vehicle crept forward until it rear-ended the pickup truck in front of it.

"Stay low!" Kahn yelled, getting out of the car. Anna watched him squeeze round after round. Kahn must have hit his target because he suddenly switched his aim to the other side and continued to fire. At some point he got to a knee and, with shaky hands, changed the magazine of his MP5. But when he got up again, he was immediately struck twice. Kahn fell to the ground next to the sedan. Silently. As if someone had simply unplugged his power cord.

Shit! You gotta move, Anna. Gotta move.

She was a sitting duck in the vehicle, and she wasn't about to cower inside the car hoping the assassins wouldn't find her. She crawled over the console and into the front passenger seat, half expecting to get shot. She reached for Kahn's MP5, but the submachine gun sling was still looped around his neck.

Damn it! She retreated back out of sight just as a couple rounds hit the inside of the door.

The driver. His pistol!

There were pieces of brain and bones and blood everywhere. When her fingers finally wrapped around the pistol, the back door of the sedan swung open. Alejandro Mayo was staring at her, a rifle in his hands and a sick smile on his face.

"Adiós, puta!" he said. Then he fired.

CHAPTER FORTY-SIX

Coral Gables, Florida

Ojeda wasn't impressed with Alejandro Mayo. The man was a thug. And he was high. So was his brother, Santiago.

Just what I need.

The Mayo brothers weren't sophisticated like Tony or Vicente Garcia had been. Ojeda agreed with Ramirez that Anna didn't have what it took to lead the Garcia crime syndicate, but she wasn't stupid. At least he didn't think so. He respected what she was trying to accomplish. Her plan to go legit had been doomed from the start, but he gave her credit for trying.

"Don't follow too closely," he told Alejandro for the tenth time in as many minutes as he wove the BMW in and out of traffic. "If we don't take them now, we'll do it later. As long as we know where they're headed."

"The bitch dies today," Alejandro replied. "Did you hear me? She fucking dies today."

"You have to be smart about this, Alejandro," Ojeda replied, trying to appeal to the man's large ego. "You're the future head of the Garcia crime syndicate. You don't want to be caught."

"I'm not afraid of the cops," Alejandro snapped back. "You think I'm afraid of the cops? We own them."

"Did you hear what my brother said, dipshit?" Santiago asked from the front passenger seat. "We own them."

Ojeda took a deep breath. Then another. It helped with his nerves. Especially when he was dealing with idiots. It was true that Tony Garcia had had a few cops on the take, just as his father had. But contrary to Alejandro's beliefs, they couldn't get away with killing Anna Garcia on a busy street in broad daylight. Ojeda had a feeling it was the drugs talking, not their brains.

"What are you guys partying on?" he asked.

"Why? You want some?" Santiago said.

Ojeda had never consumed narcotics. He never would. He had seen firsthand the negative effects they had on people. "No, just curious."

"We're gonna take them at the next traffic light," Alejandro announced from behind the wheel.

"I'll let the others know," Santiago said, texting them from his cell phone.

Ojeda's original plan had been to ambush the motorcade at the exit of Anna Garcia's estate and then take one of the boats to exfil to a predetermined marina where another rental car was waiting for him. Unfortunately, Garcia's protective detail had acted quicker than he had anticipated following the explosion, and Ojeda was now playing catch-up.

He couldn't wait to get out of the United States.

Maybe Alejandro was right after all. Maybe they should take out the motorcade at the next traffic light. Ojeda would let the brothers prove their worth and do the heavy lifting. Once he was assured that Anna Garcia was dead, he'd find his own way out of the area and let Alejandro deal with the fallout. His job was to kill Anna Garcia, not babysit Alejandro and Santiago Mayo.

"They're stuck at the traffic light," Alejandro said. "We go now."

"Get a bit closer," Santiago said, bringing his window down.

As Alejandro positioned the SUV to allow his brother to fire at the Ford sedans, a second BMW did the same by pushing a smaller vehicle out of the way with its bumper while the third BMW stopped a few car lengths behind it. Santiago was the first to open fire, and the sound was deafening in the enclosed space of the BMW.

Ojeda climbed out of the SUV and took cover behind the engine block of the BMW. One of Alejandro's men was hit and fell against a car stopped at the traffic light. Within five seconds, the situation had turned into chaos. There were at least two DEA agents returning fire, but compared to Alejandro's men—who were shooting all over the place without a care in the world—the agents were aiming their shots, careful not to hit civilians. In the background a police siren wailed. All around them, people were running out of their cars, trying to find cover wherever they could.

Ojeda slowly rose from behind the engine block and aimed at a DEA agent who had exited the front passenger side of the lead vehicle. Despite everything else going on, the agent must have sensed Ojeda's movement because he swung his MP5 toward him and had time to fire three rounds before Ojeda could pull the trigger. All three rounds found the hood of the BMW. Ojeda shrank behind the front wheel as another round hit, this one shattering its windshield. Ojeda popped up for a second, took a mental picture of the scene, then crouched again before the DEA agent could get him in his sights.

The DEA agent was directing his fire at one of the other BMWs. The moment the agent's MP5 went quiet, Ojeda got up from behind the vehicle and steadied his rifle on the hood. The DEA agent was reloading. Ojeda believed he would come back up right about . . . now! Ojeda pulled the trigger twice. The DEA agent dropped like a half-empty flour sack. It didn't matter if the agent was wearing body armor. Unless he was wearing ceramic plates, the FN FAL 7.62 rounds would penetrate anything.

To his right, Santiago and Alejandro had joined forces with the remaining two men of their group, and they were all advancing toward the Ford sedans. There was no way Anna Garcia was going to survive the assault. She was as good as dead. The job hadn't been done as cleanly as Ojeda would have wished, but it was done nonetheless. Or about to be. It was time for him to leave.

Sensing movement behind him, Ojeda spun around, his rifle up. Two men were advancing together in a combat crouch. These weren't local cops. They were operators. Both were tall and longhaired with unkempt beards. The man on the left saw him and fired three shots just as Ojeda squeezed the trigger.

CHAPTER FORTY-SEVEN

Coral Gables, Florida

Simon Carter felt Hunt's reassuring presence to his left. They had only pistols, but Carter was confident they would win the fight. He and Hunt had trained together for years while they were both with the DEA rapid response team. They knew what the other would do in any given situation. They trusted each other, and it was with no fear that Carter advanced toward the two Ford sedans.

The ambush had started less than twenty seconds ago, and already the firefight had died down. That wasn't a good sign. In front of him, four men were carefully making their way toward the Ford sedans. To his left was another shooter hiding behind one of the BMWs. A few more steps and he'd have a clear shot at the man while passing between the vehicles.

There. The man had seen him, too, but Carter was quicker. He fired three times. A round buzzed overhead. Carter flinched. He had jerked the trigger on his first shot, so he wasn't sure if all three rounds had found their target. The shooter had disappeared out of sight. To his right, Hunt engaged the four men with rapid shots to their center mass. Two fell immediately, one ran for cover, and the other one turned around and raised his rifle.

Carter and Hunt fired together multiple times, all their bullets striking their target in the chest. Carter inserted a fresh magazine into his pistol while Hunt approached the man they had just shot.

"This one was Santiago Mayo," Hunt said.

Carter nodded. "I'll check on my first target," he said and veered left, his pistol extended in front of him. He didn't want to get flanked by a target who refused to die.

———

Ojeda winced in pain. His shoulder was killing him. Where had these two men come from? He cursed himself for his own stupidity. His head wasn't in the game. It hadn't been in the game for this entire trip. And now he'd been shot. Twice! Instead of bitching about the Mayo brothers' incompetence, he should have focused on the job at hand.

With blood pouring from his shoulder and upper chest, Ojeda knew people were looking at him, but he didn't care. He needed to get away from there and find a way to the airport. From there, he could go back to Venezuela and see his father. But his legs had become so heavy he wasn't sure he'd be able to. He gulped for air. He looked over his shoulder. The man who'd shot him was fifty feet behind him, shouting something. But it was as if Ojeda didn't understand English anymore.

Ojeda's legs gave way beneath him, and he fell forward. He tried to break his fall with his hands, but only his left arm responded. His head cracked on the pavement. It was such a surprise and such a sharp blow that he almost lost consciousness. It took all of Ojeda's energy to simply roll over to his right so that he could at least face his attacker.

Where's my rifle? For the life of him, he couldn't remember where he had left it.

"Where do you think you're going?" the bearded man asked.

That was a good question. He didn't remember that either. How strange was that?

Ojeda's eyes moved to the man's hands. *SIG Sauer P226.* Suddenly it came back to him. He knew where he was going. For some reason, he really wanted to let the man know he was on his way to his father's seventieth birthday. He was proud of that.

He opened his mouth to speak, but blood drowned his every word. He tried to swallow it, but there was too much.

Papa, I'm sorry, was his last thought.

CHAPTER FORTY-EIGHT

Coral Gables, Florida

Anna winced at the sound of the gunshot and closed her eyes. Blood showered her face, and she felt an immense weight on her chest. She opened her eyes. Alejandro was slumped on top of her.

Oh my God! I'm not dead.

She pushed him off, and he rolled into the space in between the back seat and the front seat of the sedan. Who had shot him? Kahn was dead. The driver was dead. Maybe it was another DEA agent from the second car. Using her sleeve, she wiped the blood off her face so she could see better.

"Anna? Anna?" a voice she knew well called out.

"Here! I'm right here!" she shouted, the relief almost choking her.

A moment later, Pierce Hunt appeared. Even with his long hair and ragged beard, she'd recognize him anywhere. She'd never been happier to see someone in her life. Her eyes teared up, and right there she swore that she'd one day marry that man.

"Are you okay?" Hunt asked, his voice quivering. "Can you walk?"

She nodded. "Yes."

"Good. That's good, Anna," Hunt said, but he wasn't looking at her. His eyes were scanning the surrounding area. "Get out of the car, please."

Anna did as he instructed.

"Okay. Follow me. Stay close. Grab my shirt, and don't let go."

There was nothing in the world that would make her let go of him. *Nothing.* His mere presence gave her strength. With Hunt by her side, she was unafraid. She was in complete control.

"Do you have another gun?" she asked, her head on a swivel.

"I wish," Hunt replied.

Police cruisers, sirens wailing, were coming from all directions now.

"Pierce!"

Anna was familiar with that voice too. *Simon Carter.*

"Right here, Simon!" Hunt shouted back.

Carter approached them, his pistol at the low ready. An agent she had never seen before was right behind Carter. He was sporting a black DEA jacket and carrying two more in his arms. He offered them to Hunt and Carter and introduced himself to Anna. "I'm Special Agent Kleiner."

"Thanks for saving my life," Anna said, shaking his hand.

"These two did the heavy lifting," Kleiner said. "I'm just here to cover their asses."

Carter holstered his pistol and looked at Anna. "You almost gave this guy a heart attack," he told her. "Glad you're okay. Because you're okay, right?"

"I'm fine," Anna replied, but her mind was racing. "We need to let Tom Hauer know about the attempt on my life. Sophia, and by extension Leila, Jasmine, and Chris, will need extra protection too."

"I just hung up with him," Kleiner said. "He knows. Nothing will happen to your kids. Now, let me go deal with the locals."

He approached two MDPD officers who were heading toward them. They had their pistols in their hands, but they were pointed to the ground.

"What about the guy you went after?" Hunt asked Carter.

"He didn't make it. But I got his phone. It's locked, though."

"Any idea who it was?" Anna asked.

Carter, who had taken a picture of the deceased man, showed his screen to Anna.

"That's him. That's the guy who was waiting for me after my meeting with Jorge Ramirez," she said.

"Damn it!" Hunt snapped, making her jump. "His name's Luis Ojeda. He works for Ramirez. I wish I could have talked to him. I'm sure he knew where Ramirez is."

Anna sensed Hunt's frustration. "If you have his phone, maybe there's a way we can still find out."

"How?" Carter asked.

"Give it to me."

Carter handed her the phone.

"Where's the body?" she asked.

"Not far. Follow me."

Anna followed him while Hunt joined Kleiner to talk with the police officers. There were already four police officers around Ojeda's body, but they didn't seem to mind her kneeling next to him. Anna placed the phone in front of Ojeda's face. The phone unlocked.

She looked at Carter. "Voilà."

With the phone now unlocked, she played with the settings for a minute and then gave the phone back to Carter.

"Face ID is now disabled," she said. "The new PIN is 1234."

"Can Hauer access the phone remotely?" Carter asked.

"Depends on the level of encryption they added on the phone," she replied. "It's one thing to access a phone remotely. It's an entirely different matter to actually read the encrypted files on it. I could probably crack the encryption within an hour or two."

Carter gave her a funny look.

"I have a master's degree in computer science," Anna explained.

"Got it, but I think I'll give it to Hauer and let him decide what to do with it. Hopefully it will help us find Ramirez."

"Sure."

Hunt waved at Anna and signaled for her to join him. She took a quick look around her. A lot of people had abandoned their vehicles. Fire trucks, ambulances, and police cars were still arriving on the scene with their lights and sirens. Thankfully, she didn't see any civilians lying down in the streets. One woman, seated on the sidewalk, was being treated for a leg injury by a paramedic.

Is it finally over? Is this the last act? With the Mayo brothers dead and her leaving the organization for good, who was going to take control of the Garcia crime syndicate?

Mauricio is the perfect fit. With him at the helm, the organization would collapse quietly and, most importantly, without violence.

As Anna made her way to Hunt, she had a feeling she wouldn't like what he was about to say.

"What is it?" she asked him, afraid he was about to tell her he was leaving. Again.

"Carter and I need to go, Anna."

I knew it. I freaking knew it!

"Why? Where?"

"Venezuela."

"How are you gonna get there? Venezuela is on the brink of collapse, Pierce. The entire country is a mess."

"A DEA asset has left something for us down there," Hunt said. "We need to put an end to this amphetamine crisis, and we think the answer is in Venezuela."

"Pierce, I need to tell you—"

Hunt interrupted her by placing a finger on her lips. With his thumb he wiped away the tears falling silently on her cheek.

"We'll figure everything out when I get back."

"What am I supposed to tell Leila?"

"You two are good again?" Hunt queried, his voice filled with hope.

"Yeah, we're good. She's a strong girl. There's a lot of you in her, you know?"

Hunt looked tired, but he was smiling. Anna could tell he was relieved at her answer. "Tell her that her daddy loves her very much and that he misses her. Tell her that I'll see her very soon."

Anna swallowed hard and gripped both of Hunt's hands. "Promise me you'll be careful. Promise me you'll get back to me."

Hunt answered by gently kissing her. And then he was gone.

CHAPTER FORTY-NINE

Miami Executive Airport

Hunt spent thirty minutes checking the gear Daniel McMaster had provided for him and Carter. Everything was there, including a new satellite phone. Knowing that Leila, Sophia, and Anna were well taken care of cleared his mind and allowed him to focus on the mission.

It would be his first time in Venezuela, and he hoped to be in and out quickly. Hauer had given him the coordinates of the USB drive, and the secretary of defense had linked with the director of National Reconnaissance in order to provide full satellite coverage for the duration of the mission. Dorothy Triggs had passed along the message that her two CIA officers would be waiting for them upon their arrival at the Obando Airport, a small airport in Colombia. It was only thirty kilometers from the Venezuelan border, which worked perfectly since they would be entering Venezuela on foot.

The flight to Obando Airport was a nonevent. Hunt spent the flight studying maps of the region while Carter familiarized himself with the new laptop Linda Ramer—the director of the Intelligence Division—had added to their kit. The laptop had the decryption key for the drive Hauer's asset had left buried in the jungle. Since the laptop could connect to the DEA secure network via satellite, Ramer had assured them that it would take less than two minutes to upload the data and transmit it back to the DEA headquarters in Virginia, where intelligence analysts were standing by to review it.

The laptop's best feature was that it could read the drive from up to five hundred feet away. DARPA—the Defense Advanced Research Projects Agency—had come up with this technology a decade ago. It had proven itself reliable and had facilitated many exchanges of information between intelligence officers and their handlers. Instead of meeting face to face, a handler equipped with the right laptop and decryption key could download the contents of a secured drive from a coffee shop across the street or even from a hotel room a block away.

Hunt grabbed two bottles of water from the plane's galley and lobbed one to Carter.

"I'm surprised the Colombians are letting us use their airstrip," Carter said. "I was under the impression our relations with them were of the glacial type."

"I can guarantee that the CIA didn't deal with the Colombian government to secure landing permission."

"You think they dealt with the FARC? I thought those guys had demobilized last year. Aren't they a political party now?"

Carter wasn't wrong, but there was more to it than met the eye. The FARC—the Revolutionary Armed Forces of Colombia—had formed during the Cold War. Funded mostly through different kidnap and ransom schemes and the production and distribution of illegal drugs, the guerilla movement had ceased to be an armed group in 2017, choosing to disarm itself and to give its weapons to the United Nations. A month later, and in accordance with the peace deal, the FARC had officially reformed into a political party named the Common Alternative Revolutionary Force. Unofficially, thousands of FARC dissidents continued trafficking drugs.

"Certainly with the FARC, but I'd bet they had to negotiate with the other regional actors and guerilla groups like the ELN and the EPL."

"It's gonna be hell to differentiate who's the good and bad guys, Pierce. I don't like this at all."

"As far as I'm concerned, brother, you and I are the only good guys."

"What about the CIA officers?"

"I'm not sure yet. We'll have to see how it goes."

———

It was a cloudy afternoon with a minor crosswind, but the Citation X touched down smoothly, and the rollout used less than half the runway. They taxied to a small private hangar where a black Toyota Prado waited. Hunt could see the silhouettes of two people in the SUV. Once the jet came to a complete stop, he unbuckled his seat belt and walked to the front of the cabin to open the hatch and drop the folding steps. He waited for the Cessna's engines to wind down before climbing out. By the time he reached the concrete floor of the hangar, a man and a woman were waiting for him.

The woman was tall, athletic, and dark skinned, with long black hair tied in a high ponytail. Hunt guessed she was closer to forty than thirty, but he wasn't about to ask. The man was slightly shorter, bald, and barrel chested, with thick and powerful arms and legs. He set his pale gray eyes on Hunt and grinned from ear to ear.

"I don't believe this," Hunt said, matching the man's grin. "Charlie Henican."

Hunt offered his hand, but Henican refused to take it. Instead, he wrapped his arms around Hunt and hugged him like a long-lost brother.

"You two know each other?" Carter asked from behind.

"Charlie and I went to hell and back together, didn't we?"

"We certainly did."

"Rangers?" Carter asked, referring to Hunt's prior service before the DEA.

"That, too, but I was in Delta when Pierce and I had our little escapade in Gaza," Henican replied.

Carter cocked his head to the side and looked at Hunt. "Cole Egan?"

"You told him the story, Pierce? The whole story?" Henican asked.

257

"He knows," Hunt said.

In 2007, Hunt, Henican, and Cole Egan had been part of a small contingent of Rangers and Delta Force operators sent to Gaza to train and assist President Abbas's Palestinian security forces in their underground struggle against Hamas terrorists. But all hell had broken loose when two members of Hunt's team were killed and Cole Egan was taken prisoner. Hunt's team had been ordered not to intervene, but within two hours of Cole's apprehension, Hunt, three other Rangers, and Delta operator Charlie Henican had mounted a rescue operation using intelligence Hunt had collected through methods some might have labeled unorthodox. The operation was considered a military success, but the psychological scars of what he'd done—how far he'd gone to save a teammate—were still there, forever scorched in his mind. Very few people knew the whole story, and even fewer knew how much of his soul Hunt had lost on that mission.

Twelve years later, Cole Egan was dead, and Charlie Henican was standing next to him in a hangar in Colombia about to embark on an operation where they would once again play well outside the regular rules of engagement.

"What am I missing here? What are you guys talking about?" the woman asked, annoyed that she was the only one with no clue about what was being discussed.

"Pierce Hunt, meet my boss, Harriet Jacobs," Henican said.

Hunt saw recognition in Jacobs's eyes. "You're that DEA guy that took down the Black Tosca in her own house," she said. It wasn't a question.

"I have absolutely no idea what you're talking about," Hunt replied, but he was smiling.

"And what's your colleague's name again?" Henican asked.

Carter introduced himself and shook both CIA officers' hands.

Henican made a grand gesture of looking at his watch. "All right, why don't we grab your gear from the plane and get going? We'll brief you on the way."

CHAPTER FIFTY

Caracas, Venezuela

General Euclides Peraza was having an early dinner with his family when one of his aides poked his head into the dining room. Peraza was happy with the distraction because he hadn't eaten anything. Not that his wife's beef stew wasn't good—he knew it to be delicious—but he feared throwing up due to his heightened anxiety.

"I'm sorry to disturb your dinner, sir, but Colonel Arteaga is on the phone, and he's asking for you."

Colonel Arteaga had never called him at home. Whatever this was, it was important. Peraza's wife of twenty years disagreed.

"Eat your dinner, Euclides," she said. "We never see you anymore. Always working."

"Mom's right, you know," his fifteen-year-old son added, his eyes glued to his new iPhone. "Even when you're here, you're not really there. You know what I mean?"

Peraza slammed his palm against the table.

His son jumped in his chair. "What? What did I do?"

"Have the decency to look at me when you address me," Peraza said. "And when me or your mother talk to you, stop looking at your phone and listen. Is that understood?"

"Why are you being so rude?" his son asked. "What have I done to you?"

Peraza had a thousand things begging for his attention. He had no time to deal with a rowdy teenager. "You talk to him," he said to his wife. "I have to go."

Peraza stormed out of the dining room. In the hallway, his aide waited for him with his secured phone.

"Yes?" Peraza said into the receiver.

"My sincere apologies for calling—"

"What is it, Colonel?" Peraza cut in, still angry about his son's attitude.

And where did he get that phone? I certainly didn't buy it for him.

"One of our agents inside Colombia reported the arrival of a single private jet from Florida. Carrying two passengers and two crew members. It landed at the Obando Airport thirty minutes ago. Our agent was able to take a few shots of a vehicle exiting the hangar."

"Get to the point, Colonel!"

"We believe that Pierce Hunt was aboard the plane."

That was noteworthy. *Pierce Hunt.*

Peraza had read all about him. A former DEA special agent, Hunt had become a celebrity among American law enforcement for punching a Chicago reporter who'd tipped off the Black Tosca about a DEA raid. The reporter's video of the raid—and especially, his clash with Hunt—had made headlines around the United States and had collected millions of views on YouTube.

That was the public story. But Peraza also knew that after Hunt's daughter had been kidnapped by the Black Tosca, Valentina Mieles and her right-hand man and cousin, Hector, had been dead within forty-eight hours. Hunt had slaughtered practically everyone connected with his daughter's kidnapping.

Pierce Hunt was a dangerous man. His appearance in Colombia near the Venezuelan border couldn't be simply brushed off. Hunt wasn't in Colombia for sightseeing. Could it have something to do with Peter

Godfrey's death? Or had the Americans figured out Peraza was the architect behind the new drug that had already killed so many? That was possible. But knowing and proving that Operation Butterfly was Peraza's design were two different things. With the Russians investing heavily in Venezuela, the UN Security Council would never authorize a foreign military intervention in Venezuela. The two Russian Tu-160 strategic bombers at Maiquetía airport were a clear indication that the Russian and Venezuelan governments wouldn't be pushed around by the international community.

The DEA—or whoever Hunt was working for—had sent him to avenge Peter Godfrey without the US taking official action. It couldn't be anything else. Was Hunt after him? Was Peraza's own family now in danger?

"Do you still have eyes on Hunt?" he asked.

"We don't, and, as you know, General, the border with Colombia is porous. There are a thousand ways for him to get in," Arteaga said.

Peraza was well aware of the border problem. Only seven official crossings were manned along the 2,220-kilometer-long border. There were, however, over three hundred clandestine trails—or *trochas*—that were used by smugglers. Control over these trails was contested by various armed groups, including the EPL and ELN. The four-kilometer walk across the border was treacherous, but with the right smuggler and a bit of money, there was no doubt Hunt could be in Venezuela by the end of the day.

"I'm wondering why he chose to enter this way," Peraza said, thinking out loud. "He must know I'm in Caracas. How many vehicles did your man see leave the airport?"

"Just one."

"Something isn't right here," Peraza said, playing with different scenarios in his head. "It would be almost impossible for a single man to successfully get to me, at least here in Caracas."

Of course, a sniper willing to sacrifice his life for the perfect shot could pull it off, but Hunt wasn't the type. No, Hunt was here for something specific.

"What do you want me to do, sir?" Colonel Arteaga asked.

"Find Hunt and whoever else is with him, and bring them to me. Dead if you must, but I'd much prefer he was still breathing."

"Yes, sir. I'll personally see to it."

Peraza handed the phone back to his aide. "Have my car ready in ten minutes," Peraza told him. "And once my son and wife are done with their dinner, bring them to La Tumba. I want them to be comfortable but safe."

The aide snapped to attention and did an about-face, the sound from the heels of his highly polished boots echoing as he crossed the marble floor. Peraza peeked back into the dining room. His wife still looked pissed off. She picked up the unfinished plate he had left behind. His son hadn't moved an inch, except for his fingers dancing on the screen of his cell phone. He wondered if he was overreacting by moving them.

I'm sure the Black Tosca felt pretty safe in her big mansion until Pierce Hunt broke through her defenses, slaughtered her bodyguards, and went on to pump two rounds into her abdomen.

Then there was the situation in Florida. The news Ramirez had delivered wasn't optimal either. With the deaths of the Mayo brothers and the betrayal by Anna Garcia, the Garcia crime syndicate had ceased to be an effective proxy for distributing his improved and soon-to-be-ready amphetamine pills. The organization's structure was still there, but without someone they knew at the head of the table, its men wouldn't follow. As good as Jorge Ramirez was, he couldn't lead such an organization using fear alone.

Ramirez's latest report had mentioned that he was looking at two different criminal organizations that could act as distributors. One of them was an outlaw motorcycle gang based in Texas, and the other one was the California-based 18th Street gang. Ramirez was on his way to Los Angeles to speak with one of the latter's lieutenants, and Peraza expected to hear back from him by the end of the day.

Operation Butterfly had suffered a setback, but not a fatal one. Peraza didn't see the need to bother President Capriles with the news. As influential as he was, Peraza knew better than to antagonize the president with his failures. He wouldn't be the first general to *disappear* after embarrassing Capriles. Peraza had to be smart and play his cards perfectly.

Starting with finding and stopping Pierce Hunt.

CHAPTER FIFTY-ONE

Near the Colombian and Venezuelan border

Hunt folded the map on which Henican had charted the best route to their objective. He and Carter had been studying it for the last forty-five minutes, doing their best to memorize the terrain. Hunt laid the map on the middle seat beside him.

"If someone identifies himself as Queen Bee, you don't shoot," Henican said from the front passenger seat. "Understood?"

"Who's Queen Bee?" Hunt asked. "It's the second time I've heard that call sign."

"No clue, brother. Just got the note myself," Henican said, tapping the military-grade laptop he held.

"From who?" Carter asked.

"Last-minute instruction from Triggs," Henican said. "You can bring it up with her if you wish."

"I'll do just that."

Henican shrugged. "Go right ahead, brother."

Hunt grabbed his satellite phone and dialed Triggs's number.

"This is Triggs."

"This is Charlie-One," Hunt said. "Who the fuck's Queen Bee?"

"Way above your clearance, Charlie-One. You have no play here. Goodbye."

Hunt, speechless, looked at his satellite phone in disbelief. "She hung up," he said out loud to no one in particular.

"Yeah, she does that sometimes," Henican said. "Do you guys have any other questions?"

"How do you keep track of who's who in this zoo?" Hunt asked. "How are we supposed to differentiate friendlies from enemies?"

"It's impossible to do so," Harriet Jacobs answered from the driver's seat of the Toyota Prado. "And frankly, once you're in Venezuela, there are no friendlies."

Knowing whether he could trust the CIA officers he and Carter would work with had been Hunt's biggest worry coming in. That concern had vanished the moment he'd seen Charlie Henican at the airfield. The former Delta operator was one of the most courageous soldiers Hunt had worked with. Very few operators would have risked everything to follow Hunt on the rescue operation in Gaza as Henican had done. Hunt trusted the man with his life. If Henican thought the best and safest way into Venezuela was the route he and Jacobs had traced on the map, Hunt would follow it.

The coordinates Hauer had given them indicated the drive Hauer's asset had left behind before he'd been captured was five miles across the Venezuelan border. The narrow dirt road they were on now was bumpy and followed the natural lay of the land. But it was lightly traveled. Hunt had seen no other vehicle since they had left the airfield. He looked at his DAGR—defense advanced GPS receiver. They were about four miles from the Venezuelan border.

"We can get you a bit closer, maybe a mile or so, but we'll risk being spotted," Jacobs said. "There are fewer patrols here than nearer the border."

"It's fine here," Hunt assured her. He preferred walking an extra mile rather than risking that his ride home would be caught in the open by hostile forces. He didn't want to end up like Hauer's asset.

"Okay," Jacobs said. "Let me find a hiding place for the truck."

A few hundred feet farther down the road, she backed the Toyota into a spot where the jungle wasn't as heavy. They all climbed out of the SUV and spent the next five minutes concealing the vehicle from the road. They didn't want to attract undue attention.

Hunt and Carter double-checked each other's gear, a practice drilled in by years of service, and did a final radio and weapons check. Hunt retained his Charlie-One call sign and Carter was Charlie-Two. Jacobs and Henican were Papa-One and Two respectively. Tom Hauer and Dorothy Triggs were following the operations from the TOC at the DEA headquarters, but the only ways for Hunt and Carter to communicate with them was either via the satellite phone that Hunt carried with him or through Papa-One or Two.

"If for some reason the boat isn't where it's supposed to be, you get back here, and we'll find another way in," Jacobs said.

"Got it," Hunt replied.

Part of the trip involved crossing the Atabapo River. The river formed the international border between the two countries. The 131-kilometer-long river was one kilometer wide at its greatest point. To facilitate the crossing, Henican and Jacobs had positioned a small inflatable near the river. The boat had a small battery-driven outboard motor and two paddles. In order not to attract unwanted attention, the plan called for Hunt and Carter to cross the river only once darkness had fallen.

"Hey, Pierce," Henican said before Hunt left, "I don't care what the orders are. You call me, I'm there."

"I never doubted it, Charlie," Hunt said. "Just make sure you're here when we get back, all right?"

Hunt and Carter silently disappeared into the jungle.

CHAPTER FIFTY-TWO

DEA Headquarters
Arlington, Virginia

Tom Hauer was nervous, rocking back and forth from his toes to his heels. The satellite feed Secretary of Defense Flynn had arranged for them was good, but it didn't help with his anxiety. Hunt and Carter were about to embark on a dangerous game of cat and mouse. The NSA had noticed a recent uptick in military communications within Venezuela, and Hauer had considered pulling the plug on the operation, but there was just too much at stake to chicken out now. The operation was a go.

Dorothy Triggs looked at him with serenity. She even smiled.

"It's your first, isn't it?" she asked him.

"First what?"

"Black op in a country where there's absolutely no support."

"This is the DEA, Dorothy, not the CIA. We do sanctioned covert operations across the globe, but nothing like this. In Afghanistan, we had a safety net. If the Venezuelans catch them—"

"They catch them," Triggs said, her voice firm. "That's why it's a deniable unit, Tom."

"You expect me to—"

"Stop it," Triggs warned him, raising her voice just a little. "I didn't make the rules; the president did. Hunt isn't at his first rodeo, is he?

Carter is a capable operator. They'll be fine. Stop worrying so damn much."

Triggs was right. He had to trust Hunt and Carter to get the job done. How Triggs was able to maintain her composure was a mystery to Hauer.

It's your men that just entered the lion's den, Tom. Not hers. That's why.

"Nimitz, this is Papa-One, radio check, over," came in Harriet Jacobs.

"Papa-One from Nimitz, you're five by five," replied the special agent in charge of the communications for this operation. "And we have a good satellite feed, over."

"Good copy, Nimitz. Papa-One out."

Hauer watched the screen on which the satellite feed was displayed. Hunt and Carter were making good speed and had already traveled the four miles to the Atabapo River. Once they reached the opposite shore and secured the boat, they had a stretch of five miles to the USB drive Peter Godfrey had buried. Then they had to trek the same nine miles back to the vehicle where Jacob and Henican were waiting. With an average speed of two miles per hour, it would take them approximately nine hours to do the round trip, plus any additional time they needed at the destination to transmit the data stored on Godfrey's drive.

Triggs walked up to him and offered him a cup of coffee.

"It's gonna be a long night," she said.

"I know."

"They're capable men, Tom. Trust them."

Trust wasn't the issue. Sometimes being capable wasn't enough.

"Sir!" the special agent in charge of the communications called. "We might have a problem."

And here we go.

CHAPTER FIFTY-THREE

Venezuelan border

Pierce Hunt got down to one knee and signaled Carter to join him. Hunt's GPS showed that they had traveled just under four miles. They were one hundred feet away from the river.

"What's up?" Carter whispered.

"Let's take two—then we cross over."

"If we find the boat," Carter murmured.

Hunt took a defensive position while Carter drank from his canteen.

"Charlie-One, this is Papa-One, over," Jacobs said in his ear.

"Go for Charlie-One."

"Nimitz advises there's movement across the river, about a mile east of your position. Nimitz says it could be a combat patrol of approximately a dozen men. They're walking away from you. I say again, they're moving east and away from you."

"Good copy, Papa-One."

"What do you want to do?" Carter asked, putting his canteen away. "You want to go for it now or wait till they're farther away?"

"We go now," Hunt said without hesitation. He lowered his NVGs into place and turned them on.

The inflatable was exactly where it was supposed to be. Hunt and Carter each grabbed a side and carried it into the water. Carter went back to pick up the motor. Hunt took it from him and fixed it to the stern in less than two minutes. The battery-powered motor started on the first try. Hunt drove the boat while Carter took a firing position on the bow. Even though the motor was almost silent, Hunt cut it about two hundred feet from shore and tilted it on its housing until the propeller was cleared of the water. He and Carter quietly paddled the rest of the way. Hunt jumped into the shallow water and dragged the inflatable to shore while Carter covered him.

It took a little more than ten minutes to cover the inflatable with brushwood and leaves. While Carter finished up on the boat, Hunt carried the motor fifty meters away and concealed it, making sure to mark its location on his GPS.

"Charlie-One from Papa-One," Jacobs said.

"Go ahead for Charlie-One," Hunt replied.

"Nimitz reports a second patrol of approximately twenty men approaching from the south. The patrol is approximately one and a half miles from your position."

"Charlie-One copy, Papa-One."

Hunt looked at Carter through the uncanny green glow of the NVGs. "What are you thinking?" Hunt asked.

"I think we should push through," Carter replied. "If the boat gets compromised, we'll just have to improvise and find another way out."

Hunt agreed. They couldn't wait forever. The night was their friend, and they needed to take advantage of their superior equipment. After another quick hydrating session, Hunt sneaked through the thick growth like a panther, Carter following six feet behind. Even though he had easy access to his GPS, Hunt mostly navigated using his mental compass.

After an hour of walking, it began to rain. The rain continued for thirty minutes, drenching both men with warm water and slowing their progress. When it finally stopped, the relentless dripping from the thick jungle growth gave Hunt the impression that it was still raining. He was sweating copiously, and his muscles were stinging and protesting every step, but he carried on. So did the mosquitos, munching on his flesh. An hour later, Hunt called for a five-minute break. This time he checked his GPS.

"We aren't moving fast enough," Hunt said to Carter. "If we continue like this, we won't make it back before sunrise. And I don't want to cross the river during daylight."

It was near pitch black in the jungle. The dense overhead growth easily filtered out most of the moonlight, making their progress more difficult.

"Charlie-One, this is Papa-Two, over," Henican came in.

Hunt's body tensed. "Go ahead for Charlie-One."

"The patrol that was east of you has split into two groups of six men. One of the groups has turned around, making their way back toward your position. They're a little less than half a mile away."

"Good copy, Papa-Two. We'll lie low until we figure out where they're going," Hunt said. The patrol was directly in their path. There was no point continuing forward and walking directly into a Venezuelan combat patrol.

For the next hour, Hunt became one with the jungle floor. Lying on his stomach on the wet muck, he had turned off his NVGs in order to heighten his other senses. The sounds of the night creatures and the odor of rotting plants slowly became normal to him. Mosquitoes fed off him, and mysterious insects crawled on his hands and face.

Just like the Rangers. He wondered how Carter was doing. The big man was less than four feet to his left, but with only a few moon rays making it through the overhead growth, Hunt could hardly see his bulk.

Then Hunt heard a noise—a sound that was out of sync with the environment. A sound that didn't belong. A sound different than the natural jungle sounds he had become accustomed to. He heard a faint click as Carter readied himself to fire.

The jungle had heard it, too, because everything turned quiet. Forty or so seconds later, the jungle progressively reverted back to its usual cacophony of sounds. Maybe he had been mistaken.

"Charlie-One from Papa-One, over," came in Jacobs, her voice barely a whisper.

Hunt, unwilling to make a sound, broke the air once by clicking the transmit button.

"Charlie-One, Nimitz advises that six hostiles are less than two hundred feet from your position. Unless they divert, they'll walk right on top of you."

Ha!

Hunt tapped the transmit button of his comms unit twice, wordlessly acknowledging this latest communication from Papa-One. There was nothing they could do but wait. And be ready.

CHAPTER FIFTY-FOUR

Venezuelan jungle

Colonel Carlos Arteaga wasn't a paper pusher, and because of that, he'd probably never make it to the rank of general. But Arteaga was fine with that. General Peraza took great care of him and his family. His wife was happy, or at least she told him she was, and his five children attended the best school in Caracas. Their bellies were filled twice a day, three times during the weekends, and they had a nice car and enough money to fuel it when necessary, which was better than most of his countrymen could say about their lives. He didn't need more than that.

Well, that wasn't entirely true.

He'd always been an opportunist. That was why he had a backup plan. But as long as General Peraza's heart was in the right place and they were making progress toward improving the lives of the Venezuelan people, Arteaga would tag along for the ride. When and if that ever stopped, he'd reevaluate.

For now Arteaga saw it as his job to please and protect the general from people who meant him harm. So when the general told him he was sending his wife and son to La Tumba—the SEBIN headquarters—for protection, Arteaga knew that General Peraza took the Pierce Hunt threat seriously. So Arteaga had decided to travel south to personally supervise the search for Hunt.

At first, Arteaga had been confused. It had made no tactical sense for a lone operator to sneak into Venezuela so far south of Caracas. Even if there was more than one operator—Arteaga was persuaded Hunt wasn't acting alone—the journey to Caracas would be risky. Perhaps Hunt had help from someone within Venezuela, but it would still be impossible for him to get to General Peraza. He was too well protected.

A buzzing inside the small tent distracted him. Despite all his years in the field, Arteaga still reviled mosquitoes as much as when he was a young infantry officer in training. God must have been feeling testy when he created mosquitoes. Arteaga tried to swat the offending insect between his hand and forearm, but it was too late. The mosquito had escaped. He couldn't make the same mistake with Hunt.

What if Hunt wasn't after General Peraza? What if he was going after something or someone else? The only thing linking Hunt to Venezuela was Peter Godfrey. Could it be that the Americans had sent Hunt on a rescue mission? That they didn't know that Godfrey was buried in a shallow grave ten miles outside of Caracas?

Maybe.

Arteaga studied his map. His troops had caught up with Godfrey and his two DEA wannabe saviors only a few miles from here. Were the Americans here to retrieve the remains of one of their own? Arteaga had left the first DEA man where he had fallen. By now, there wouldn't be anything left of him worth picking up. The jungle would have seen to that. What about the second DEA agent? They had thrown his body on the side of the road. There would be nothing left of him either.

What about the ambush site? Could that be where they were headed?

Arteaga replayed in his mind the events on the night of the ambush. He had given Godfrey and his escorts thirty seconds to surrender. What would he have done in Godfrey's shoes, knowing he was about to get captured?

I'd hide the intelligence I'd collected, hoping someone would come to pick it up so four years of my life wouldn't go to waste.

Of course! If Godfrey's plan had been to exfil from Venezuela, he had probably carried on his person all the intelligence he had collected while working for General Peraza. If Arteaga had to guess, he'd say that Godfrey had buried a flash drive or a similar device somewhere close to the site of the ambush. Whatever was on that drive was important enough for the Americans to risk sending operators into Venezuela to retrieve it.

"If that's where you're going, then that's where I'll be waiting," Arteaga thought out loud as he ran his finger over the map. He called two of his subordinates inside the tent and briefed them on what he wanted them to do.

Once he was done, there was only one question.

"Yes, Captain Palacios?"

"What about additional troops, sir? And could we get air support?"

"General Peraza trusts us to apprehend, or kill if we have to, a small American patrol consisting of no more than four people," Arteaga told him. "This isn't a regular mission, Captain. There will be no reinforcements and no air support."

The captain nodded. Once the two officers had left the tent, Arteaga combed through his rucksack for his tubes of face paint. He camouflaged his face with various shades of dark-colored grease paint and looked at his reflection in the small combat mirror he carried in his pocket. Satisfied that all the exposed areas of his skin were darkened, he replaced the tubes in his rucksack, grabbed his rifle, and exited the tent.

If all went well, he'd be home in time to have breakfast with his family.

CHAPTER FIFTY-FIVE

Venezuelan jungle

Hunt swore silently, but he didn't dare move. Five minutes ago, he had turned his NVGs back on. And now, they had just died on him, and he had no idea why. He had spare batteries in his pack, but he couldn't move, couldn't make a sound. The Venezuelan soldiers were too close, and they were disciplined. They were walking in single file, spread five feet apart, and they were being fairly quiet. They were all there. The six of them. Nimitz had confirmed it.

Hunt couldn't see them clearly, but he could feel their presence. He sensed their movement and made out their dark, ghostly shapes as they progressed through the jungle, not even ten feet away from where he was and getting closer. Hunt had decided they wouldn't engage the soldiers if they didn't have to. Even with surprise on their side, two against six weren't odds Hunt liked. Moreover, Hunt didn't think suppressed assault rifles were standard issue for Venezuelan frontline troops. That meant that they would have to neutralize the six of them before one Venezuelan soldier could return fire, because if even one unsuppressed shot was fired, it was game over for Hunt and Carter. They'd never make it back to the river, let alone Colombia.

Sixty seconds passed, but to Hunt it felt like an hour. Had the patrol stopped? Hunt couldn't tell without turning his head. Doing so would alert anyone standing close. A mosquito entered his ear canal, scratching his eardrum and making Hunt's hairs rise up on the back of his neck. Something tiny was crawling inside his nose, but he ignored it, forcing himself to concentrate on the sounds around him.

Then he felt movement between his feet. Hunt's heart jumped five beats ahead, his veins pounding at his temple. A soldier had just stepped between his legs and stopped! The soldier's next step would hit Hunt. It didn't matter where. His leg, his calf, his foot. It. Didn't. Matter. When that happened, the element of surprise would be lost, and he and Carter would be gunned down.

Goddamn it! He was in an impossible position. Had the soldier seen him? Was he just messing with Hunt's mind, his rifle pointed at his head and only waiting for Hunt to make his move before pulling the trigger?

Hunt's training told him to remain still, but his instincts were screaming for him to act. If he sprang into action, would Carter react immediately? There was no way Hunt could take the six soldiers on his own, certainly not before they fired a shot. And without his NVGs? That was impossible. But so was doing nothing.

In the end, his trust in Carter won.

Using his left leg, Hunt rammed it with all his might behind the soldier's knee while using his right leg to sweep at his ankle. The soldier plunged forward, slamming into the wet muck. Before the soldier realized what had happened, Hunt jumped on him, his tactical knife in his right hand, and plunged the blade into the man's throat twice in rapid succession. To his right, Carter's M4 spat twice.

———

Simon Carter had no idea why the patrol had stopped there. With his NVGs, he had seen their approach. These six men were professional soldiers—of that Carter was sure. They were in control of their environment, and despite the darkness, they seemed at ease in the jungle. They weren't strangers visiting someone else's playground. This was where they trained, worked, and fought. This was their home.

The soldier was literally two steps away from him and about one foot from stepping on Hunt's leg. Hunt wasn't moving. Not an inch. The silence was deafening. It was so quiet Carter could almost hear the trees breathing. The whole jungle was tensed, waiting to see what would happen next.

Then the soldier took a step, his left foot landing squarely between Hunt's legs.

Oh shit. Here we go. It was impossible for Hunt to have missed that. Still Carter didn't see his friend move.

Hunt is one cool cucumber. He didn't even twitch.

Knowing Hunt, he was probably analyzing the situation. When Hunt was cornered, his first move was to attack with everything he had. Always.

So when Hunt made his move, Carter was ready. He had already pictured in his mind where the five other soldiers were positioned. Before Hunt's right leg had finished sweeping the soldier's ankle, Carter had already rolled to his left and sat up. He raised his M4 to eye level and fired twice at the closest soldier. The soldier wasn't even down before Carter was already firing at his next mark, hitting him once in the back of the head. He swung his M4 methodically to the right, resting his sight on the chest of his next target, who was still unaware of the mayhem around him. Carter squeezed the trigger twice and then moved to the next soldier half a heartbeat later and shot him in the face, right below his nose. To Carter's right, from the corner of his eye, he saw the remaining soldier raise his rifle and knew to the depths of his soul that anything he tried would be futile.

I'm dead.

———

The muzzle flash of Carter's M4 provided Hunt with just enough light to identify his next threat. Hunt didn't need to think about what he had to do. Since Carter was working his targets efficiently from left to right, the soldier farthest to Carter's right was the one his friend wouldn't have time to take out. Hunt flicked his knife so that he was holding the blade and threw it overhand at the soldier, who was standing fifteen feet away. The knife struck the soldier just above his plate carrier. The soldier stepped back, dropped his rifle so he could bring two hands to the knife embedded in his upper chest, and fell to his knees.

———

For an instant, Simon Carter was confused as to why the soldier hadn't fired. Then he saw the knife. In the green glow of his NVGs, he saw the soldier's face: a mask of shock. Carter double-tapped him in the mouth, ending the man's misery.

The entire firefight had lasted less than eight seconds.

———

Hunt looked at Carter, who had just shot the last soldier. "You okay?"

"Yeah," Carter replied. "What do we do now?"

"Let's move from the X. We need to bug out."

"Roger that."

"But let's see what these guys were carrying," Hunt said, already combing through the tactical vest of the last man Carter had shot.

Hunt found a handheld Garmin GPS and a map. He pocketed both. The search of the other bodies revealed nothing else of interest.

"Lead the way, Simon," Hunt said. "My NVGs are dead."

In order to cover more ground more rapidly, Hunt placed his left hand against Carter's back. There was a possibility that the Venezuelans had called in the location, and Hunt didn't feel like being there if mortars started to fall.

"Papa-One, this is Charlie-One," Hunt called on the comms system.

"Go ahead for Papa-One," Jacobs came back.

"Charlie-One and Two engaged an enemy force of six. Six enemy casualties. Charlie-One and Two are fine. We're continuing to our objective. Over."

"Good copy, Charlie-One. We'll relay your sitrep to Nimitz."

Twenty minutes later, Hunt called for a short break. There were a couple of things he wanted to do before getting closer to their objective. First he changed the batteries in his NVGs. He tried to power them on. No success. There was no point trying to fix them in the dark. He'd go low tech for the rest of the mission. Next, Hunt put on the tactical headset he'd taken from the dead Venezuelan soldier and almost turned on the radio. He stopped himself. What if the radio had a GPS tracker? It wasn't worth the risk. He removed the headset and replaced the radio in his rucksack.

Hunt drank some water and gobbled a protein bar, making as little noise as possible. Once he was done, he took Carter's place as security and let his friend eat and drink.

"Charlie-One, this is Papa-One, over," Jacobs came in.

"This is Charlie-One."

"Charlie-One, be advised that Nimitz confirmed a heavy presence around the objective. It looks like the Venezuelans are setting up an ambush. They know you're coming."

"Copy that, Papa-One. We're two miles out from our objective."

Hunt turned toward Carter. "The way I see it, we have two advantages."

"I'm listening," Carter said.

"The Venezuelans have no idea we don't actually need to have the drive in our possession to download its contents."

"True. And what's the second thing?"

"We have an eye in the sky."

CHAPTER FIFTY-SIX

Venezuelan jungle

Colonel Arteaga tried to control himself, but he was growing more frustrated and angrier by the minute. Captain Palacios's patrol had missed their last three radio checks. It was possible that they had had to go silent, but he doubted it. An uneasy feeling crept over him.

Hunt took them out.

Arteaga had sent four more six-man patrols to the problematic area in an effort to reestablish contact with Captain Palacios but had kept twenty men with him at the ambush site. For the last ninety minutes, they had been methodically combing the ground for any signs of a hidden object. They were on their second pass when a young soldier found it buried three inches into the ground.

On first look it appeared to be a regular USB drive, but it felt different to the touch. It was a bit heavier than normal, and Arteaga's gut told him he should just destroy the device and be done with it. But Peraza's orders were clear. He wanted to know what Peter Godfrey had downloaded. Arteaga slipped the USB drive into the breast pocket of his combat shirt.

Then he set his trap.

CHAPTER FIFTY-SEVEN

Venezuelan jungle

Hunt wished he could talk directly with Nimitz instead of passing through Papa-One and Two. It would have been easier for all parties involved. But the comms were what they were, and he had to deal with that.

It had taken them just over five hours to travel the last two miles. With Nimitz's help, they had been able to avoid the numerous patrols. Twice they had heard gunfire in the distance, reminding them that Venezuela wasn't a country at peace. Even though they hadn't encountered any more patrols, the trek to the objective hadn't been easy. Just moving through the jungle had brought endless scratches and a dangerous number of insect bites. Constantly wet from the draining heat and occasional showers, Hunt felt he was wearing a second skin of sweat and dried blood.

To connect with the drive, they needed to get closer. Five hundred feet was the maximum range, but the USB drive was buried, and this might affect its range. Getting closer was going to be an issue. The Venezuelans knew how to set an ambush. It was only their eye in the sky that made it possible for Hunt and Carter to approach without being caught in a cross fire.

"Two hundred and fifty feet," Jacobs said in his ear, counting down the distance between Hunt and the next Venezuelan soldier.

Since they had only one working pair of NVGs, Hunt had ordered Carter to stay behind with the laptop and the rest of their gear. The fact that Hunt wasn't tech savvy had played a part in the decision too. Carter was to move only when Hunt told him to.

"Two hundred feet."

All around Hunt was darkness. Even with the NVGs, his senses were as sharp as a razor's edge. His mind took in every noise, every smell, and catalogued them swiftly. He moved silently and with caution, stopping every few seconds to listen.

"One hundred feet."

Hunt could feel the adrenaline flowing. Sweat streamed from every pore in his body, making jagged patterns on his dirt-encrusted face. The seconds ticked by like days.

"Fifty feet. Right in front of you," Jacobs said. "You should see him now."

And he did. The jungle was thinner here. A Venezuelan soldier was standing next to a tree, his AK-103 rifle tightly clutched and ready to fire, stretching one leg at a time. When Hunt was twenty feet away from the soldier, he silently drew his knife. Hunt was almost on him when the soldier stiffened, probably sensing a presence behind him. Hunt didn't hesitate. He grasped the man's face, jerked his head to the side, and plunged his knife into his throat while placing a knee in the man's back, bending him backward. Ripping his knife outward, Hunt severed the man's jugular. He felt the gush of warm blood on his hand as he carefully lowered the man's body to the ground.

"Target down," Hunt whispered, keying his radio. "Move up, Charlie-Two."

"Copy, One. On my way."

Hunt wiped his blade on his trousers before sheathing his knife and shouldering his M4.

It took Carter ten minutes to reach Hunt.

"All right," Hunt whispered. "Give it a shot."

"How far are we from the device?"

"Four hundred feet, I'd guess." Hunt scanned the jungle.

Hunt yearned for the laptop to connect with the USB key, because if it didn't, they would need to get closer.

And closer means I'll need to take out at least two more soldiers.

The computer screen emanated very little light, but Hunt didn't want to leave anything to chance, so he covered Carter and the laptop with a waterproof tarp he'd taken from Carter's bag. Hunt heard the faint hum of the laptop as it powered up.

"Charlie-One, this is Papa-One. You have two sentries approaching your position. Approximately one hundred feet due north of you."

Hunt turned his head in that direction, slowly bringing up his M4 to eye level. He scanned the jungle.

"I have a connection," Carter said softly. "I can't believe it."

Hunt couldn't believe their good luck either. Now he just had to wait for the other shoe to drop.

"Papa-One, this is Charlie-One. Over," Hunt said, getting down to one knee next to Carter but keeping his M4 up.

"Go ahead, Charlie-One."

"We're connected to the device. Are you getting anything on your end?"

"Stand by, Charlie-One. I'll ask Nimitz."

Hunt saw movement through his scope. Two men, slowly and vigilantly approaching in a combat crouch, scanning left and right with their rifles. They didn't have night vision, but the way they moved told him they were at ease in the jungle and that any careless sound he made would pinpoint his location and bring down a barrage of effective fire on his position.

Hunt keyed his mike. "Two tangos approaching."

The two men stopped, as if they had heard Hunt talk. Had they? They then retreated a few steps and took cover behind a large tree.

What are they doing?

"Charlie-One from Papa-One. Nimitz confirmed they're getting the data. Another three or four minutes and you'll be done."

"Good copy," Hunt said under his breath.

Three or four minutes? *Damn it!* They had told him it would take no more than two minutes. Technology—it never worked as advertised.

That was when the first mortar illumination round exploded overhead, completely blinding Hunt.

Then all hell broke loose.

CHAPTER FIFTY-EIGHT

Venezuelan jungle

Colonel Arteaga and Captain Pietri were making their way to Sergeant Chourio's position. The young sergeant hadn't returned the last radio check, and Arteaga had the impression that Chourio had fallen asleep on duty. If that was the case, he'd be put on bread and water rations for the next three months.

Something moved inside his shirt. At first Arteaga thought a small snake or a large furry spider had found its way between his body armor and his shirt. He stopped, took a few steps back toward a large tree trunk, and took cover behind it. Captain Pietri joined him seconds later.

When Arteaga tried to grab the offending creature, he realized it was the USB drive vibrating. Not only was it vibrating, but a tiny blue light flashed at the very top. It took Arteaga less than two seconds to figure out the reason.

"The Americans are here," he said to Captain Pietri. "And they're close."

"How do you know, sir?"

Arteaga showed him the USB drive. "Someone's connected to it. I want illumination rounds now. We need to find the Americans."

While Captain Pietri called the small mortar team and gave them their firing orders, Arteaga tried to shut down the USB key.

How does this thing work? He tried to push on the blinking blue light, but to no avail. *I knew I should have destroyed this thing.*

Arteaga jumped when the first illumination round exploded. He hadn't expected his mortar team to be so efficient. He closed his left eye to safeguard his night vision, but he was too late. His night vision was gone.

Captain Pietri was on the radio, and Arteaga could hear him shouting orders to his men. Pietri raised his rifle and cut around the trunk they were using as cover. More 60-mm mortar illumination rounds went off around them, lighting the area so much it almost looked like daylight.

Pietri's AK-103 barked three times. Arteaga replaced the USB drive in his pocket and crawled next to Pietri. He was about to squeeze the trigger when Pietri's head snapped back, spraying him in the face with a fine mist of blood.

Arteaga rolled to his left and fired his AK-103 in the general direction of the shooter. More silent rounds slapped into Pietri's body, forcing Arteaga to retreat behind the tree.

———

Hunt flipped up his NVGs. He didn't need them anymore.

He and Carter weren't in the best position. Their left flank and rear were exposed to enemy fire. One of the men had taken advantage of Hunt's confusion to fire at him. The rounds whipped over his head, shredding the vegetation behind. Hunt hastily returned fire, then hit the deck as more rounds flew above him. Hunt pulled the trigger once more, but this time he'd taken the extra half second to aim. His round hit the man in the forehead. A second man rolled away from the first and fired a long burst, his bullets raking the wet jungle floor all around Hunt. He heard Carter grunt just before he squeezed the trigger, sending bullets toward the new threat.

"You okay?" Hunt asked Carter.

"I'm fine, goddamn it!" Carter crawled away while keeping the laptop open and in front of him. "I just lost the tip of my pinkie! Fuuuck!"

A soldier emerged from the jungle and ran to the tree where the second man Hunt had seen was hiding. The soldier didn't make it. Hunt sighted on the man's chest and fired. The soldier collapsed almost on top of the first man Hunt had shot.

"Papa-One from Charlie-One. We're under contact at the objective."

"Copy that. Nimitz says they need another minute. Maybe two."

Behind him Carter fired his rifle on full automatic. Hunt spun around in time to see two soldiers jumping out of sight behind a fallen tree. He ripped a frag from its pouch and pulled the pin. He tossed it behind the tree. One of the soldiers tried to dash to cover, but Hunt shot him four times in the back. The grenade exploded, sending shards of wood in all directions.

"Let's go, Simon! We're moving!" Hunt yelled as more rounds stippled the ground and trees around him. They needed to get back into the jungle, where the night was their friend. Here they were outnumbered and outgunned. The Venezuelan soldiers had been slow to react, but the minute someone took charge, he and Carter were toast.

———

Arteaga swore out loud. Captain Pietri was dead. Arteaga was the only officer left. It was on him to mount a counterattack. But first, he grabbed the USB drive, placed it on the ground, and stomped on it with the heel of his boot. The damn thing didn't break. Instead, it sank into the muddy jungle floor. Frustrated, he pulled his pistol and was about to fire when the blue light stopped flashing.

My God! The Americans had done it. They had downloaded the drive remotely. He couldn't let the Americans escape. If the world ever learned about Operation Butterfly, it was all over for Peraza and

Capriles. The future of his country depended on his ability to stop them. Or did it? It didn't have to be this way. There was an alternative.

Was it finally the time to play his best card?

Arteaga thought of his wife and his five children. What would they want for Venezuela? What did they expect from him? Because, deep down, it was for them and other families like them that he had decided to serve in the armed forces. To protect *their* rights. To protect *their* lives. Not to protect some wannabe dictator.

Then something clicked in his mind. All wasn't hopeless. At least not for him. Maybe not even for Venezuela. He just had to rise up. Maybe there was an opportunity here. He just had to seize it. If that was the case, then doing nothing and letting the Americans escape was the *right* thing to do for his country.

For *his* Venezuela.

CHAPTER FIFTY-NINE

Venezuelan jungle

Hunt couldn't believe what Jacobs was telling him.

"What do you mean they're not pursuing? We killed a bunch of them. Of course they're after us."

"I don't know what you want me to say, Charlie-One. But you're in the clear."

Hunt and Carter had been on the run for the last ninety minutes, taking only a short two-minute break to drink the last of their water. Both were exhausted, and Carter hadn't stopped bitching about his pinkie finger.

"We're half a mile from the river," Hunt said. He didn't want to celebrate too soon, but things were certainly looking brighter than they had been just a couple of hours ago. He didn't know if Hauer—or President Reilly—would be happy about the outcome of their mission, but Hunt was sure glad it was almost over.

The inflatable and the battery-powered motor were where they had left them, and the crossing went without a hitch. On the Colombian side, Henican was waiting for them.

"You really look like shit, Pierce. Seriously. This ain't a joke, man," Henican said, even refusing Hunt's offer for a man hug. "I don't think Harriet will let you sit in the truck. Even less in the plane."

Then, turning to Carter, he said, "We have a first aid kit for your finger in the plane, but you won't see a doctor before we're back stateside."

"That's fine," Carter said. "It doesn't hurt that much, and there isn't much we can do. It's not like we could grow it back, right?"

"What do you mean it doesn't hurt that much? You didn't stop moaning and bitching for the entire way back."

"Oh, that? It was just to get on your nerves."

72 HOURS LATER

CHAPTER SIXTY

The Oval Office
Washington, DC

Tom Hauer had expected to see the SecDef, the attorney general, and Dorothy Triggs already seated in the Oval Office when he arrived, but he was alone. The president was behind his desk, speaking on the phone, and gestured for him to move closer.

"Very well, Mr. President. I'm glad we could come to an agreement," President Reilly said, giving Hauer a big thumbs-up. "Sounds good. We'll see each other in a few weeks then."

President Reilly hung up. "That was the president of Russia," he said, inviting Hauer to take a seat with a flick of his hand.

"Yes, sir," Hauer said, not exactly sure why he was here by himself with the president.

"Your team did an excellent job, Tom. I'm very pleased."

"Thank you, sir."

Even though Hunt and Carter had been unable to download the entire contents of the drive, enough intelligence had been recovered to pinpoint who the main actors were: President Capriles and General Euclides Peraza. The United States had issued warrants for their arrest. Large sums of offshore money belonging to over two dozen Venezuelan generals had been seized, and two relatives of President Capriles had been arrested in France for drug trafficking. They were awaiting trial from the interior of a jail cell, courtesy of the French Republic.

"Do you know Pierce Hunt well?" President Reilly asked.

"He's not a personal friend, if that's what you're asking, Mr. President. But yes, I know him well enough."

"So you were aware of his relationship with Anna Garcia, correct?"

Hauer sighed. He had a feeling that not being stricter regarding the Anna Garcia situation was going to cost him his job. Maybe today. Maybe another day.

"Yes, sir, I knew about it. I didn't agree, nor did I encourage—"

"Tom," Reilly said, lifting his hands in the air. "You're not in any trouble here. It's just you and me. This isn't a court of law."

If that was supposed to make Hauer feel better, it didn't work. Hauer kept his mouth shut, waiting for the president to continue.

"Can you drop the case against her?"

That was a shocker. "I . . . yes, sir. It's certainly your prerogative, sir. I'm not sure this is the best way, to be honest. But I'm curious. Why are you sharing this with me, Mr. President?"

"Because I know that the DEA is the agency in charge of putting the file together for the federal prosecutors. I don't want you to waste human resources on this. I think she played fair, and in the end, she collaborated with us. What do you think?"

"I'll go with whatever you say, Mr. President. I know Hunt would be pleased with this outcome."

"All right then," President Reilly said, getting up. "Thanks for coming, Tom."

"I serve at your discretion, sir. It's always a pleasure." Hauer shook the president's hand.

What the hell was that? Hauer wondered a few minutes later, as he waited for his car. *What just happened?*

President Reilly poured two glasses of scotch and offered one to Dorothy Triggs. "What do you think?" Reilly asked.

"He's not ready," Triggs replied, swirling the single malt in her glass. "He's a lawman. He has only limited experience in running clandestine operations. We can't expect him to run someone like Hunt. And did you see how he reacted when you asked him to drop Anna Garcia's case?"

Reilly chuckled. "Yes. I did see that. But he ran Hunt in Afghanistan," Reilly reminded her.

Triggs nodded. "But can you imagine what Hunt could have done with the CIA's backing?"

"What you're really saying is that you want Pierce Hunt. Am I right?" Reilly asked, taking a sip of his drink.

"I think he'd fit perfectly with us. I don't think Hunt is being used to his full potential with the DEA."

"In the end, Dorothy, it will have to be Hunt's decision."

"Of course."

TWO MONTHS LATER

CHAPTER SIXTY-ONE

Palm Cay Marina
New Providence Island, the Bahamas

Pierce Hunt couldn't remember the last time he'd been so happy. He backed the stern of his Cobia 296 into the boat slip and cut the engines.

Leila helped him tie the boat to the dock and started to wash down the boat with the hose. It had been a great day on the water. A father-daughter day. A real one. The seas were calm, and the fish had almost jumped into the boat. They had caught four yellowfin tuna and six mahi-mahi. But the day hadn't been all about fishing. Fishing was just an excuse to get on the water and spend some time with his only daughter. He'd never be able to catch up with all the time he had lost, but he'd savor every moment he spent with her.

"Anna is gonna love this, Dad," Leila said, holding the biggest of the six mahi-mahi. "We'll have more than enough to do a trio, don't you think?"

"A trio?"

"Yes. Blackened, grilled, and fried."

"I'm not sure about the fried one, baby, okay?"

"What about a carpaccio?"

"Perfect."

My God! She was a grown-up now. *What about a carpaccio?*

Hunt hadn't even known what it was until Leila had explained it to him. He wasn't the fancy type. He was more of a steak-and-potato kind of guy. But he was glad his daughter could appreciate the finer things. She deserved it.

They had gone together to visit Jack Cameron's grave. Anna hadn't come, though. That would have been weird for everyone. Leila was still struggling once in a while with Jack's death, and she still communicated with his parents, but overall, she was doing just fine. Hunt was doing just fine.

———

Hunt's eyes had been on Anna for the last twenty minutes. She'd fallen asleep on the sofa while he massaged her feet. She had cooked the fish perfectly. They had invited their neighbors over, and even with fourteen people feeding on the four yellowfin tuna, there were plenty of leftovers, and everybody went home with a little box. They had shared a total of ten bottles of wine, so he could understand why Anna was snoring. The girls were tired, too, and had gone to their rooms on the third floor.

The prosecutors had dropped all charges against Anna for her organization's role in the amphetamine distribution and the other crimes they were aware of the Garcia syndicate having committed. Anna had stepped back from the organization completely; Tasis had taken over and dissolved what remained by selling all the properties belonging to the Garcias. The last sighting of Tasis had been thirty days ago at the Miami airport, where he had boarded a flight to Costa Rica.

Since the Venezuelan mission, Tom Hauer hadn't contacted Hunt or Simon Carter. Hunt was curious why Hauer hadn't called, but he didn't worry too much. His retainer as a contractor was still being deposited every fifteenth of the month. It wasn't much, but it was enough to make the payments on his boat and to pay the insurance.

Anna stirred. Hunt picked her up and took her to their bedroom on the second floor.

Their bedroom. He still loved the sound of that.

Hunt was happy with their decision to move to the Bahamas. Anna had sold the Garcia house and had given the proceeds to charity. With the zero-interest loan Moon had offered him, Hunt had purchased the beachfront property. It wasn't a big place, but the three-bedroom townhouse was perfect for them. He gently put Anna on the bed and removed her socks and pants. The new phone she had bought was on the nightstand. These days, Anna used it as an alarm clock and not much else. Hunt unlocked it, set it to airplane mode, and canceled the 6:00 a.m. alarm. He kissed her on the forehead, and for a moment she opened her eyes.

She smiled at him. "I love you, Pierce Hunt," she said before closing her eyes. "Come to bed. Please."

How could he resist such an invitation? "I'll lock the doors and turn off the lights," Hunt said. "I'll be right back."

Hunt made his way back down the stairs, but he knew something was wrong before his foot touched the floor.

In a flash his right hand moved to the small of his back, where he kept a Glock 26.

"Stand down, Mr. Hunt," the woman in the living room said. "My name is Dorothy Triggs—"

"I know who you are, goddamn it! Just tell me what you're doing in my house," Hunt barked. This was his house. This was Anna's house. Leila and Sophia were sleeping upstairs. Hunt didn't know what kind of game the deputy director of the Directorate of Operations was playing, but he wasn't a player.

"Have you watched the news recently?"

"I try not to," Hunt replied. "I watch plenty of fishing shows, though."

"That's why you were so good today with your daughter. Seems like you two had a terrific day, wouldn't you say?"

"What do you want?"

"First of all, I'd be grateful if you could lower your weapon."

Hunt holstered his Glock. "I was about to go to bed, so say what you're here to say, and be on your merry way."

Triggs pointed her finger toward the sofa. "Can I?"

"Be my guest."

"Thank you. You're not sitting down?"

"Talk. Please."

Triggs shook her head, as if she was disappointed with his attitude. "If you had watched the news, you would know that Venezuela has changed drastically in the last two months."

If she was expecting him to ask her to elaborate, she was going to be disenchanted real fast.

"Very well then," she continued. "President Leopoldo Capriles and General Euclides Peraza were both arrested for corruption and embezzlement of public funds."

"Your point?"

"Who's the new president?"

"Some career military officer, I believe," Hunt replied.

"His name is Colonel Carlos Arteaga. Ring a bell?"

"Is it supposed to?"

"Let's just say that I kind of helped him reach his full potential," Triggs said.

Hunt was intrigued, but he didn't want Triggs to know. "What does this have to do with me?"

"He's the officer with whom you had your little shootout in the jungle. Where Simon Carter lost the top of his left pinkie? You certainly remember that."

How could he forget? Carter kept talking about it. He and Emma were scheduled to fly in the next day for a three-night stay. Hunt had stacked the fridge with beers, knowing his friend's weakness for the local Bahamian brew.

"Again, what does it have to do with me?"

"Colonel Arteaga asked us a favor."

"Is Colonel Arteaga Queen Bee?" Hunt asked, his eyes drilling into Triggs's.

Triggs's face hardened at the mention. "Yes."

Hunt nodded, as if he had known all along. "What kind of favor?"

"The kind of favor you're very good at, Mr. Hunt."

"Is that so?"

"He'd like you to hunt down a man named Jorge Ramirez."

"Jorge Ramirez?" This came from Anna, who was halfway down the stairs. Hunt wouldn't be surprised, or upset, if she'd been listening from the get-go.

"Miss Garcia," Triggs said with a charming smile.

"Who are you, and what do you want?" Anna asked. She didn't sound friendly, and Hunt could see that Anna was trying to take a hint from him to figure out if Triggs was a friendly or not.

In all honesty, he wasn't sure either. Hunt introduced Triggs to Anna. No hands were offered.

"What were you saying about Jorge Ramirez?" Hunt asked.

"When Ramirez realized that the Spider was in trouble, he refused to return to Venezuela. Ramirez had made multiple alliances with different cartels and gangs to distribute the same amphetamine pills that were used in the United States four months ago. We don't know where his labs are located, but we think he might be five or six months away from being able to manufacture vast quantities of that very dangerous drug. But this isn't our biggest concern right now."

"Seems pretty big to me. Those amphetamine pills are ultra-addictive."

"You aren't wrong, but the more pressing issue is that Jorge Ramirez knows that Colonel Arteaga is our Queen Bee. Documents seized at his house in Caracas showed that he has known for quite a while."

"For more than four months?" Hunt asked, his mind going back to the raid in Paraguay and the dead CIA case officer they'd called Ms. Red.

"For a year. Maybe more."

Hunt sighed. Ramirez had been in Paraguay. And that was how he'd gotten away—by claiming he was the Queen Bee. Hunt was sure of it.

"So your problem is that you're afraid Ramirez will let the world know that the new Venezuelan president is an American puppet?" Anna asked.

"No, that doesn't bother me much. The Venezuelan people were tired of Capriles's despotism. They don't care who's pulling the strings as long as they can eat once or twice a day and have access to enough medicines to keep their children healthy."

"So what are you afraid of then?" Hunt asked.

"What terrifies this administration is the fact that Ramirez knows about a few questionable actions President Arteaga had to take to keep his cover."

"Like what?"

"We're not sure."

Triggs's response was too evasive for Hunt's taste. "Like what?" he repeated, his voice hardening.

He could see that Triggs was uncomfortable. "There's a possibility that Arteaga might have ratted out other American and allied forces agents in order to solidify his tenure within the Spider's network."

"You must be kidding me," Hunt said, sensing his anger growing and his blood beginning to boil. "Now I know what's keeping you from sleeping at night."

"Americans can't learn of this," Triggs said. "But what scares us the most is that Ramirez could use this information to blackmail President Arteaga into doing his bidding. That's unacceptable. We don't want Ramirez to have that kind of power."

"Why are you here and not Tom Hauer?" Hunt asked.

"This would be a CIA operation—"

"Not interested. Not for me. Thanks for coming. Bye now," Hunt said, gesturing toward the door.

"Why are you acting like that?" Triggs asked.

"I like working for Hauer. He's straightforward. He's a no-bullshit guy, and he's honest. I trust him."

"All very nice," Triggs said with a smile. "But at the CIA we have many more gadgets. Many more resources. And much, much more money."

"Still not interested. So please go."

But Triggs wasn't done. She had one more card to play. And it was a big one. "You're friends with Charlie Henican, yes? The former Delta operator?"

Hunt didn't like where this was going. "You know I am, so why are you asking the question?"

"Wouldn't you agree with me that you owe Charlie? Especially after what he did for you in Gaza?"

Hunt felt the blood drain from his face. "Something happened to Charlie, right?"

"I'm afraid so," Triggs replied. "His assignment was to take out Jorge Ramirez. He missed his last ten check-ins."

"Fuck me."

"Maybe another day. But in the meantime, I'd be grateful if you could give my proposal some serious thought," Triggs said, standing and making her way to the door. "I'm told you're good at hunting people down."

ACKNOWLEDGMENTS

The trick when writing a series is to make every story unique but with the same feel as the others. I hope you, the reader, enjoyed *Trained to Hunt*, as this is the only thing that matters. The experience you have while reading is of the utmost importance to me. I hope you enjoyed the ride. Heartfelt gratitude for picking up my books. I owe you the world.

I have so much appreciation for my amazing, insightful, and marvelous team at Thomas & Mercer. They do everything right. Everything. They are truly a world-class team. Special thanks to my editor, Liz Pearsons. Her feedback and constructive criticism are critical to who I am as a writer. Thanks for believing in me. I am forever grateful for your vision and unwavering support. Thanks to Gracie Doyle, editorial director of Thomas & Mercer, and to Sarah Shaw, my author relations manager, for making me feel part of the team since day one. A warm thank-you to my awesome publicist, Ashley Vanicek. I know how hard you all work to bring my books to life.

Thank you to the amazing Caitlin Alexander, developmental editor extraordinaire. This is my second book with her. I'm a much better writer because of her. I'm also indebted to Eric Myers, my friend and agent at Myers Literary Management, for everything he does for my career.

As always, thanks to my sweet wife, Lisane, who deserves as much credit as I do. She's my biggest fan and best friend. Without her support, Pierce Hunt would have never seen the light of day. Thanks, too, to Florence and Gabriel. You're my angels. You make everything fun.

ABOUT THE AUTHOR

Photo © 2013 Esther Campeau

Simon Gervais was born in Montréal, Québec. He joined the Canadian military as an infantry officer and was commissioned as a second lieutenant in 1997. In 2001, he was recruited by the Royal Canadian Mounted Police and became a federal agent. His first posting was in Toronto, where he served as a drug investigator. During this time, he worked on many international drug-related cases in close collaboration with his American colleagues from the DEA. His career switched gears in 2004, and he was placed with a federal antiterrorism unit based in the Ottawa region. During the following years, he was deployed in several European and Middle Eastern countries. In 2009, he became a close-protection specialist tasked with guarding foreign heads of state visiting Canada. He served on the protection details of Queen Elizabeth II, US president Barack Obama, and Chinese president Hu Jintao, among others. Gervais lives in Ottawa with his wife and two children.